The Kit Aston Novellas

The KIT AS

AND OTHER STORIES

Jack Murray

Jack Murray

Books by Jack Murray

Kit Aston Series
The Affair of the Christmas Card Killer
The Chess Board Murders
The Phantom
The Frisco Falcon
The Medium Murders
The Bluebeard Club
The Tangier Tajine
The French Diplomat Affair (novella)
Haymaker's Last Fight (novelette)

Agatha Aston Series
Black-Eyed Nick
The Witchfinder General Murders
The Christmas Murder Mystery

DI Nick Jellicoe Series
A Time to Kill
The Bus Stop
Trio
Dolce Vita Murders

The Kit Aston Novellas

The French Diplomat Affair

The FIRST Kit Aston NOVELLA

Jack Murray

Jack Murray

Copyright © 2018 by Jack Murray

All rights reserved. No part of this publication may be reproduced, distributed, or transmitted in any form or by any means, including photocopying, recording, or other electronic or mechanical methods, without the prior written permission of the publisher, except in the case of brief quotations embodied in critical reviews and certain other non-commercial uses permitted by copyright law. For permission requests, write to the publisher, addressed 'Attention: Permissions Coordinator,' at the address below.

Jackmurray99@hotmail.com

This is a work of fiction. Names, characters, businesses, places, events, locales, and incidents are either the products of the author's imagination or used in a fictitious manner. Any resemblance to actual persons, living or dead, or actual events is either purely coincidental or used in a fictitious manner.

ISBN: 9798781939176
Imprint: Independently published

Prologue

Eiffel Tower, Paris: 21st February 1924

Madness.

He was late. Very late. Damn strike. He should have foreseen this. The French were always striking over something. He sprinted along the pathway, dodging in and out of couples and families walking in the park. Children laughed and pointed at the silly man running with one hand holding onto his hat. How big a fool he looked he could only guess. How big a fool he was for not planning better this morning of all mornings only time would tell.

Time.

Twenty-five minutes to eleven. Up ahead he saw it and his heart sank. The queue to get into the Eiffel Tower seemed to extend for miles. He cursed the sun and the gently spring-like day that had brought the crowds out to the park. He arrived and stood behind a group of Americans. They were a big presence. Literally. Noisy and seemingly built on a different scale from him.

One lift came and went. Then another. The third lift arrived, and the queue moved forward like a centipede in search of a leaf. Ten minutes to eleven. Maybe, just maybe. More movement, then a halt. If ever a process was designed to shred the nerves of the most unruffled individual, it was queuing when you were already late.

At last he was into the lift, squeezing in much to the irritation of an American lady. *If you weren't so big, we'd have fit a lot more on* thought the man sourly.

The lift began to rise at a disappointingly unhurried lick. All around the man, voices cooed as the Champ de Mars slowly hove into view, an expanse of green against the white, grey, and tan buildings of Paris. Higher and higher they rose, but too slowly for the man. Pressed against the door, he looked at his watch. Four minutes to eleven. They reached the first level which required a change of lift.

He was out of the lift in a flash, only to be confronted with yet another queue. His heart sank as he gazed at what lay ahead of him. This wouldn't do. Thinking quickly, he announced in French, 'I'm a doctor, let me through.' He repeated the statement in English putting on what for him felt a remarkably silly French accent. The London stage wouldn't be beckoning any time soon, he thought, as disgruntled tourists parted but not without some suspicious grumbles. The man ignored them and made his way to the front of the queue speedily and with a slight degree of guilt. He arrived as the lift doors opened.

He could have cried at the speed they rose. Have the French something against speed and efficiency, he wondered. It was all he could do to stop himself clubbing the doors in frustration. But the frustration he felt was more with himself. *Idiot. Idiot. Idiot.*

And maybe he really was an idiot. Certainly mad. Being here. Paris now. What utter folly. However, he knew he had to come. To be sure. To be, absolutely, certain beyond any shadow of doubt. He knew he would never have been able to live with the doubt. Better to be a poor fool and live without the regret. His stomach felt empty. Had he felt this scared before, back then, back there when the guns had stopped?

He looked out at the expanse of Champs de Mars beneath him. Scurrying around the long walkway, the crowds seemed like ants. At one side, he could see the Seine snaking its way around the tower. He looked at his watch for the tenth time in the last minute.

Five minutes past eleven.

He was officially very late. On a fool's errand to boot. Idiot, idiot, idiot.

The lift bumped to a halt. A lady fell into him, but his eyes were elsewhere. He followed the crowd out of the lift into the light, wanting to scream, 'get out of the way'.

At last he stumbled out onto the top deck of the Eiffel Tower. It was colder. At this height the air stung his face. He was shivering, but not through his reaction to the icy temperature. Fear gripped him. He held his breath, his heart thumped wildly. Would she be here?

Jack Murray

1

5 Years earlier

Calais, France: January 30th, 1919

The final whistle had blown. The war was over. Not the War. It had finished four months previously. This was war by other means, played out on a soccer pitch between two highly motivated and, as it transpired, still quite violent companies in the British army stationed in France.

Harry Miller trudged off the pitch, or to be more precise, limped, courtesy of a highly illegal challenge from the opposing full back, who had grown tired of Miller's trickery on the wing. The tackle had successfully reduced Miller's influence on the game but was too late to save the full back's team. Miller's team won 3-1.

Following their showers and some degree of rapprochement with the opposition, Miller and his colleagues sloped off to join the rest of the company to do what they had spent the last two months doing: nothing. Miller was bored, his army pals were bored, everyone wanted to go home.

Home was across the channel, tantalisingly close but, for the majority, a place they wouldn't see for a long time yet. The process of demobilisation of the British army was now a lot clearer since Churchill had become involved, but this was cold comfort for those who were not either long serving, older, wounded or required for key branches of industry.

It was early afternoon, and the sun was hidden behind a grey blanket of cloud. Thankfully the rain was holding off but there was a bite in the air. Miller looked around at his fellow soldiers sitting on the grass at the camp. There was a sense of ennui among all. The football was finished, and nobody was listening to the drill sergeant. Every so often one lucky sod would be called out to be shipped back to Blighty. If there was any resentment from the other soldiers, they hid it well. Instead, good news for a close colleague was greeted happily. Mostly. Miller watched one such soldier shaking hands and receiving slaps on the back. The soldier beside Miller commented on the departure.

'Lucky bugger, I wonder what he does.'

Miller didn't know and said as much. The conversation closed. Just ahead Miller saw another soldier becoming agitated. The waiting around was a source of tension. Most soldiers recognised that demobilising around four million men could not take place overnight. They had to wait their turn. But not all soldiers were so patient. Rumours were spreading in the camp that a mutiny had taken place at another camp nearby. Talk was of nothing else. A soldier a few yards away from Miller was past the point of waiting. Miller had seen of few of these types. Trouble was looming. The soldier beside Miller touched his arm and indicated he was seeing the same signs.

'I don't like the look of this,' said the soldier nodding towards the vocal group.

'Me neither,' replied Miller.

Up ahead the agitated soldier was on his feet and addressing a group of younger soldiers around him. From what Miller could hear, he was saying they had to do something about the lack of food. He talked also of the treatment of fellow soldiers at other camps who had been arrested. His message seemed to be hitting home and other soldiers began to yell out support. Miller and the other soldier glanced at one another. The atmosphere was febrile.

'Should we do something?' said the other soldier. 'Young fool will cause a riot.'

Miller rubbed his chin then stood up and walked over to the young soldier.

'Listen, mate, we're all in the same boat. We all want to go home, but you'll have to wait your turn. No use in bellyaching. They're going as quickly as they can. We don't know why the other chaps were arrested and it's not so bad here.'

Miller could hear a few soldiers shouting out support for him, so he continued.

'Why don't you sit down and wait for the call?'

This seemed to quieten the group of young soldiers who had been so vocal a few moments earlier. The agitator remained silent and walked over to Miller with his hand held out. Miller smiled and reached out to shake hands. As the soldier gripped Miller's hand, he yanked him forward. Seeing he was about to be hit, Miller tried to evade the punch and was caught a glancing blow on the chin. The blow stunned him momentarily but then he regained his balance and had his arms up ready to attack.

Within seconds more soldiers were on their feet attacking Miller. Blows rained down on him. He fought back gamely, vaguely aware his companion of a few moments ago was taking on a few of the other soldiers to help him. The sound of shouting from the participants as well as onlookers alerted the military police, who were getting used to these situations.

The military police waded in and extracted the combatants, including Miller, and hauled them away from the scene forcefully. This brought cheers and some laughter from the watching soldiers, who had enjoyed the show as a welcome respite from their boredom.

Miller and the other soldiers were thrown into a makeshift building which was serving as a cell. There was no floor, just dirt. The sound of the door locking seemed to bring everyone to their senses. The original agitating soldier looked sheepishly at Harry and held out his hand. Miller looked suspiciously at it.

'Sorry, mate, that was a dirty trick. I was a bit carried away.'

Miller was in no mood to disagree with this, but neither was he the sort to hold a grudge very long. They shook hands. The other combatants all apologised also to Miller and his companion.

Miller turned to the man he had been speaking with earlier and who had tried to help him.

'Name's Harry, by the way, Harry Miller,' said Miller shaking hands, 'Thanks for your help back there.'

'Guha, Amit Guha,' replied the man with an enormous smile and a slight movement of his head. He was a little older than Miller, of a similar height but more lightly built. Even during the scuffle, Miller had noted with approval the quick movement of his comrade matched with a fearlessness in coming to his aid.

'You seemed pretty handy back there, Amit,' noted Miller with a smile.

'Sadly, I've had plenty of practice,' replied Guha, his smile became more rueful as a dozen images came into his mind. Miller nodded but made no comment on this. He looked down at the arms of the Indian. He was a corporal. Miller guessed he must have been an exceptional soldier to have received such a promotion.

The rest of the afternoon passed quickly as Guha told Miller more about his time in the War.

'I came over to France at the end of 1914 with my regiment the Garhwal Rifles. It was winter. My goodness we were cold. We only had summer clothing. I'm not sure the officers knew what to do with us at first, but I think we showed we were up for the fight,'

'Why are you here? It's not your war,' pointed out Miller.

'I wanted to come because Bapu said we should,' replied Guha, still smiling.

'Bapu?'

'Mohandas Gandhi, our leader. He said that it would help bring us closer to independence if we support the British at this time. So I volunteered. I did my training in France and my first time with the Germans was at Neuve Chapelle. My regiment were right in the thick of it, I can tell you. We lost so many men, but we won. After that, I think the British looked at us differently. In fact, immediately after Neuve Chapelle I was transferred from my regiment into the 25th Infantry.'

'How did that happen?' asked Miller, genuinely curious about the Indian's story.

'The 25th were to our left but when we were in the middle of it all, it was very confused. At one point I saw a British officer fighting hand to hand with two Germans, I went to help him. When I arrived, we were fighting four of them but between us we did it. When we'd finished, he looked at me, asked me my name and then disappeared. A few days later I was called to see my commanding officer. The man I'd rescued had requested my transfer to his battalion. It turned out that he was a lord, so much influence. He wanted me to be his batman. I wasn't sure, but my commanding officer said that it would be the best thing for me and for us. I think he meant our country.'

'Who was this lord then?' asked Miller, laughing.

'Captain Lake. He was a wonderful man.'

'Was?'

'I don't think he was killed. A few months later he was transferred also. I stayed on with the 25th, this time as a soldier,' said Guha. He stopped at this point, a faraway look in his eyes. Miller didn't need to ask what he was thinking. Finally, Guha continued but his words came more slowly as he tried to regain command of himself, 'We saw so much fighting. The Somme, Passchendaele, Arras. Never ending death. So many.' His voice trailed off at this point.

Several of the men involved in the flare up were listening by this stage. Like Miller, most were in their mid-twenties. None had particularly wanted to go to war but had felt duty bound as more of their friends enlisted. Now all were desperate to return home. So many had fallen. They had made it.

Early evening and the military police finally looked in on the unhappy group. One captain and a sergeant entered the makeshift cell. The group immediately stood to attention when they entered, a move suggested by Miller to placate the authorities and mitigate any punishment. It appeared to catch the captain by surprise. He walked along the line saying nothing. When he had finished his review, he stood before them. The tension in the room thickened the atmosphere.

'What happened today was tantamount to mutiny,' said the captain. Miller could feel his heart sinking. 'Mutiny in the British army is an offence punishable by death.'

The captain smiled cruelly as he registered the looks on the faces of the men before him.

'Yes, that's how we treat mutineers. Now, I suggest when you leave here, you bear it in mind. You let everyone you speak to in this camp be aware of the punishment, because I promise you, if this re-occurs, there will be no trial. We will act summarily. Do I make myself understood?'

'Yes, sir,' said every man in the room.

The captain turned to his sergeant, 'Get their names and then let them go. All except this man.' The captain pointed to Miller. Guha looked at Miller in surprise. The man who had originally started the fracas walked forward.

'Sir, the fight was my fault. I was bellyaching.'

'Enough,' ordered the captain and walked away.

Miller glanced at the other soldier and nodded. The soldiers began to troop out, leaving their names with the sergeant as they left. Guha made one last effort to make a case for Miller to the policemen.

The captain looked at Guha dismissively, 'You're a corporal. You should've known better. Leave your name and go. Be thankful we don't take this further.'

Miller was left alone. Outside he could hear Guha continuing to make a case for Miller but to no avail. Most of the men he had fought with were like him: young, poorly educated, in low paid jobs or even lower paying crime. A few of the boys he'd met admitted as much. There weren't many of them left now. None of his original gang. They were wiped out at the Somme. Memories trickled into his mind. At first the images flickered like firelight on a wall. The pictures began move slowly. He saw friends shredded by gunfire as they marched slowly into a wall of lead. He'd known relatively few men from the sub-continent but was touched by the Indian's interest and impressed also. He wondered if he'd see him again.

Ten minutes later, the captain returned. There was a faint trace of a smile on his face. This doesn't bode well, thought Miller.

'Get your things. You're going home.'

Although in shock, Miller didn't need a second invitation. He re-joined Guha and told him his news. The group he'd formerly been fighting came over to congratulate him. There seemed to be no hard feelings towards him. Miller picked up his belongings, and with a salute to the other men, bid them farewell.

2

Crystal Palace Demobilisation Dispersal Centre: 10th February 1919

Miller took a boat over from Boulogne to Dover. He wasn't a natural sailor and was relieved the crossing was relatively calm. He joined the soldiers on the deck as the white cliffs of Dover hove into view. He felt like crying, and not from happiness. However, the soldiers on the boat began to cheer and Miller was hit by several hats that had been thrown into the air. A band played 'See the Conquering Heroes' as they disembarked. Miller marched down the gangplank and onto the wet grey concrete of Britain. Home. To what, he wondered?

A day later, Miller was on a train to the Dispersal Camp in London. From the train he marched with the other soldiers to the camp. The soldiers were ordered to stand to attention in the parade ground. In batches of twenty to thirty they were moved into the makeshift huts to be processed. After an hour of standing in the cold, it was Miller's turn. He marched forward with a batch of other soldiers. The Lance Corporal glanced at Miller's Z22 form and then looked Miller up and down. The form confirmed Miller was suffering from no disability and would, therefore, be making no claim for any injuries arising from his service.

'Move along,' said the Lance Corporal, who had already lost interest in Miller and turned his attention to the next soldier. Miller looked behind him. There were another twenty soldiers behind him and as many ahead. The Dispersal Camps were getting through several thousand a day, yet it still wasn't quick enough for the soldiers waiting to return.

'Strip, gentlemen,' ordered a sergeant, who gave no impression that he believed them to be gentlemen, 'Put your belongings in your helmets and walk to the baths.'

This was the first hot bath Miller had taken in nearly a year. It felt wonderful. He was beginning to enjoy his return. It would be short lived.

When he came out of the bath, he found out they'd run out of uniforms. Their old uniforms were too dirty or lice-infested to keep. Miller and hundreds of other men were forced to parade naked until arrangements were made. In response the soldiers began to march around the camp singing, 'We want some food, we want some money.'

The officers looking on felt some sympathy for the men. After years of war, the men deserved better than this. They let the men blow off some steam. A few hours later, clothing had arrived.

'About time,' said Miller to the sergeant, as he stepped forward.

'Tell me about it,' replied the sergeant. 'Right, son, you have a choice, keep your uniform for twenty-eight days and then hand it back. We'll give you money to buy your own clothes. If you lose or damage it, anything you'll be fined. Alternatively take some civilian clothing from us now, you can keep your overcoat for the moment.'

Miller opted to keep the uniform and receive a clothing allowance on top of his demobilisation account. The process ended with Miller receiving a postal draft which he could cash, a Z18 form showing what he had done in the army and Z11 form confirming he was no longer in the army and giving him a rail ticket to his home. Third class.

He'd served nearly four years. He'd seen friends maimed, killed, or go mad. He'd killed for his country. The postal draft was for nineteen pounds, eighteen shillings and four pence.

It was to be paid in instalments.

A wave of anger passed through Miller and then he felt it dissipate to be replaced by a profound emptiness. Miller had spent four years of his life wanting nothing else but for the War to end and to return home in one piece. But what was he returning to, he wondered again, as he made his way out of the Dispersal Centre? Beside him, the soldier waiting to exit seemed to be of similar mind.

'Back to a land fit for heroes. We'll see about that.'

Miller nodded, 'You have a trade to return to?'

The man nodded, 'Yes, my old garage said they'll take me back.'

'That's good,' smiled Miller.

'You?' asked the man.

'I was self-employed,' replied Miller. He'd been a burglar.

'Hopefully your old customers will want you again,' said the soldier optimistically.

I doubt it, thought Miller before saying, 'I might look to change trade, see what opportunities there are.'

They parted a few minutes later with wishes of good luck on both sides. He took one last look behind him, then Miller stepped out of the front door a free man, a civilian once more. He shut his eyes and breathed in the air. Was it his imagination that it felt cleaner? He opened his eyes and exhaled.

The first sight to greet him was two policemen. One of the policemen was familiar, a sergeant named Fredericks. Miller stopped for a moment, unsure if they were there for him or not. There was no reason why they should be. He'd done his bit. Although he had previous run ins with the police, there was never any evidence to link him to the crimes he had committed. He felt certain they were not there for him.

'Miller,' said Sergeant Fredericks, 'come with us.'

-

The police cell was small, there was little light; the camp bed mattress was thin and lumpy, a vast improvement on the last four years, reflected Miller with a smile. He lay back in the bed and made himself comfortable. Knowing the police as he did, they would let him stew for a while, little suspecting that he would have no problem sleeping in such a situation.

The two-hour nap was ended when Fredericks came into his cell and gave the sleeping Miller a none-too-gentle shake.

'I could've done with another hour's kip,' pointed out Miller.

'You won't be laughing soon, son,' said Fredericks, a sneer appearing on his face, 'If you think running away to France was going to solve your problems, you were mistaken.'

'You mean fighting a war to protect the likes of you, sarge,' replied Miller, walking out of the cell before Fredericks could reply.

Charles 'Chubby' Chadderton looked at his in-tray with something approaching distress. He was working twelve-hour days at the War Office trying to sort the process of demobilisation. He had no problem with the new approach outlined by the recently installed War Minister, Winston Churchill, but the logistics were ridiculous. Returning between three and four million soldiers to civilian life or stationing them in Germany, was not a task for the faint-hearted.

A former soldier himself, invalided out of the army after losing a hand, he had tremendous sympathy with the men he was trying to re-deploy. He had been at the War Office for a couple of years now but knew well the desperation to return home to their families and loved ones. His department was overwhelmed by the demobilisation process.

It was five o'clock. He was sorely tempted to call it a day and retire to his club for a well-earned gin and tonic or three. He took one more look at the pile of papers on his desk. One more hour he thought. He owed it to the men. Rising from his desk his long, thin, and certainly not chubby frame moved rapidly to the office door. His long-suffering secretary, Miss Brooks looked up.

'Miss Brooks, I think you can leave now. It's late. If you could get me a cup of tea, please, before you do, it would be a kindness.'

Chubby returned to his seat and began to read though the pile in front of him, paper by paper. He hardly noticed Miss Brooks return with a cup of tea and a biscuit. Rather than disturb him she placed the cup down and silently left the office for the evening.

It was another two hours before Chubby decided to call it a night. He noticed the tea and biscuit for the first time. It was cold. Just as he was about to leave the phone rang. Chubby looked down at the phone, unsure if he should escape or pick it up.

A moment's hesitation then, 'Hello, Chadderton here.'

'Who?... Oh yes, I remember now...He's where?'

3

Harley Street, London, 10th February 1919

Kit Aston struggled to his feet. His doctor stood beside him and watched Kit rise from the chair. For a moment he looked like he might lose his balance, but the mission was finally accomplished. The two men were in a surgery in Harley Street, London. It was a large room lined with books on one wall and paintings on the another. It could have been Kit's club, Sheldon's, such was the unashamedly male décor.

'Well done, Kit. You'll no longer need the crutch soon,' said the doctor, smiling with genuine delight, even pride.

'Thanks to you Frank,' said Kit with a grin.

'Nonsense, Kit. You did it. How does the new limb feel?' replied Dr Frank Hannah. He was approaching sixty. Grey whiskers running from his ears and above his mouth. His jovial nature was apparent from his Falstaff-like frame and an expression of contained vivacity. As family physician to the Astons for nearly forty years, he had long since dropped the formal use of titles and was on first name terms with all.

'Much better. The weight is better distributed. Lighter to walk on but gives you a decent base also. Definitely a big improvement on my previous peg leg.'

'Glad to hear it. By the way, your father's due to see me in an hour. Fancy sticking around to see the old man?'

Kit looked doubtful, 'Is Marge with him?'

'Yes, I believe so,' replied Hannah, knowing this would effectively hasten Kit's exit. It did. Kit smiled and shook his head. This made Hannah smile also. He shrugged and smiled as if to say, "I tried". A few minutes later Kit had successfully negotiated the stairs accompanied by Dr Hannah and was out onto Harley Street. The two men parted with a friendly handshake.

Rather than hail a taxi, Kit decided to road test his new leg. The weather was far from warm, so he buttoned up his overcoat and put on his hat. The sky suggested the rain would hold off, so he set off in the direction of Belgravia to his apartment in town.

-

The walk took the best part of thirty minutes and by the end Kit was feeling decidedly less warm towards his new acquisition. His knee felt sore where the prosthetic limb was attached. He fell upon his sofa, removing the limb with something approaching ecstasy. The apartment was empty. Since the death of his manservant Hargreaves a month previously, Kit had made do on his own, spending a lot of time at Sheldon's. In fact, it had become a second, or strictly speaking, third home to him.

Many of his old pals, who had joined when he did, were no longer there - a consequence of marriage, the War, and yet more marriage. His oldest friend, Lord Olly Lake was still in Russia. Not surprisingly he had heard little of him in the last year. His presence was unknown to the Russian authorities and would certainly have been considered unwelcome. Kit himself had narrowly escaped Russia the previous year as the Bolshevik secret police had closed in and rent apart the British spy networks in the country.

Although many of his generation were no longer there, Kit enjoyed the company of many of the older members. Few had been involved directly in the War, but many had lost sons or nephews. This reduced conversation on the topic. If many were aware of Kit's injury, few made mention. This suited Kit. Although personally reconciled to what had happened, he was in no mood to discuss it with others. The subject was a book he preferred to remain closed and unread.

Kit dined alone at the club, occasionally being joined by other members. Following dinner, he usually retired to the library to read the evening papers or sit and chat with friends. This evening he sat alone reading the latest on the Paris Peace Conference and the discussions about forming a League of Nations as a forum to stop future major wars. It made eminent sense to Kit. The War had been a catastrophe. There was no other way of describing it.

Presently Kit felt a hand on his shoulder. He looked up and saw Lord Peter Wolf.

'Mind if I join you?' asked Wolf.

Kit happily assented as he was feeling a little bit bored. He knew Wolf in passing and liked him. He was a man of around sixty with dark, intelligent eyes and greying hair which contrasted with his tanned skin. His manner was an attractive mixture of open-mindedness mixed with unconscious certainty. Meeting him again, Kit reflected how he would have made a good senior officer in the War, unquestionably better than a few he'd served under.

'You look as if you've been on the Riviera, Peter,' said Kit.

'I have. You should be a detective, Kit. I spent most of the winter down at my place at Cap Ferrat, near Monte Carlo. You're always welcome by the way, Kit. I came back before Christmas. Call me old-fashioned but I do love Christmas in England.'

'I don't blame you, Peter,' smiled Kit. Looking down at the newspaper he asked Wolf, 'What do you think of Paris?'

'Fascinating stuff. I haven't been over although Lloyd has asked me a few questions from time to time.'

Wolf was referring to Lloyd George, Britain's Prime Minister, the man who had led the country to victory in the War. Although Kit knew better than to inquire what the Prime Minister and Wolf had discussed, he was immensely curious. Thankfully Wolf did not leave him hanging and expanded a little.

'Can't say too much of course, but it sounds like a different type of war being waged now between us, France and the Americans. It would be fair to say peace is a rare commodity in Paris now.'

'Is there anything in particular causing disagreement?' asked Kit.

'At a high level, it's pretty clear there's precious little consensus on the overall strategy for peace. I don't think much consideration was given to it before the War ended. Lloyd and Clemenceau are paying lip service to Wilson on the League, but the real game is carving up Germany's colonies, the Austro-Hungarian and Ottoman empires and how much Germany should pay.'

'My goodness, it sounds like a good old-fashioned land grab,' exclaimed Kit.

Wolf nodded in agreement, 'It is, Kit. Wilson, or more to the point, his man Edward House, isn't stupid. They're wise to this and they want the League to be the forum to handle all of this and decide what to do with Germany itself.'

Wolf could see the worry on Kit's face and waited for him to put words to what was on his mind.

'We seem to be storing up trouble for the future.'

'We are,' nodded Wolf looking grim, 'It feels more like a bandage than a proper strategy for repairing Europe.'

'Well let's not dwell further,' smiled Kit. 'It's all too depressing. How's business? I gather you converted one of your factories to armaments a year or two back.'

'It's true, but it wasn't my idea, I hasten to add. My partner David suggested it. By the end of the War we'd three factories making parts for the likes of Vickers or Harland and Wolff,' explained Wolf. 'David has absolute genius for spotting this kind of opportunity. I'm more of a salesman.'

Kit laughed, 'Well the idea that you can make something, and people will beat a path to your door is probably fantasy. Business requires people like you, Peter, as much as it needs a David Lewis. I wish I'd invested when you suggested it back in thirteen.'

David Lewis was the reclusive other half of Lewis & Wolf, the transnational corporation which had interests in armaments, clothing, and food. Kit had not met him before but had heard talk of his visionary intelligence. They chatted a little longer before Kit decided to retire for the night. As he was leaving, a concierge from Sheldon's approached him holding a silver plate. On the plate was a telegram addressed to Lord Aston. Kit thanked the man and read the telegram with something close to astonishment.

KIT. IN PARIS AT THE CONFERENCE. MET THE MOST RAVISHING GIRL. I AM IN LOVE. COME URGENTLY. SHE HAS BEEN ARRESTED FOR MURDER. SPUNKY.

4

Wandsworth Prison: 11th February 1919

The warder banged on the door of the cell, waking up Miller. He was in the top bunk, shivering. Like his accommodation at the police station, the remand centre was far from being his first choice, but it remained an improvement on the trenches. The ground was dry, it was relatively quiet, and the absence of rats was a relief. The future was a worry, though.

Miller's career in burglary had been a family business. His father had started around twenty years previously, evading capture all this time. Miller's older brother, Dan, had joined their father, first as lookout and then on safes. Miller had taken an active interest in the business. It seemed exciting, left him free during the day and beat working for a living. He left school at fifteen to join his father and brother. His career trajectory followed his brother's, first as lookout and then safes. Miller proved to be a highly talented addition to the 'firm'.

The burglary business provided a steady, if not lucrative, income for the family. They did not flash any wealth accrued, nor partake of any vice that might give away the source of their wealth. The family approach was highly professional. It was more than a job; it was a career. At least for Miller's father and Dan. Miller was under no illusions about crime providing a long-term solution for his life. After a few years, the excitement began to pale. The morality of his actions left him remarkably untroubled but the risks he was taking, both physically and with his liberty, began to prey.

In the months before Princip's shot had unleashed hell on Europe, Miller was actively looking to move on from crime and take up a more honest trade. He had an interest in motor cars and used his free days to work part time in a garage learning the mechanic trade. Night-time was reserved for the family's commercial activities.

The onset of War disrupted the Millers like almost every other family in the country. Even Dan, reckless, roguish Dan, heard the country's call. Both the Miller boys joined up, six months apart. Dan joined in late fourteen and Miller in early fifteen. He was twenty-one years old. By twenty-two he was neck deep in dirt and dead bodies.

-

The keys clanked against the metal door. Moments later it was opened, and a guard pointed to Miller.

'You, down now.'

'I don't think I heard a please, Mr Guard,' replied Miller, smiling.

Seconds later Miller was grabbed and roughly thrown to the ground. It was as much as Miller could so to stop himself beating the hell out of the guard. He wouldn't have broken sweat doing so. Miller glared at the guard and tensed his body. The guard glared back at Miller but moved back half a step. Miller relaxed a little. Why make things worse?

'I hate thievin' scum like you,' snarled the guard, 'You think swanning off to war was going to keep you out of the nick?'

Eyes ablaze, Miller was on him in a flash. In a moment the guard was on the ground with Miller's hand on his neck and the other poised to strike. The fear in the guard's eyes stopped Miller from doing what every fibre of his being screamed at him to do. Standing up, he dragged the guard upright like he was a ragdoll and threw him against the wall.

'I want you to understand something, mate, thousands of good men died to protect a pathetic wretch like you. You can say what you like about what I did before the War, mate, but nobody, and I mean nobody, swanned off there, and clearly not you.'

Seizing him by the lapels, Miller manhandled him off the wall, threw him out of the open door into the corridor. He followed him out. Standing in the corridor looking on were two men. The head of the remand centre, Mr Asquith, and another man Miller did not know. He was tall, expensively dressed, maybe a few years older than he.

The head of the remand centre glared at the guard and said, 'Get out of my sight, Wilson, I'll deal with you later.'

'This way, Miller,' said Asquith. He turned and led the three men down the corridor. Miller noted the limp from the unknown man. They entered a small room. Asquith nodded to the other man and then departed leaving the two men standing looking at one another.

'It's Harry, isn't it?' said the man. His voice seemed friendly. Miller's assessment of him was accurate: this was a member of the upper class.

Looking the man in the eye, Miller nodded. Miller's first thought was to wonder if he'd done a job in the man's mansion. The Miller family tended to target townhouses of the wealthy. Richer pickings and they could afford it.

'Let's sit, Harry,' said the man, 'It's more civilised.'

Both men sat down. Miller remained silent waiting to hear what the man wanted.

'I gather you're something of a cat burglar. Sounds exciting. If you're wondering if our paths have crossed in this regard, let me put your mind at rest.'

Miller smiled in relief. The man seemed affable with a relaxed smile. It certainly didn't appear that Miller's past was a problem; anything but.

'If it's alright with you sir, I won't admit anything. I met an American chap last year. They have something over there called the fifth amendment. I think I'll take the fifth if that's alright with you.'

The other man's smile widened at this, 'Yes, I'm familiar with this idea. Eminently sensible in my view. No point in incriminating yourself unnecessarily.'

Miller wondered if the man would introduce himself, but for the moment no name was being offered.

'Mr Asquith and I heard everything that transpired in the cell, by the way. I like the way you stood up for the men. People like that chap Wilson sicken me also.'

Miller nodded but said nothing to this. He wondered what part, if any, the man before him had played in the War. His reference to the men suggested he knew something of what had happened in France. And then there was the limp.

'I'm being rude. I haven't introduced myself. I'm Kit Aston,' Kit reached out to shake Miller's hand.

Miller was surprised. He had heard of Kit Aston. Who hadn't? The lord who'd fought at the front. Multi-decorated for his bravery and a leader widely admired by the men who fought with him.

There was silence for a few moments. Miller could see how the aristocrat seemed to be wrestling with his emotions. Finally, he spoke again.

'I wanted to meet the man who saved my life.'

The look of astonishment on Miller's face was such Kit wondered for a moment, if he had the right man.

'You were the man who was in the middle of No Man's Land?' said Miller in disbelief. Miller had been certain the man was a goner. He'd heard nothing since that night and had assumed his efforts had been in vain.

'Yes, it was me. I'm not sure who's the bigger fool. Me for being there in the first place or you for coming to get me.'

'I thought you'd bought it. You were in a pretty bad way,' explained Miller, glancing involuntarily at Kit's leg.

Kit could see the direction of Miller's gaze and smiled. He reached towards his wooden cane and gave his leg a rap with the cane. Miller's eyes widened as he heard the noise of wood on wood.

'Buggered up my tennis game, that's for sure. Can still play golf, though,' smiled Kit. Miller noted that the lord did not seem unduly troubled by his disability.

A look passed between the two men. Both knew what the last four years had been like. What they had seen, no man should ever have to see. What they had done, no man should be asked to do. They'd made it through. In that moment an agreement was reached tacitly. The subject would not be raised again between them.

Kit glanced around at the surroundings. The room was sparsely furnished and painted an unprepossessing grey.

'Not quite the Ritz, is it? How are they treating you?'

'You'd know more about the Ritz than me, sir, but the service does leave a lot to be desired. The bed's comfy, though, and the food's an improvement on some of the establishments I went to in France.'

Jack Murray

'It was pretty frightful, the food, wasn't it,' reminisced Kit with a smile. Then his face became a little more serious and he looked at Miller, 'I'm going to take you out of here Harry. It's the least I can do. Furthermore, when you've been to see your family, I'd like you to consider working for me. I need a manservant. I could use you Harry if you're interested.'

'I don't have any experience, sir.'

'We'll fix that. If you know how to drive, can learn a bit of cooking, you're halfway there already. The pay's good, the accommodation will be a decided improvement on the last few years and there'll be a bit of travel. Have a think about it and let me know.'

'I can tell you now, sir.'

Belgravia, London: 13th February 1919

Two days later, following a reunion with the family, Miller made his way to Belgravia. It was a rainy afternoon. He looked at the scrap of prison paper containing the address provided by his new employer. The building in Belgravia Square seemed a world away from his family home in Peckham. All around him were people, conspicuously wealthy people who seemed to be a different race. They were taller, better looking and, inevitably, expensively attired. Not just a different race, he thought, a different world.

Miller loved the bustle of south London, the energy, the noise the sense of life. Here, the streets seemed quieter and cleaner. The air smelled sweeter. The foul-smelling stench of horse manure, fish from the markets and other fluids that Miller didn't want to think about permeated the air in Peckham. Looking around him, it was clear there were no beggars or street sellers to sully the eye or assault the ear.

He walked ahead, unimpeded by rubbish or evidence of canine digestive yields. Yes, he thought, this is another world. He wondered if it would ever be his world. It wouldn't be long before he found out. He walked up the steps to the apartment building where Kit lived. If walking the streets around Belgravia was the starter, Kit's apartment provided the main course. Miller had been in beautiful houses before, professionally speaking, but the time of night he was visiting did not afford him the opportunity to stay and enjoy his surroundings. The idea of living in this apartment seemed like a dream.

The apartment was enormous and seemed to take up the whole of the second floor of the building. Miller felt lost in its size and splendour. All around him were works of art and books. His quarters were enormous consisting of a large bedroom and a small living area.

'I hope you'll like it, Harry,' said Kit when the tour had finished.

'Not bad,' said Miller with a grin, glancing out the window, 'Do you have anything south-facing, sir?'

Kit roared with laughter, 'I'll take that as a yes.'

Next Kit took him to a wardrobe. Inside were some clothes which Miller took to be his uniform.

'I had some livery made up for you. Guessed your size. I hate formality, these are fairly un-showy. I hope you don't mind. They're just dark suits. Nothing too Victorian.'

'Don't worry, sir, I'm used to uniform by now,' said Miller. He ran his hand along the cotton shirt and then the trousers. He hoped Kit had guessed the correct size as these were a world away from the rough, lice-ridden clothes he'd worn during the War.

Kit left him to get dressed. When Miller had finished dressing, one look in the mirror told him Kit had a good eye. The clothes fit perfectly. He sat on the bed and bounced on it a little. Then he lay down on it to try it for size and to check how comfortable it was. The mattress was firm but with just enough give to make it as joyous an experience as he could remember. The thought of entertaining female guests in this apartment crossed his mind. He swiftly cast it away. First things first. There would be time and occasion enough in the future.

Miller re-joined Kit in the main living room.

'Fits beautifully, sir. Thank you.'

'I shan't ask you to do a twirl,' replied Kit with a smile.

Kit motioned for him to sit on one of the leather sofas that sat facing one another. They were separated by a coffee table upon which sat a small chess set. Miller felt his body melt into the arms of the sofa. It still felt like a dream but the look on Kit's face suggested it was time to get down to business.

For the next half hour, Kit took him through his duties which, after years of latrine duty, sounded none too onerous. Any nervousness Miller felt about going into service were dispelled by Kit's friendliness and uncomplicated lifestyle. One question on Miller's mind was answered at the end.

'As you may have gathered, I am part of the idle rich. I have no job, no business, and no official role since I left the army. I can't abide being idle. Thankfully things crop up from time to time in which my friends call upon my help. It can be interesting work. Not without risk. I hope that won't be a problem. One such thing came up last night.'

Kit handed over the telegram from Spunky. Initially, Miller was unsure if he should read it, but Kit nodded his permission.

'I won't ask how he obtained his nickname. What do you intend doing, sir?'

'We go to Paris tomorrow. I've made the arrangements. You're going to the Peace Conference, Harry.'

'Bit of a change from the nick, sir,' laughed Miller.

'I suspect there were more honest people where you were, Harry,' replied Kit.

'Can I tell them politicians, never again?'

'You have my permission, Harry. Let's hope. By the way, there's one other inhabitant in the apartment. I'll be back in a moment.'

Kit went to his room. As Miller was sitting waiting, he heard barking. Kit emerged holding a Jack Russell, who was intent on making his presence known.

'This is Sam,' said Kit introducing the little terrier. Sam extricated himself from Kit's arms and spent the next minute in front of Miller barking. He didn't seem too enamoured by the new arrival.

'Glad you two have hit it off so well,' said Kit doubtfully.

'Recognises a crook when he sees one, sir,' laughed Miller.

'Less said about that. Anyway, perhaps if you feed him, he might become friendlier. Kit led Miller into the kitchen and showed him where Sam's food was stored. The prospect of food seemed to calm the little dog down.

Miller served the food into a bowl. Sam looked at it with some suspicion, looked at Kit, who nodded. Sam tore into the food

'Needs time,' said the two men in unison.

How old is he, sir?' asked Miller, looking at Sam rip into his food.

'He's ten. I've had him since Cambridge,' responded Kit.

'Always been so friendly?'

'No. He's softened a bit over the years,' laughed Kit.

Leaving Sam to his victuals, Kit took Miller through what to pack for their impending trip to Paris and the arrangements for transport. Kit was relieved to see how quickly Miller picked up on his instructions. It augured well for the future.

When Miller had finished, Kit suggested he take the rest of the evening off and retire as they had an early start in the morning. Miller took Kit up on his suggestion. He spent the most comfortable night of his life on his new bed. He had one thought as he felt sleep overtake him: *I will make this work.*

Hotel Majestic, Paris: 14th February 1919

Aldric 'Spunky' Stevens adjusted the monocle on his good eye. The other eye sported an eye patch courtesy of a German shrapnel wound earned few years earlier. The odd combination of monocle and eye patch was set off, finally, by a dark, thin moustache. The overall appearance was either faintly piratical or alarming depending on your point of view.

Spunky thought his look just the right side of dashing. His success with the opposite sex was testament either to Spunky's charitable assessment of his looks or a combination of extraordinary confidence allied to a liberal, if not princely, allowance from his father, and his willingness to spend said allowance, generously.

Spunky's wound had ended his military career and hastened his move into the world of spying, or as he preferred to think of it, Intelligence. Spying, for Spunky, was a tawdry activity, full of duplicity and unpleasant people whose sole motivation was financial. They were like workers on the factory floor whereas he was in the boardroom, so to speak, turning their lead into gold.

Those who did not know him assumed he was a particularly ridiculous example of the silly ass Englishman. In many respects Spunky lived up to this description, happily and unwittingly. However, despite a personality that seemed dedicated to female conquest, drinking and yet more female conquest, a sharper brain lay hidden, well hidden in fact, beneath the blustering bonhomie.

Spunky had a genius for logistics. Show him data on factory output of widgets in the Ruhr and Spunky could translate this into aircraft numbers and timings on when they would be in the air. He turned statistics into meaningful information for a grateful military top brass.

Jack Murray

He predicted Britain and its allies would ultimately triumph over Germany because it had access to money. The growth of the wartime German economy had been decelerating since 1914 because of dwindling supplies of new labour. He recognised how Germany's decreasing access to raw material inputs, thanks to Britain's dominance of the sea, was putting enormous pressure on the enemy's finances. Compared to Germany, the allies had access to almost limitless resources to win the War, at least according to Spunky's estimates using the data coming from Britain's agents. This made him a gift for the recently formed British Special Intelligence Service led by Mansfield Cumming, known by close operatives as "C".

Spunky's approach to love was akin to a Maxim machine guns to targeting. Far, wide, and rapid fire. Although very much a man for the ladies, Spunky was not immune to romance. Just occasionally he would become more sniper than artillery.

Perhaps it was the prospect of spring in the air, maybe it was the ferment of compromise and rapprochement, although on reflection, Spunky realised there was precious little of it at the Peace Conference, or perhaps it was Paris itself. Something had happened to Spunky: he was in love. Or jolly close to it, anyway.

All in all, it was a tad inconvenient that the object of his affection had been arrested for murder. If the Dreyfuss affair was anything to go by, common sense, fair play, and tiny matters such as, for example, evidence, were a precious commodity. Spunky had little or no confidence in French impartiality. To give the police their due, the evidence in this case did seem superficially and troublingly material. Even more reason why it was important his great chum, Kit Aston, should get a shift on and throw his weight behind the cause.

Such thoughts lay heavily on Spunky as he sat alone amongst hundreds of Parisiennes and conference attendees watching a musical, or operetta, as they liked to call it here, called Phi Phi. He was enjoying the show immensely. On more than one occasion, Spunky had to clean his monocle to ensure a better view of the young ladies, many of whom seemed to have forgotten items of their clothing. In such ways did Spunky fill in his free time, trying to overcome the desolation of losing his love to the foibles of French justice.

The British empire brought a delegation numbering well over four hundred officials, advisers, clerks, and typists to the Paris Peace Conference. This veritable army of officialdom occupied five hotels in Paris, although Prime Minister Lloyd George wisely stayed away from the hotels choosing instead a luxurious flat in Rue Nicot, with former Prime Minister and able lieutenant in the meetings, Foreign Secretary Arthur Balfour, one floor above.

Spunky took residence at the largest of the hotels, the Majestic, near the Arc de Triomphe. Although not, as the name suggested, the pick of the crop, it suited Spunky's purpose nicely as it was very much a social centre. One of the reasons for its popularity was an arcane ruling by the British that officials could not have their wives stay with them. They stayed elsewhere. A similar rule did not apply to the voluminous number of female typists and even female journalists.

Spunky's strategy delivered wonderfully well. The presence of the debonair Spunky among such attractive and congenial company was an opportunity that an old hand, such as he could not fail to take advantage of. Consequently, he had enjoyed a few romantic interludes before he met her. The one. Or to be more accurate, the latest one.

Angela Malcolm was an attractive blonde in her mid-twenties, working as a typist for a small team liaising with the French delegation on detailed policy issues. Her fluency in French was matched by the speed of her shorthand, the nimbleness of her typing and the imaginative deployment of her unquestionable physical attributes in the cause of her latest amour.

They had met late afternoon at one of the regular series of dances enjoyed by delegates at the conference, a break from meetings to decide the future of Germany, the map of Europe but not the Middle East. Love dawned somewhere between the end of the second waltz and the commencement of a brisk foxtrot.

When Spunky attempted to sweep a girl off her feet, he went full tilt, charging gamely towards the enemy fire, guns blazing, although he stopped short at poetry. Champagne dinners followed at the Charles V, just beginning to return to its former pomp. Miss Malcolm was swept along the tide of romantic entertainment and Perrier-Jouet. She duly played an equal, active, in fact highly energetic and, on occasion, exotic, part as evening turned to night. All this crossed Spunky's mind, the next afternoon, as he sat dejectedly awaiting the arrival of Kit in the café of the Hotel Majestic.

At four in the afternoon, Kit made his appearance as arranged. He waved to Spunky as he approached the table. Kit noted with amusement how Spunky's attention seemed to have been diverted momentarily by a young nurse at a nearby table, *Plus ça change.*

'What ho, Kit,' said Spunky with a smile and a cheery wave, when he finally caught sight of his friend.

They shook hands and Kit sat down. Spunky attracted the attention of a waiter and ordered Kit a pot of tea. Then it was down to business.

'You look well, Spunky, so tell me more about what's happened.'

'You know me, Kit, I'm not the sort of chap to make an ass of myself at the first flutter of an eyelash, but my word, Angela is a real looker. Takes my breath away. Perfectly constructed too, I might add. And the best of it is, she's a suffragist, would you believe?'

'She has a real catch in you, Spunky,' said Kit sardonically as Spunky's eye was momentarily distracted by a young woman passing their table.

Spunky ignored the jibe and continued with a forensic analysis of her many qualities, mostly physical, before Kit finally interrupted to point out the most pertinent fact about the otherwise adorable Miss Malcolm.

'So, you mentioned she's in jail for murder, Spunky. Perhaps we should move on to this.'

'Good point, Kit, old chap. I like it. The old bloodhound is on the scent, what?'

'Not quite, you chump, I know nothing of the case or, indeed, the context for it. Perhaps we should start wide,' said Kit.

'Then zero in on the essentials,' finished Spunky, nodding his head sagely.

'Let's start with what's happening here,' suggested Kit, gesturing around him, 'at the conference'.

'Not sure what you've heard, but there's precious little sign of peace here, I can tell you. Nominally the conference is about punishment, payment, and prevention. The reality, in

Clemenceau's case, is more like pontificating, posturing and plunder. The state of play runs something like this. Everyone has come to the conference expecting to get a bit of the German pie, including Bulgaria, who fought with the blighters in the first place. They're claiming they hastened the end by declaring for peace early. Funny thing is, they probably will gain some land. Rumania has a claim on a piece of farming land called Banat. Serbia, or Yugoslavia, wants it too. Rumania have now occupied Transylvania, which tells you all you need to know about the Austro-Hungarian empire's position. If they think they can call upon an army of the dead, then they've been reading too much Bram Stoker.'

'The Balkan map is going to be re-drawn as Yugoslavia. This has offended Italy who wanted some of that land and don't like the idea of a strong south Slav state. So, they're doing everything they can to support Rumanian, Austrian, and Bulgarian demands. That's a mess.'

'Then we have the mandates,' continued Spunky.

'Which are?' asked Kit

'All those bits on the map that, in our humble opinion, aren't fit to govern themselves. That's everywhere outside of us and the Americans, if you ask me, and I'm not sure about the latter sometimes. Wilson can't even keep his own Congress under control.'

'Obviously, we want to protect the empire, and we want to make sure no one else can develop one, so we're broadly supportive of Wilson's idea that the League should have control on this. Bit like a trustee, I suppose. These are the mandates. We must keep an eye on France in the Middle East as well as Japan and China in the Far East. They're looking at some Russian territory.'

'What of our Russian former friends?' prompted Kit.

'Oddly Wilson and the Americans were sympathetic to their taking part. They sent some men over there, no doubt wined, dined and, well, you can imagine they were made very comfortable, lucky beggars. But Clemenceau and Churchill, I have to say, are adamant the Bolsheviks are the enemy, if not now then probably in the future. We both know they're right on that score.'

'Despite some misgivings about Wilson - he's a bit pious - he and Lloyd George get on pretty well and I think we're broadly supportive of the League. Wilson's completely obsessed with his League idea, by the way, which is just as well. Leaves the rest of us free to get on with the job in hand.'

'And France?' prompted Kit.

'Fair play to Clemenceau and the French, they don't discriminate based on colour or creed - they've given everyone the pip. In fact, the one thing uniting this conference is hatred of the Frenchies. Just to be reasonable to them for a second, shoot me if I'm longer, Clemenceau just wants France to be secure. I can see his point when you look at a map and lo and behold, there's Russia and Germany staring manically over your fence into the garden, holding a big pitchfork. Can't be very comforting. He's pointing this out to any man and his dog who'll listen. Personally, I think he's overplaying it, he just wants Alsace-Lorraine back. It's rich in coal and full of Germans. Sounds lovely. I don't think I'll be holidaying there anytime soon. Oh, and of course, the *piece de la resistance*, he also wants bags of money from Germany. And I mean bags.'

'France did lose lots of men.'

'True, Kit, and lots of factories and lots of everything, but we all did though. And no one has paid more towards this War than us.'

'Really?'

'Oh, Kit, come on, we bankrolled it for years. We were funding France and Russia, so much so, the Americans had to give us a wedge also. And let's face it, we're not getting anything back from the Russians any time soon. Especially since Reilly or whoever, tried to bump off Lenin. Now the Americans think they have the whip hand because we're all in their debt to some degree.'

'It sounds like a lot of fun,' laughed Kit, 'Well I think that's the context taken care of. Maybe you should tell me more about Miss Malcolm and what exactly happened.'

7

Kit and Spunky decamped to a quiet Italian ristorante at the latter's suggestion. The ristorante was full of Italians and clearly run by them, if the level of noise emanating from the kitchen was anything to go by.

'Can't stand the beastly French food,' explained Spunky. 'Italian is much better, and we get on better with them. Well, away from the meetings, anyway. Disagree with them on everything except food. They're wonderfully indiscreet and they can't stand the French, which is a plus.'

'I was going to ask about your role here,' smiled Kit.

'Information gathering, I leave to the worker bees, as you know,' pointed out Spunky airily.

'Such as me,' pointed out Kit, smiling affectionately.

'Quite so, Kit,' agreed Spunky, 'Actually while I have you here, all of this wonderful Italian food has given me an idea.'

Kit groaned inside. Spunky was perennially claiming poverty and coming up with various money-making schemes to fund his exorbitant lifestyle. So far, gambling appeared to be the only one that he was pursuing. Not without success, thought Kit, but it felt like his friend was playing Russian Roulette with providence.

'Not one of your hair-brained business ideas, Spunky. You're the son of a baronet, for goodness sake,' pointed out Kit.

'Bastard son, Kit, if you remember, and not the only one at that. The old man's generosity knows its bounds, unlike his libido. Anyway, pizzas, Kit.

'Pizzas?'

'Pizzas. Italians eat mountains of them, and I've acquired a taste for them myself. They're devilishly easy to make and very tasty. I was thinking a string of pizza ristorante's up and down the country would make a veritable skinful of money. What do you think?'

Kit's face expressed all the scepticism he felt. Spunky looked at his old friend and shook his head.

'The trouble with aristocrats is you lack a commercial nose,' admonished Spunky.

'I'm not sure how credible you are as an Italian restauranteur, Spunky old chap.'

'I was thinking *Stefano's* would be a good name, close enough to Stevens, don't you think?'

The conversation moved on to the main topic of interest. The murder. Kit cut short a rerun of Spunky's lyrical admiration of Miss Malcolm's physical qualities to focus on more material issues.

'Angela started work with the service three months ago. She's bilingual. Her father was French.'

'Was?'

'The old boy didn't make it through. I think he and the mother, who is English by the way, had separated by then, Angela stayed in England with the mother. Not sure why they split, but given he's French, I can think of at least one good reason.'

'So, what was her role here?' probed Kit.

'The biggest sticking point for the conference is how to make Germany pay. The Americans want reparations to be low to allow Germany to get back on its feet. They should be based on the damage they've done.'

'Is there a problem with this?'

'Well yes, to be frank. It would mean all the money would go to France and Belgium, we'd end up with bugger all despite a million men dead or maimed.'

'I see, so we want Germany to pay a lot more.'

'Yes, but not as much as the French. I think they want to turn the Germans into slaves for the next few generations based on the demands they're making. The problem is Lloyd George is under a lot of public pressure from the Daily Mail and the like to make Germany pay. This isn't helped by the split among his advisers. Do you remember Keynes? He's here. He's advocating lower reparations and opening up trade in Europe.'

'Makes sense. Last thing we want is to cripple Germany and start another war if they fall to the Bolsheviks.'

'You would think. Unfortunately, there's a couple of real hardliners whispering in Lloyd's ear too, Cunliffe and Sumner. They want to squeeze Germany until the pips squeak. Lloyd's stuck in the middle of this and we need to get some alignment or bang some sense into the French, hence this series of meetings we've been having with them and the Americans.'

'So, Angela was acting as a translator at these meetings?'

'No, taking notes. She's great with her hands, Kit, believe me,' said Spunky wistfully.

'I don't doubt it, Spunky, but tell me, exactly what happened?'

'Well, bloodhound, this was the third session for the group. Obviously, I wasn't there. I heard all this second hand. Angela went to get some water for the various officials. She poured water into each of the glasses. The French chap, in question, Monsieur Mantoux took one drink and then keeled over.'

Spunky slammed the table for added effect, causing several diners to look around and Kit to glare at his friend. A sheepish Spunky turned away from the rest of the room.

'So he was poisoned. Did the police check the contents of the glass for poison?'

'They did. And found nothing.'

Kit looked aghast at his friend, 'On what grounds was Miss Malcolm arrested then?'

'Well there you have the British point of view in a nutshell. Everyone has been keeping a lid on it, but I can tell you, Lloyd is livid. He thinks the French are going to use this to undermine our opposition to excessive reparations as well as all the other trifling matters like the Middle East. It's a damn sticky situation here, Kit, particularly for poor Angela. You know they still have the guillotine here. We need your bloodhound qualities on the case.'

'Tell me about who else was in the meeting,' suggested Kit.

'On the French side, aside from Mantoux, there was his attractive secretary, mademoiselle Deschamps and then two advisers, Courtois and Simon. Both are relatively young, neither fought in the War, don't seem the type, to be honest. Look like they graduated from the Sorbonne last year.'

'On the American side you have Miss Morris, who tries to look like a spinster with a cat. Fluent in French, spent many summers here apparently. I wouldn't be surprised if she bats for the other side if you catch my meaning. The head man is Terrell. Not everyone's marmalade but a sharp mind, knows what the game is and wants to block French manoeuvres. Then we have one other, I hesitate to use the word, gentleman, chap called Hart.'

'Why do you say that?'

'Let's say he set his cap, or should I say cowboy hat towards Angela,' said Spunky rolling his finger around the lip of his wine glass slowly, 'this was one war the Americans lost. Yes indeed, Kit old chap, the Union Jack flutters gloriously once more...'

Kit held his hand up and interrupted, 'Good show, Spunky. Kept the British end up, did you?'

'Horrible fellow, loud, abrasive, thinks America rules the world. Needed taking down a peg or two.'

'And on the British side, apart from Miss Malcolm?' continued Kit.

'Leading our delegation to the meeting is Monk, who is anything but if the stories are true, and then two arrogant fools, Fink-Nottle and Geddes. Always getting them mixed up. Monk is a steady hand on the tiller, well regarded by Balfour, which is good enough for me. Can be left on his own, doesn't need to be nannied. So there you have the layout. That's the list of suspects, if that's how you want to think of them, bloodhound.'

'I'll be allowed to speak to them and Miss Malcolm also?'

'Yes, I've arranged for you to see Angela tomorrow morning.'

'Excellent – how is she holding up?' asked Kit.

'She's an absolute brick. We built empires with girls like that'

And a well-drilled artillery against spears, thought Kit. The evening ended and they made a short walk back to the hotel. Paris was as cold as London, thought Kit as they strolled along the Champs Elysees past lovers, beggars and soldiers. Paris seemed to be regaining its special atmosphere that had been absent since 1914. The women Kit saw, were well-dressed, the lights of the shops and the night spots glowed alluringly. It felt good to be back in very different circumstances to the last time he had been to the city.

At the hotel, Kit and Spunky went to the hotel café for a nightcap. A waiter came over to Kit and handed him a note. Kit took a moment to read the note then looked up at Spunky.

'Good lord, my man's been arrested for brawling.'

'Really, I would have thought Hargreaves a bit old for that sort of thing. Still, shows you never can tell.'

'He's somewhat dead as well, Spunky. It's my new man Harry Miller, the chap who saved my life at Cambrai.'

Spunky nodded, 'Ah yes, remember now about poor Hargreaves. Sorry. Well let's get your man out of the clink.'

'Don't worry, Spunky, best I handle it. You turn in.'

Just as they were about to rise, Spunky put his head in his hands and said, 'Oh no.'

Kit looked concerned for his friend, 'Spunky, what's wrong?'

A few moments later a man appeared clutching a bottle of champagne and gave Spunky the sort of over friendly pat on the back that would have had many a man asking the culprit to name his seconds.

'Don't think you can hide like that, Spunky old chap,' said the new arrival, 'Lord Aston, what a pleasant surprise. What brings you over to Paris? Rescuing damsels?'

Kit looked up and realised the reason for Spunky's dismay. Percy Pendlebury looked down at the two men, exhibiting all the benevolence half a bottle of consumed champagne could create. Pendlebury was a newspaper gossip columnist who revelled in revealing high society liaisons and lapses, living proof that you could run with the hare while stealing its golden eggs. Pendlebury removed his cloak with a flourish and threw it over a nearby chair.

'Go away, Percy,' said Spunky gloomily, looking up at Pendlebury.

'Nonsense, old chap, just arrived,' replied Pendlebury, ignoring Spunky's entreaty and sitting down, 'So what's the skinny?'

'I have no comment to make, Percy, nor has Kit,' said Spunky rising with Kit.

'I say, chaps, don't be like that,' replied Pendlebury holding up the champagne, 'You wouldn't let a man drink alone?'

'Watch me,' replied Spunky, giving a mock salute before adding under his breath, 'Fathead.'.

Pendlebury shrugged and called out to the two men as they departed, 'So be it chaps, but I'll be reporting on this French diplomat affair, whether you want me to or not.'

Jack Murray

8

Harry Miller strolled along the Champs Elysees towards the Arc de Triomphe. He'd seen pictures of the monument, but the scale of the street and the size of the monument impressed him more than he could say. At the same time, he couldn't help thinking about the lives ruined. No memorial, no matter how impressive, could ever convey the loss, the pain suffered by so many. However, its existence, and its scale was recognition, at least, that many hundreds of thousands of lives are blighted by war, and not just those on the battlefield.

Miller ducked down a side street near the crest of the Champs Elysees. It seemed full of life and there were many restaurants. Over the years in France, Miller had picked up a smattering of the language. Much of his life at or near the front had been spent waiting. As a way of filling in the many empty hours he had begun studying French. One or two of his comrades taught those who were interested. It was a respite from the War, at least until the rumble of guns reminded him of where he was and what lay ahead. Reading the menus staked to the billboards outside the restaurant was not a problem. One restaurant also had a menu in English. He walked inside.

The interior was large, with dark wood panelling and large mirrors on the walls. There was a dozen or so tables in the middle with seating along the walls. Miller caught the attention of a waiter who pointed to an empty table for two. The restaurant was crowded, the noise levels high, thanks mainly to a group of Americans sat nearby. Miller glanced in their direction. The laughter of the American table filled the space, suffocating the good humour of other patrons, as far as Miller could tell.

The waiter came over, took one look at Miller, and said, 'English?'

'*Oui, mais je parle Francais un peut,*' responded Miller. He glanced involuntarily at his clothes, wondering how the waiter could tell from one look he was English. Are we so badly dressed, he wondered?

'I prefer to practice my English,' said the waiter with a smile.

Miller sat down and reviewed the menu. A few minutes later, the waiter returned, and he made his order. Miller sat back to enjoy the buzz all around him. English accents filled the air, aside from the Americans. At the table beside his, he sensed two young women looking at him. Finally, one of the young women took up the courage to speak.

'Hello there, yours is a familiar accent.'

She was a Londoner. Miller smiled at her, 'I'm from Peckham, you?'

'Clapham, Ida's from Croydon. I'm Ethel, by the way.'

She reached over and shook Miller's hand. Ethel was about Miller's age. Her smile was friendly, her accent like his. Ethel's companion seemed quieter. While Ethel was on the right side of plump, Ida was slender, and on Miller's second surreptitious glance, pretty.

At her suggestion, Miller joined them, 'I hope you don't mind; we're getting a bit concerned about that bunch of Americans over there. They keep looking at us.'

'You're both attractive girls, can't fault a man for that,' said Miller, laughing, 'We're all guilty as charged on that score.'

Both girls laughed. They chatted more. Miller found out that they were nurses stationed at a nearby hospital for British soldiers. Each had arrived towards the end of the conflict to deal with thousands of casualties coming back from the field stations. Listening to them describe their daily duties, Miller realised the word hero didn't just apply to those who had been at the front. It made him feel guilty as he realised how little thought he had given to the hospitals. Many had served. Suffering and pain were not reserved solely for the fallen and their families.

As the evening wore on, Miller became increasingly aware of what had concerned the two women. The attentions of the group of Americans were apparent not just in the looks being thrown the nurses' way but also in some ribald comments. On more than one occasion the nurses restrained Miller from going over to have a word, as he described it.

Finally, the loudest of the group made his unsteady way over to where Miller and the nurses were seated. He clapped a none too gentle hand on Miller's shoulder, leaned down so that everyone could enjoy the full impact of alcohol on his breath.

'Hey ladies, when you've finished with the loser here, you're welcome to join the guys.'

He gesticulated somewhere in the general vicinity of where the other Americans were seated. Miller glanced over at the other men. They seemed somewhat alarmed by their friend's behaviour, but none were making a move to prevent him. Miller guessed they were subordinates. He understood their dilemma and nodded to them that there was nothing to worry about.

Finally, one of the drunk's party called out, 'Hey Howie, leave them alone, let's split this joint.'

Howie waved them away. He was on a mission now. Turning his erratic gaze away from the two women and onto Miller, he said in a caricature of an English accent, 'I say, old chap, would you mind pushing off?'

Miller rolled his eyes at the ladies and ignored him. However, he was aware the man was large and well built. If it came to a fight, Miller knew how to handle himself. With his speed and agility, he fancied himself against the larger man. It helped that he wasn't drunk also He hoped it wouldn't come to this. He'd had his fill of fighting. Seconds later, the choice was taken out of his hands.

A powerful hand grabbed Miller's shoulder and pulled him away from the table. In an instant Miller was on his feet, pivoting round to face his opponent. He ducked one punch from the American and landed one of his own in the stomach. It felt like his hand connected with concrete. The American was more impressively made than he had suspected.

The American's next punch was more successful although Miller managed to avoid the full force by weaving away in time. Just as well. His eye felt like it had been hit by a sledgehammer, even though it was only a glancing blow. Miller jabbed two quick punches at the American, careful not to hit too hard. It would be easy to break a hand on this man's face. Each connected with the

American's eye. Both men would have something to show for the evening's entertainment.

By now the café was cheering on the two pugilists. It wasn't difficult to tell, thought Miller, who the crowd was rooting for. The next punch from the American was an attempted haymaker which Miller easily slipped. Such was its force, the momentum carried the big American forward and out the door, conveniently opened by the waiter who had served Miller earlier.

Miller nodded to the waiter and said, '*Merci beaucoup.*'

'*De rien.*'

He followed the American out of the café to finish off the job, only to find him being helped to his feet by two stern looking Gendarmes. Both took out truncheons and held them threateningly. Miller decided challenging their authority would not be his most inspired idea and held his hands up. The American was getting to his feet slowly. Miller could see a swelling over his left eye. He could also feel a stinging on his own eye.

Behind him he heard the two nurses arriving on the scene along with an irate café owner. He was gesticulating at Miller and the big American and speaking too rapidly for Miller to understand, but it wasn't difficult to guess the gist of it.

-

'I hope you're not going to make a habit of this, Harry,' said Kit as he greeted his manservant at the police station.

Miller smiled ruefully, 'I would have preferred to avoid it, sir, but I hadn't much of a choice.'

'What happened?'

Miller briefly explained the circumstances leading up to the fight. He could see on Kit's face a mixture of amusement and irritation at the actions of the big American. He also seemed very interested in the two nurses.

'I don't suppose one of them was called Mary by any chance?' asked Kit hopefully.

'No sir, Ida and Ethel.'

Kit looked disappointed and he could see the concern on Miller's face.

'She was the nurse at the station after you picked me up in No Man's Land. Have I mentioned what a damn fool you were?'

'In passing sir,' smiled Miller.

'Anyway, what were they like?' said Kit.

'I would say more my sort than yours, sir, if you don't mind me saying.'

Kit looked a little disheartened by this before returning his attention to Miller.

'You'll be glad to know I've straightened this little mess out with the gendarmes, I'll also see the restaurant right. I don't blame you, Harry. In fact, once again if I may say, I think your actions speak well of you. It sounds like you know how to deal with these situations.'

'I prefer to avoid them. But if push comes to shove, sir, I won't be running off into a corner.'

'Good to know. Anyway, let's hope this little fracas hasn't caused a breach in Anglo-American relations,' smiled Kit.

It was now well after midnight. Kit led Miller out of the cell and into the reception area at the station. As the two men left the police station, Kit noted a plain clothes detective looking at them. He had clearly just arrived as his raincoat and hat were still on. His eyes followed them all the way out, a gendarme clearly explaining who they were.

'I wonder who that was, sir,' said Miller as they arrived at the street.

'You saw him too, then?'

'I have a feeling he knew who you were, sir,' pointed out Miller.

'Me too, Harry. That said, my presence and role here is not exactly a state secret. I suspect I may be meeting our friend again soon.'

The Kit Aston Novellas

9

Hotel Majestic, Paris: 13th February 1919

'So, you've sprung John L. Sullivan then?' said Spunky by way of greeting as Kit arrived to join him at breakfast.

Kit laughed and explained the circumstances leading to Miller's arrest. Both agreed that Miller had done everything expected of him and put up a damned good show, high praise indeed from Spunky. When they had finished breakfasting, they left the dining room just as Percy Pendlebury was arriving.

'Off somewhere, chaps? Need company?'

'We'll let you know Percy,' said Kit, smiling at the journalist.

Spunky and Kit walked outside. The doorman hailed a taxi. They climbed into the first one and much to the surprise of the cabman, Spunky asked to be taken to jail.

'It's the same one Harry was in last night,' announced Kit as the taxi pulled up outside a few minutes later. He wondered about the police detective he'd seen earlier that morning.

Inside the reception area, Kit and Spunky had to wait nearly half an hour before they could see Miss Malcolm. With some dismay, Kit noted how many soldiers were there, either coming to collect colleagues or be released. He reflected on how difficult it would be for them to be assimilated back into civilian life. This was a challenge Britain was facing also, not just France. The wait seemed to make Spunky unusually agitated. From time to time he rose to his feet in impatience, ready to march over to the desk to demand immediate attention.

'These French chaps are colossally inefficient, have you noticed? Just like their food, needlessly complicated, over affected and takes forever to arrive. I'm going to have a word.'

'Sit down. If there's one thing guaranteed to extend our stay, it's officialdom seeing their best endeavours bearing fruit,' pointed out Kit.

'Sage advice, old fellow,' said Spunky resuming his seat.

Kit looked at his friend with amusement and decided to add another sage point while the going was good, 'Spunky, old chap, I think it best if I see her on my own. Do you mind?'

'Understand perfectly, bloodhound. Send her my love, old boy,' said Spunky cheerily. His confidence in Kit's abilities knew no bounds but, worryingly, it added to the pressure he was feeling.

Finally, a gendarme arrived and led Kit through to the holding cell housing Miss Malcolm. The door opened, and Kit found himself looking at the girl who appeared to have stolen the heart of his friend.

Angela Malcolm was as attractive and as agreeably proportioned as Spunky's highly detailed description had led him to believe. His friend's assessment that she was bearing up well also seemed true on first acquaintance. Very accurate, in fact. As Kit entered the holding cell, she rose slowly and gazed at him coolly.

'Miss Malcolm,' said Kit, extending his hand, 'I'm Kit Aston.'

Angela Malcolm nodded in recognition and shook his hand. She looked at him up and down unashamedly. If she liked what she saw, she did not say but her face wore a permanent half-smile. Kit found her smile both difficult to interpret and undeniably alluring. Her blonde hair was shoulder length and fell over her eyes. This added much to her sensuality and no little to the sense of mystique.

'Thank you for taking an interest in my case,' said Miss Malcolm, evenly, 'Aldric mentioned you had some experience in these matters.'

Her voice was slightly deeper, her delivery slow. The overall affect was very pleasant suggesting not only someone who had been privately educated but who found the whole experience amusing. Kit was surprised to hear his friend, called Aldric, but then realised it could hardly be any other way. Both sat down and after assuring her of Spunky's continuing admiration, Kit began the interview.

'I gather your father is French,' said Kit by way of opening their conversation.

'Yes, but he left us, my mother and me, that is, when I was relatively young, I didn't know him very well, then the War came,' explained Miss Malcolm. She had no trace of any accent other than English concluded Kit, but he was curious to hear her French.

'You lost him in the War,' asked Kit in French.

She confirmed he had died at Verdun two years previously. Despite being over the conscription age, he had volunteered immediately after Germany had invaded Belgium.

All of this was said in faultless French, but although Kit did not have the same expertise in this language as in Russian and German, he detected an Englishness to her pronunciation. He wasn't sure if this was natural or feigned. Either could have been true with this young woman. Returning to English, Kit asked her to explain her role at the conference.

'I came over from the start. There weren't many fluent French speakers capable of simultaneous translation and shorthand. I was in demand,' she said, the half-smile reappearing. Kit was conscious that he was being assessed every bit as much as he was assessing her. She continued her explanation.

'Agreement on the reparations is a tricky area and there's little consensus on how we calculate and distribute what Germany must pay,' explained Miss Malcom, 'Sir Jonathan wanted someone who could pick up on the nuance and tone of what our French counterparts were saying not just in the translation but also in our notes. Hence my promotion to this role. I must say I've found it all fascinating.'

'I'm sure you have,' smiled Kit, 'These are historic times. What gets done here will impact the rest of the century for good or ill. Can you tell me more about the morning in question, please, Miss Malcolm?'

Miss Malcolm went on to describe what had happened.

'We all entered the room together.

'Was it locked or already open?' asked Kit.

'It had been locked previously, so I was not in before anyone else. Everyone sat down at their usual places. Sir Jonathan asked me to pour everyone a glass of water. I tend to do this at each of the meetings. I did as he bid, then Monsieur Mantoux seemed to have a seizure, seconds later he was face down on the table, dead.'

Kit noted that Miss Malcolm remained calm and did not appear to be upset in retelling what had happened. He found this admirable but at the same time strange. Perhaps, he reflected, the world really was changing, and the weaker sex were no longer prepared to play the role of the hysterical, frivolous female or coquettish female. Whatever Miss Malcolm's allure was it was not based on anything so obvious as fluttering eyelashes.

'Why have they arrested you?' pressed Kit.

'I don't know, Lord Aston', replied Miss Malcolm. Kit looked at her and knew she was lying. Even more interestingly, he sensed Miss Malcolm knew this also.

'One last thing,' said Kit, 'Is Malcolm your mother's maiden name?'

'Yes, my father was Delaroche.'

The rest of the interview was short and established two things in Kit's mind. Firstly, Miss Malcolm was not telling the whole story and secondly, she was remarkably calm given her situation. Kit was sure the two observations were related.

Kit re-joined Spunky at the front of the police station. Much to Kit's surprise, Spunky was talking to the same plain clothes policeman Kit had seen in the early hours of the morning. Spunky introduced the two men.

'Kit let me present Inspector Briant. He is leading the investigation on Angela. Inspector Briant, my friend Lord Aston.'

As Spunky had spoken in English, Kit did likewise, not wishing to tip his hand he understood French well.

'Inspector Briant,' smiled Kit, shaking the Frenchman's hand.

'Lord Aston,' said Briant. His face remained grave, partly a result of the moustache which was heavy enough to disguise any smile, 'A pleasure to meet a hero of the War.'

'There were millions of heroes, Inspector, as you know,' said Kit in response.

'*Oui, d'accord,*' responded Briant nodding his head, 'I understand you are here to look at the investigation.'

'I'm sure the Sûreté have matters under control,' said Kit.

'But yet you are here, Lord Aston,' pointed out Briant shrewdly.

'Lord Aston is representing His Majesty's Government, Inspector,' interrupted Spunky, 'I hope we can enjoy full cooperation in this matter which involves a British subject.'

'She's also a French subject, Monsieur Stevens,' replied Briant.

The introductions over, Kit and Spunky departed. The meeting with Miss Malcolm and Briant had left Kit with an uneasy feeling. There was a lot more to this matter than Spunky was aware of and he suspected both Briant and Miss Malcolm knew much more than either would ever admit.

The next appointment was with the head of the British delegation, Sir Jonathan Monk. The meeting took place in the same room in which the French diplomat had met his end. Kit had enough time to survey the room. There were no other doors apart from the one they had entered. It was on the fifth floor of the hotel, so access from outside would have been difficult. The only keys to the room, according to Spunky, were with Monk himself with spare keys held by the cleaning staff in the hotel.

Kit had not met Monk previously, but Spunky's assessment was of a very intelligent individual who was an ideal representative in such delicate discussions. He was a 'lifer' at the Foreign Office, but an economist by training. He counted Keynes among his friends, which told Kit a great deal about his attitude to Germany's reparations.

When Monk arrived, Kit was surprised at his relative youth. Kit judged him to be no more than forty-five. He was good looking with a distinguished manner that never strayed as far as pomposity. A serious man conducting serious business on behalf of his country, was Kit's immediate assessment. After the initial introductions, Spunky left the two men to the room.

'I won't detain you too long, Sir Jonathan, I recognise how busy you must be.'

'It's not a problem, Lord Aston. This is a sad business, and I don't for one second believe Angela has done anything wrong. Take as long as you need. I'll help you in any way that I can.'

Kit asked for a summary of what he had seen during the fateful meeting. Monk's summary tallied exactly with Miss Malcolm's. He confirmed he was the only key holder also and the room had been locked prior to his arrival. Kit ascertained further Monk clearly had a great deal of respect for Miss Malcolm and repeatedly complimented her professionalism. He could offer no reason as to why Miss Malcolm might want to kill the diplomat. Nor could he shed much light on everyone's whereabouts prior to the meeting.

As delicately as he could, Kit teased out more about the atmosphere between the parties in the room. It was apparent Monk had little time for his French counterpart, nor had the Americans.

'They, particularly Mantoux, are blocking everything. In my view reparations should be fair and proportionate. Enough to allow Germany to rebuild. We must avoid the Bolsheviks getting a toehold in Germany. Mantoux is obstinate to the point where you would think he didn't care if there was more conflict. Even Clemenceau recognises there is a point at which the Germans will just say *nein*. Frankly if the Bolsheviks did take over in Germany, France will have a much bigger headache to deal with than they've ever had before.'

'You say the Americans are with us on this?'

'Yes and no. Yes, they dislike French obduracy. They hated Mantoux. But they're holding Wilson's line about the League being the forum for all of this. We're with the French on this. We'll get our way in the end. It may be American money everyone owes, but it was our men, French and British, who bore the brunt. Russians too, but they've effectively cut themselves off from this.'

The issue of what everyone was doing prior to the meeting was beginning to take on increased significance in Kit's view and he took it up with his next two appointments, the other British delegates. The motive remained unclear but Kit's instincts, which he trusted implicitly, were telling him Briant could offer more in this area.

The meetings with Fink-Nottle and Geddes were next. Spunky had been none too impressed with them but Kit resolved to form his own judgement. Too often Spunky had been disparaging about people Kit liked, for reasons surpassing understanding but possibly related to a certain sniffi-ness on his friend's part for the middle class or potential love rivals.

The first man mentioned by Spunky, was certainly not in the latter category. Julian Fink-Nottle was young and clearly bright. Kit earmarked him as a man who would go far in the Foreign Office. His interests were foreign affairs, diplomacy, and newts, in roughly that order. He arrived at the meeting with Kit wearing an ill-fitting suit, a shirt that looked like he'd ironed it himself in the dark and a bowler hat that was once black. Kit wondered what public school he'd been to.

He added little fresh to what Monk had told him on the murder but did enrich Kit's understanding about the mating habits of semiaquatic salamandridae. It was clear poor Fink-Nottle would be hard-pushed, even in as licentious an environment as the Paris conference, to match up to the colourful courtship manoeuvres of the pleurodelinae.

Gerald Geddes was, an altogether, different proposition to Fink-Nottle. Kit guessed immediately he combined Spunky's two dislikes. Slightly older than Fink-Nottle, he was infinitely worldlier. As tall and as well made as Kit, his hair was dark but with hard grey eyes that were taking Kit's measure every bit as much as Kit was examining him. His Saville Row suit was pinstriped and clung to his muscular frame. From his side pocket, he took out a silver cigarette case and offered one to Kit, who declined.

Geddes seemed like someone who should have fought in the War, but, according to Spunky had not. He had remained at the Foreign Office throughout the conflict. Looking at the man before him, Kit could tell he had been involved in the War, but perhaps not on the front line. There was little value on attempting to tease out what his role had really been. A thought occurred to him about how much Spunky really knew of the operatives working for Intelligence.

'What did you make of Mantoux?'

'A blocker. I won't miss him,' replied Geddes.

Geddes made no attempt to express the usual sentiments death required from people. Yes, thought Kit, you've been around death before.

'Do you think Miss Malcolm murdered Mantoux?'

'The charge is ridiculous,' stated Geddes.

'I know, and I think the Sûreté know this also, but that wasn't my question,' pointed out Kit.

'She's a cool customer, but murderer?'

This still wasn't an answer to his question, but Kit let it slide for now. Getting Geddes to give a straight answer was proving trickier than catching smoke.

'What do you make of her?' asked Kit.

'You've met her?' asked Geddes in response. Kit nodded, so he continued, 'The same as you, I suspect'.

'What do you think she's keeping back?'

Geddes was momentarily surprised by Kit's directness. Slowly he began to smile.

'Your friend Mr Stevens was, shall we say, courting her?'

Kit did not respond and waited for Geddes to continue.

'She's an attractive girl. I imagine many men would admire her,' said Geddes.

'You?'

'No, call me an old-fashioned sort of chap, but I prefer monogamy from the women I'm seeing,' replied Geddes, still smiling calmly.

Geddes smiled at the reaction from Kit. 'Who else was she seeing?' prompted Kit.

'Our esteemed and inaccurately named leader, Monk, for one.'

10

Kit updated Spunky on the initial meetings but tactfully neglected to mention the question mark over the extent of Miss Malcolm's ardour for his friend. Instead, he chose a different tack and suggested Spunky might be of great service if he could find out as much about Miss Malcolm as possible. This would have the dual benefit of establishing both the veracity of her story and, perhaps, if Geddes was not merely spreading tittle tattle, create seeds of doubt in Spunky's mind.

'I'd like to know more about Fink-Nottle and Geddes,' added Kit.

Spunky snorted at this, 'One's a fool and the other's full of himself if you ask me.'

Having met the two gentlemen in question, Kit agreed with this assessment but felt more background information on them would not go amiss.

'What is Geddes here to do?' asked Kit.

'He's some sort of German expert at the Foreign Office.,' answered Spunky, not without a hint of derision.

'I'll bet his experience is first-hand,' said Kit enigmatically. They parted soon after as Spunky claimed to have a lunch appointment in Montparnasse.

'I gather it's where all the up-and-coming artists are. I might find the new Picasso or Matisse.'

'I can't think of anything more horrible, Spunky,' laughed Kit, whose tastes were decidedly old fashioned.

'That's the whole idea, Kit old chap,' laughed Spunky on his way out, 'the worse it looks the more it'll be worth in a few years. That's how the art market works. Mark my words.'

-

Kit took Miller away from the hotel for a quiet lunch in a restaurant well away from the centre. As the day was quite pleasant, they sat outside on the pavement and watched Parisiennes promenade past. There were unlikely to be many foreigners in this part of the city, so Kit and Miller could talk without fear of being overheard. At the end of the street Kit pointed out where the Bastille used to stand.

'Please do me the honour of avoiding ending up in a similar sort of place, Harry.'

'I shall try, sir. No promises mind,' said Miller with a grin.

Kit updated Miller on what had taken place in the morning at the police station.

'Two visits to the same police station within eight hours is a first for me.'

'Sorry, sir'

'No matter, Harry. I think I can use you tomorrow. We need to speak to the Majestic's staff. If anyone knows what's going on in the hotel it'll be them.'

'Not sure my French is quite up to it but one of the girls I met last night might be able to help. Ida's French is very good,' suggested Miller.

'Do you think Ida will help?' asked Kit. 'I can get Spunky to pull a few strings and get her the morning off tomorrow.'

'I'm sure she'll be happy to help. She seems a plucky sort,' agreed Miller. He wasn't sure yet if he was attracted to Ida, but he admired her tremendously. The thought of renewing a friendship with her appealed, especially in an interesting cause.

'I'll speak to Spunky when he gets back from his art speculation,' said Kit.

Miller raised his eyes to question what Kit meant. Kit shook his head and laughed.

'You don't want to know. Suffice to say, Spunky is always on the lookout for ways to supplement his income.'

-

Kit's afternoon meetings were with the American delegation. The senior American diplomats, aside from President Wilson, had based themselves at the Hotel Crillon. As Kit entered the hotel, he was immediately aware of the security. The Americans were taking no chances with anarchists.

Unlike the Majestic, the Crillon was small, and the Americans were renting offices nearby for managing their affairs. Kit assumed the meetings would take place at one of these offices. However, he was taken to the second floor and shown into one of the bedrooms. Kit noted some guards on the rooms he passed. Spunky had mentioned that the third floor was even more heavily guarded. The most senior diplomats resided there.

Kit was led into an enormous, high-ceilinged room, with white panelling on the walls. No stinting on luxury, reflected Kit as he entered the room. Three people were sat at a table, two men and one woman. The two men stood up. The younger of the two men was large and was sporting a black eye, not dissimilar to Miller's.

The older man noted Kit's gaze and smiled but with a trace of irritation.

'Lord Aston, I am Colonel Andrew Terrell,' said the older man holding out his hand, 'May I introduce Miss Evelyn Morris, and this is Mr Howard Hart. As you can see, my colleague's been enjoying the Paris nightlife.' His accent bespoke someone from the deep south.

'With one of your fellow countrymen,' added Hart, 'I look forward to getting re-acquainted.'

Might happen sooner than you think, thought Kit, who merely smiled and shook everyone's hands.

'If you don't mind, Lord Aston, I've asked that you meet us all together. Clearly, we're not accused of anything, nor do I anticipate we will be,' added Terrell meaningfully.

'I'm sure you have no need to worry on that score, Colonel. I'm just trying to establish the order of events. We want to ensure Miss Malcolm receives fair treatment with evidence that is accurate,' replied Kit but he was unhappy at the arrangement proposed. He would have preferred individual interviews.

'It's a ridiculous charge,' interrupted Hart.

'Really?' prompted Kit.

'Of course. She just poured the drinks. She couldn't have added anything without us seeing. You ask me the French don't have a clue what they're doing.'

Terrell glanced at Hart with ill-disguised irritation.

'Thank you, Howard. Perhaps we should let Lord Aston ask the questions.'

The interview added little new in terms of the immediate events surrounding Mantoux's seizure but did improve Kit's understanding of what happened in the period just before the meeting commenced. The attendees had met up in the corridor outside the room and the greetings had taken place before they had entered. Miss Malcolm was the second last to arrive. Fink-Nottle showed up as the meeting had begun, much to the irritation of Monk, who had admonished him with a stern look as he made his way round the table shaking hands.

Kit wondered what had delayed Miss Malcolm and logged it away to ask her next time he saw her. Nothing else emerged from the meeting other than confirmation of Spunky's impressions about Terrell being a shrewd individual, Miss Morris seemed a quietly efficient woman with the emphasis on quiet, and Hart being a bit of a blow hard. On more than one occasion Terrell had to rein him in. This was disappointing but understandable. However, there were moments when Kit wondered if there wasn't an element of performance in his manner. It was a look in the eye, fleeting, but enough to make Kit wonder. Hart accompanied Kit out of the room and walked with him down the stairs to the lobby.

'Would you like a drink, Lord Aston?" asked Hart as they passed the hotel bar.

Kit looked at Hart in surprise and nodded. This was unexpected given how much Terrell had wanted to control the flow of information. Kit couldn't decide if this was with Terrell's tacit permission or a display of insubordination from a loose cannon. The two men sat down and appraised one another.

'Tell me more about what you want, Lord Aston.'

'The truth.'

Hart smiled and rolled his eyes, 'How noble.'

'This is a British...'

'And French,' interrupted Hart with a smile.

'And French lady, who has been arrested on the back of precious little by way of evidence.'

'We agree on that. Why you, may I ask? Why not a member of Scotland Yard?'

This was a pertinent question and probably had as much to do with control as getting to the truth.

'I've had some experience in the past. Why do you think she's innocent?'

'She's certainly not innocent but, in this case, I don't think she's guilty of murder.' The smile on Hart's face made Kit certain that he knew more than he would communicate. Kit moved the conversation on to Paris and the Peace Conference, suspecting that further questions on the murder would not yield much more from the big American. In fact it seemed to Kit, Hart was pumping him for information.

-

Kit left the Crillon and made his way back to the Majestic. It was late afternoon, and the sun was shining which made the air pleasant, not too cold. Tempting though it was to walk, Kit elected to take a carriage back to the hotel. He was still getting used to his prosthetic limb. Rather than go directly, he asked the carriage driver to make a detour along the Seine via Notre Dame. He had arranged to meet Spunky for an aperitif in the Majestic around five. Spunky was a little late, unusual for him. The prospect of a bracer with an old chum required no second invitation and he was usually at his post when the bugle blew. As Kit waited in the bar, he spotted Fink-Nottle sitting alone near the window, reading through some documents. Kit walked over to him.

'May I join you for a moment, Mr Fink-Nottle?'

'Of course, Lord Aston.'

'I have one other question, just so that I can tie up some loose ends. I gather you were late for the meeting. Is that so?'

'Yes, overslept. Never done it before,' replied Fink-Nottle with an ingratiating smile. He seemed like a puppy to Kit, eager to please.

'Have you worked with Sir Jonathan, Mr Geddes and Miss Malcolm long?' asked Kit as the conversation ended.

'Only Sir Jonathan. I became acquainted with Mr Geddes and Miss Malcolm at the conference, but we've worked quite closely since.'

'Do you think Miss Malcolm capable of murder?'

Fink-Nottle's answer was a beat slower and less vehement than Kit would have believed from someone who claimed to have a close working relationship. It seemed to Kit few people really believed she had killed Mantoux, but he sensed they believed her capable of it.

-

Spunky finally arrived twenty minutes late, looking like he had already partaken of a moderate skinful. He sat heavily on the seat and attracted the attention of the waiter to order two more of whatever Kit was drinking. He was manifestly in a high state of pippedness.

'Productive trip, old chap?' inquired Kit.

'I tell you, Kit, these artist chappies, like to enjoy life,' said Spunky, in a slightly slurred voice.

'You seemed to have joined them,' pointed out Kit.

'You know me, I wouldn't dream of being rude.'

'How was it then? Have you found the next Picasso or Monet?'

'Well there were a number of chaps I was drinking with who show promise. I went back with them to their flats. How the other half live. Anyway, they all showed me examples of their work. Each worse than the next. Some of them didn't try to paint anything, they just splashed a lot of random colours down and voila! But it lacked that special badness that I was looking for. I mean it's one thing to be a talentless hack, anyone can be that. But I wanted was something truly hideous. I was going to draw the line at obscene although, I can tell you, I saw a few things that I might keep for my private collection.'

Kit rolled his eyes at this but let Spunky hold forth.

'Anyway, I pretty much rejected the idea of the more colourful pieces. Their banality was overwhelming, but I could see they might appeal based on the colours they were chucking on the canvas. What I wanted was something that would not be understood, something that was going to be the emperor's new clothes for this generation. And I think I may have found it.'

This peaked Kit's interest and he leaned forward.

'Chap called Duchamp. Very likeable, speaks good English I might add, pity about the American inflexions. He takes everyday objects and declares them art. Ready-mades, he calls them. I'm interested in a few of his pieces'

'Good lord, really?'

'Apparently he's a genius. I think we both know what he is, so I think I might buy a couple of items from him,' explained Spunky, 'And maybe a painting by an Italian chap called Giorgio. I'm going back tomorrow night to seal the deal, so to speak.'

As he said this, he spied Percy Pendlebury weaving between tables on his way to join them.

'Go away, Percy, there's a good chap, the adults are talking,' said Spunky.

Pendlebury ignored him and sat down.

'Is that any way to treat someone who has the most delicious bit of gossip on...'

'Thank you, Percy, can you and I chat later?' said Kit, staring at Pendlebury in the eye.

Pendlebury appeared to receive the message and shrugged his shoulders, 'Quite.'

'What's all that about?' asked Spunky. Had he been a little less sloshed, his suspicions might have been aroused, reflected Kit with relief.

'Never mind. Anyway, regarding your speculations in the art market, let's hope you've hit a goldmine, old chap. Now if we can return to business. I've met with the British and the Americans, thank you for organising. I know you're sourcing more on the background of everyone I spoke to so can you get me anything on our American friends? I understand the information may be a little patchy.'

'Consider it done. Anything else?' responded Spunky cheerfully.

'Yes, a little bit delicate, but here goes. I'd like to understand more about Miss Malcolm's movements in the twenty-hours prior to the murder,' said Kit looking meaningfully at Spunky.

'Catch your drift, old sausage, you mean when was I with Angela?' smiled Spunky.

'Well, yes.'

'Angela and I tend to take long lunches together. It's all very French. The conference works in the morning. Everyone takes a long lunch period, allows time for the Americans to prepare for the late afternoon sessions, the French and the Italians do as you may imagine French, and Italians do, the Japanese sleep and the English do a mixture of all the aforementioned or go to second-hand bookshops.'

Kit raised his eyebrows at Spunky, indicating he needed more specificity.

'Angela and I rather take the French and Italian approach. We have a long lunch and relax at a room I've booked on the left bank.'

'Sorry to probe, Spunky, but you know how important this is. Do you spend the night with her at all?'

'No, Angela prefers to keep us a secret, so I don't actually see her in the evenings very much. The last I saw of her the day before the murder was when we parted company near the Majestic just before five in the afternoon. She would have attended the meeting and then, I presume, had some dinner then off to bed.'

Kit nodded but was highly sceptical if Miss Malcolm was alone in the evening. It also reminded him about the hotel staff and Miller.

'Spunky, I need a couple of favours. Given that we have virtually taken over the Majestic, do you think someone could grant my man Miller permission to speak to some of the hotel staff tomorrow morning.'

'Won't be a problem. Does he speak French?'

'Very little, that's the second favour I'll need.'

-

Kit walked into the hotel bar and spied Pendlebury sitting on his own at a table, at peace with the world. Pendlebury adjusted his pince-nez as he spied Kit dodging a waiter en route to his table. He had spent most of his adult life with the fourth estate. Not for him the tawdry hamster wheel of news or current affairs. His calling was towards higher affairs.

Literally.

He had spent most of his years in the press courting high society and watching high society courting. Pendlebury was especially drawn to the breezier type of aristo. They were both the source and subject of his gossip columns. The victims, if they could be so described, wore their mentions in his column as a badge of honour. Some even added the newspaper cuttings to a scrapbook. On such things was social value measured.

Current affairs and politics only intruded on Pendlebury's consciousness when it was likely to interfere with the serious business of frivolity. The murder in Sarajevo by Princip had registered, even with Pendlebury, as the herald of a bad show. And so it proved. It was nearly enough to make a man a pacifist. Nearly but not quite.

The nation was not in the mood to observe the excesses of the rich enjoying life excessively. While high society did not quite shut down so much as hibernate, it certainly reduced Pendlebury's opportunities to observe the recreational activities of the rich at first hand. The occasional mentions of those lucky members of society, positively dripping in wealth by newspapers were rarely calculated to show them in a good light. The Daily Herald had made an enormous impression with stories such as 'how the rich starve at the Ritz'.

Cometh the hour, cometh the gossip columnist. A writing skill honed by years of conscientiously observing rich, bright young things making asses of themselves was not an obvious qualification for reporting on the horrors of Flanders. However, Pendlebury earned great credit with his key patrons following a series of highly successful articles depicting the sacrifices being made by the sons of the wealthy at the front.

Unfortunately for Pendlebury, this necessitated he intermingle with the horrible business of war. But this was a life-or-death matter: the very future existence of high society was at stake. Pendlebury acquitted himself well at the front owing to a naturally jovial nature, regularly upholstering himself with gin and the certain knowledge it would all be over soon, for him if not the poor blighters in the trenches.

Kit and Pendlebury had crossed paths several times in the years prior to the War. He quite liked the journalist, and the sentiment was returned. It helped that Kit had deftly avoided entanglement in Pendlebury's tittle tattle. This owed more to discretion and guile on Kit's part rather than any monastic inclinations.

'Hello, Percy,' said Kit taking a seat opposite the journalist.

Pendlebury smiled warmly and genuinely.

'Kit, so good to see you again.'

They chatted for a few minutes about the last few years and how Kit was. One of the reasons for Pendlebury's success was his extraordinary ability to remember, in detail, the names not just of his subjects but also their families and their goings on. A few gentle thrusts by Pendlebury on Kit's disappearance from society over the last year were parried, but they acted as a reminder of the need to be circumspect.

Although no one would ever have confused Pendlebury with the supreme incarnation of detectives, Sherlock Holmes, his mind could occasionally travel along similar lines. Eliminate the impossible and whatever remained, no matter how improbable was, potentially, a juicy headline.

'So,' said Pendlebury fixing his eyes on Kit, 'What's this business about the French diplomat? I've had several conversations halt whenever I appear in the vicinity. Has this chap been squiring one of our young ladies? And is this young lady known to our mutual chum, Spunky?'

Kit silently breathed a sigh of a man reprieved from a weekend with one's aunts. The only course of action, Kit accepted, was to tell the truth, the half truth and nothing but the half-truth.

'How do you do it, Percy?' said Kit, smiling in mock admiration.

'Well, you know,' said Pendlebury modestly before recovering his focus, 'Anyway, what's going on?'

'Do you love your country, Percy?'

'I say, Kit, steady on. Should you have to ask?' said Pendlebury, genuinely affronted at any question mark over his patriotism.

Kit leaned forward and looked around him to make sure no one was listening to the unmitigated balderdash he was about to unleash. The effect of this movement reaped the reward Kit had sought. Pendlebury leaned forward also, senses tingling at the prospect of some scandalous tidbit to tantalise his readers or, more importantly, his editor with. The cost of sending Pendlebury, all expenses paid to Paris for a week or two, was on the left-hand side of the balance sheet, or was it right, he wondered?

'I ask, Percy old chap, because we are in the middle of very delicate negotiations with our allies, our comrades in arms who would happily steal the shirt off our backs.'

'Why I knew it, the dirty ___'

Kit held his hand up, keen to avoid Pendlebury's detailed inventory of the manifold failings of the Gallic race.

'Suffice to say, Spunky's at the wicket and the diplomat in question is bowling googlies,' said Kit, sitting back in his seat, nodding sagely.

'You don't say,' exclaimed Pendlebury, utterly unclear as to what Kit was talking about. Before he could figure out a face-saving way of clarifying what on earth this meant, Kit continued.

'It's frightfully hush hush. Whenever Spunky hits it for six, I'll give you the full skinny. What do you say?'

You couldn't say fairer than that, although Pendlebury did. They parted as soon after as Kit intimated that the game was afoot, and it was time to play up. Pendlebury nodded excitedly, delighted to be in the middle of he knew not what.

Jack Murray

11

Paris: 16th February 1919

Ida Roberts loved Paris in the morning. The walk by the Seine just after sunrise was her time. Alone, before the world had woken up, she could stroll along the left bank, enjoy the yellow purple of the morning sky, the mirror-like calm of the river and the sight of birds, trip trapping along the water in search of food. She needed this time and peace because the next twelve hours would see her on duty dealing with the aftermath of carnage. Of bodies and minds torn asunder.

Ida was twenty-two. She had been nursing for three years. There wasn't a time when she hadn't wanted to be a nurse. It was a sad result of war that the demand in London was high. When the opportunity came to take a position at the military hospital in Paris, she grabbed it with both hands. Although she had left school at sixteen, French had been one of her better subjects. For the weeks before her interview, she spent hours in a local library refreshing her memory. During the interview she had demonstrated her language skills in the hope that this would sway the panel towards her ahead of more experienced applicants.

The time was well spent. The panel reached a rapid consensus on Ida Roberts, and she was informed immediately of her success. She arrived in Paris the previous summer. Paris was still a city living in fear of a German breakthrough, a city full of soldiers, a city at war. It was an enormous change from London. Paris felt like another world, yet it was only a matter of hours away from her home.

She arrived at the hospital just before seven. The noise of men screaming, and the smell of disinfectant acted like a slap in the face following the cool balm of the Seine. For the next two hours she patrolled the wards dealing with soldiers who were ready to make the trip back to Blighty. Her friend Ethel was a nurse on the ward where the most serious injuries were dealt with. Ida was relieved her relative youth meant that more experienced nurses dealt with these cases. Around mid-morning a doctor called her over.

'Nurse, can you go to the General Manager please? He wants to see you,' said the doctor, before adding after noting her look of concern, 'no need to worry.'

Ida hurried along to the office. She'd only met the General Manager once before, and that was on her first day. This made her nervous, notwithstanding the doctor's comment. Why would he want to see her? There was always a fear lurking in the back of her mind of having made a mistake. In a hospital a mistake had deadly consequences. With some trepidation she knocked lightly on the door. A voice called for her to enter.

The General Manager was a fearsome looking character. In his sixties, he had grey whiskers which led from his sideburns to under his nose. His ruddy complexion suggested he had arrived at his own solution for dealing with the everyday heartrending trauma of war.

He looked up as she entered. A gruff but not unkind voice inquired, 'Can I help you nurse?'

'Sorry to interrupt you, sir. I was asked to come and see you by one of the doctors,' explained Ida.

'Ahh you must be Nurse Roberts.' He smiled as he said this. She was an attractive girl and you're never too old to put your best foot forward, he thought.

'Yes, sir,' replied Ida, a little more confidently. Despite the crotchety appearance, it was now clear the General Manager wasn't angry.

'We've had a request from someone in the British delegation at the Peace Conference that you help them in a matter. They won't tell me what's needed but they say it's urgent. I told them three hours, then we need you back. We can't spare good nurses like you.'

The compliment seemed genuine bringing embarrassed colour to Ida's face.

'Where am I to go, sir?'

'Hotel Majestic. You're to meet Lord Kit Aston, would you believe?'

Ida's eyes widened. Harry Miller, who she'd met the previous evening, was the manservant of Lord Aston. She wondered if this was a wheeze to get her to go on a date. If it was, she would give him a piece of her mind. Her job was important to her. She wasn't going to be a bit of a diversion for a man passing through Paris. A part of her felt flattered, but for the most part, she felt a nagging disappointment.

'Yes, sir. Am I to leave immediately?'

'Yes, but change back to your civvies first, would you? I dread to think the impact a charming young nurse's arrival will have among all those old men,' said the General Manager, his eyes twinkling.

-

The Hotel Majestic was every bit as impressive as the name suggested. Ida walked towards the front entrance looking at the building and the people in wonder. As she went through the large entrance with its doormen opening the door for her, he felt apprehensive. Anger was mixed with an undeniable curiosity. She had liked Harry Miller, but if this was some sort of ruse it was unacceptable, and she would tell him so. Whatever he might believe about nurses, she was not that type of girl. However, even if her worst fears proved true, she knew she would probably forgive him. He'd stood up for her and Ethel impressively against an enormous American and handled him without too much trouble.

Slowly she twirled around, looking at the diplomats, the officials, and the army men. She felt like a child. This was the serious business of peace, of reconstruction and it was happening here. And she was here, too. Ida Roberts from Croydon. Her heart swelled with pride, her apprehension increasing by the second. The lobby was enormous. Its opulence marked by the shiny floor, the beautifully manicured plants with hues that harmonised with the colours of the walls and the floor. The expensively clad staff flitted around, professional not servile, efficient, and eager to assist. This was another world, yet she was in it. Her heartbeat even faster.

Then she saw him. Harry was accompanied by a tall, very handsome, and clearly distinguished gentleman. This could only be Lord Aston. All at once relief flooded through Ida. And guilt. She had been wrong to suspect Harry's motives. She looked at Harry again and smiled and knew something had changed in her.

-

'There she is sir. In the...'

'Brown coat, Harry?' said Kit, looking at his manservant with a raised eyebrow. Ida Roberts was very pretty, Kit noted, and he smiled with approval at Miller's choice of translator.

Miller looked up at Kit and shrugged sheepishly, 'Her French is very good, sir, I promise.'

Kit smiled and shook his head, 'I've marked your card already, Mr Miller.'

They both walked forward to greet Ida. As they approached her, Ida turned around and her face was a mixture of surprise and, it seemed to Kit, relief. Her smile though, was genuine and seemed to inhabit her whole person. Kit liked her before they'd even spoken. And he sensed he could trust her.

'Nurse Roberts, I'm Kit Aston. I gather you know Sir Galahad here or should I say Gentleman Jim?' said Kit returning Ida's smile.

Ida looked with some concern at Miller's eye which showed clear signs of the confrontation with the big American.

'Mr Miller was very brave, sir,' said Ida, 'The American was much bigger than him. He'll think twice about trying that again after Mr Miller sorted him.'

Kit smiled at Miller, 'Did Harry tell you how we met?'

Ida shook her head and Miller looked uncomfortable. Kit briefly explained the circumstances of their meeting in No Man's Land. Sensing something between the pair, he made sure it reflected well on Miller's bravery and his own foolishness for being there in the first place.

Ida looked at Miller afresh and with an even greater sense of guilt. It was apparent now just how highly Lord Aston regarded him. She also noted Miller's modesty in not telling the story of how he had met Lord Aston. In Ida's view, it spoke volumes for his character.

Kit suggested they move to the café where he could explain the reasons for the unusual request. After they had sat down and ordered, Kit explained more.

'This is highly confidential, Ida, but I think I've seen enough of you already to trust your discretion.'

Ida reddened slightly, and Miller looked on, almost with pride, she thought.

Jack Murray

'A French diplomat was murdered here a few days ago. It's been kept out of the press, but an English woman has been arrested on suspicion of his murder. I've been asked to make some inquiries, discreetly I may add. Our government is keen the matter remains hush hush for the moment. The last thing the conference needs is bad publicity and anti-British feeling being stoked up by the press. The French agree with this, but it is only a matter of time before it blows up.'

As they were drinking coffee, a tall middle-aged man came over clutching a camera. He wore a beret which Kit thought made him something of a caricature. Kit had seen the man before, taking photographs of the clientele of the hotel, in the hope of selling them later. Although a part of him was suspicious, he decided if the man was allowed a free run of a hotel with so many high-ranking diplomats, checks would have been made. The photographer noticed Kit's amused face and guessed it was the beret. He smiled back at Kit and shrugged.

'The beret is expected of us French, *non*?'

This made everyone at the table laugh. Kit deftly moved back out of the line of the photographer's shot in order that he take only Ida and Miller together. Kit requested a business card from the photographer. As he didn't have one, he wrote down his address which Kit pocketed. The photographer left them and moved on to other tables. They took up the conversation where they had left off.

'How terrible. Did I hear you correctly? A woman is suspected?' said Ida.

'You did. And this is where I need your help for the next few hours. Because of the confidential nature of what we're doing, I can't ask anyone else here to help. We need to speak to some of the staff at the hotel, chambermaids, barmen, doormen to understand more about the movements and the activities of the lady in question. Harry doesn't speak well enough to do this, but I gather your French is rather good,' replied Kit.

'I wouldn't go that far, sir.'

'I would, sir. She's speaking it like a local,' chipped in Miller.

Ida gave Miller a look, but it was not too stern, observed Kit and its affect was diluted by the obvious suppression of a smile.

'I'm with Harry on this. It sounds like you'll be ideal. How do you feel about playing detective for the next few hours?'

'Harry, I owe you an apology,' said Ida as they walked along a corridor towards their first interview.

'Really?' said Miller, surprised.

'When I heard from my General Manager Lord Aston wanted to see me, well, I assumed the worst. That it was really you trying to get me to go on a date.'

'I wouldn't take you away from your job, Ida, not like that. What you're doing is too important. Those poor men need you.'

Miller's voice trailed off and Ida could see he was battling with his emotions. She didn't need an explanation.

'I'm sorry, Harry.'

Miller wasn't sure if she was apologising for her misjudgement of his character or for what he'd been though in the War. A hand placed gently on his shoulder answered this question. He was beginning to like Ida very much. They entered a small room used by the chambermaids for their break. There were two ladies in the room, both were closer to sixty than fifty. The smell of cigarette smoke was overpowering. Miller glanced at Ida, and he could see she was thinking the same. Over tea, Kit had outlined a series of questions to ask the staff. If either of them thought of supplementary questions to ask based on what they were hearing, they should do so.

Beatrice and Bernice had worked as chambermaids at the Majestic for over twenty-five years. They had seen it all over this time. Both had walked in on courting couples, been propositioned, met actors, politicians, generals, good and bad people. Nothing surprised them anymore.

Miller showed them a photostat of Miss Malcolm. They recognised her immediately. One of the perks of having such a low paid and often gruelling job was the potential for gossip, tips, and rewards. They were linked.

Over the years, many famous and not so famous people had used the Majestic to enjoy illicit liaisons with members of the opposite sex. Very often, in order to buy their silence, they were well rewarded by the people whose rooms they cleaned. If not, then a little later, a story would appear in one of the newspapers hinting at an affair involving this actor, or that politician. Beatrice and Bernice didn't specify but both cackled in laughter at the memories.

'From the first moment I saw mademoiselle, I knew what she was,' said Beatrice, the more vocal of the two ladies.

'How?' asked Ida, genuinely curious.

Beatrice waved her cigarette flamboyantly, causing Miller to duck out of the way of flying ash.

'Mademoiselle, it is a certain something in the eye, how they look at you, in the way they walk, in the way they talk to men. For example, you are very beautiful, as beautiful as this lady, but you do not have what she has.'

'Oh, I see,' said Ida, not sure whether to take it as a compliment or an insult or indeed what she was missing. On balance, she thought it a compliment but was dying to know the other. However, Beatrice had not finished. Without looking at Miller she fixed her eye on Ida.

'This man, you are together?'

'Well, no,' said Ida, a little perturbed at the direction the conversation was going.

'You could have him like that,' said Beatrice snapping her fingers, 'If you were more like her.'

Bernice laughed in agreement and echoed the snap of the fingers, 'Like that.'

Miller looked on mystified but could guess by the reddening of Ida's face the conversation had moved away from the questions suggested by Lord Aston towards him.

Ida attempted to steer the conversation back to the topic in hand, 'Do you know if she was with other men.'

'Pfffffp,' said Bernice.

Even Miller could guess that meant yes.

'Can you tell us who?' asked Ida hopefully.

'One of the men is in Room 1012. The other or others we don't know, it's another hotel,' replied Beatrice. Bernice shook her head also in confirmation.

'How do you know she's with someone at another hotel?' pressed Ida.

'She never sleeps in her room. There are some nights when she has obviously been in Room 1012. But there are other nights when she was not.'

Ida explained all this to Miller after each answer, although she tactfully avoided talking about the earlier diversion.

'Ask them if she stayed in Room 1012, four nights ago, Ida.'

The answer was no.

This ended the questions. Miller and Ida thanked the two ladies and turned to leave. As they did so, Miller noted Bernice nodding to Beatrice as if to push her to tell them something.

Miller asked her in passable French, 'Is there something else you want to mention?'

'Yes, an Englishman came to see us earlier this morning? He was asking us questions about these matters also.'

'What was his name?'

'He didn't say,' shrugged Beatrice.

-

As it wasn't raining, Kit elected to walk around the corner to his next destination, Rue Jean Giraudoux. He held the card with the address in front of him as he walked, counting off the numbers as he went. Finally, he found the location, *Francois Sagnier, Photographe.* He went inside and up a narrow staircase. The door at the top of the staircase was already open but Kit knocked anyway.

'*Entrez,*' shouted a voice from inside.

Kit explained in French what he wanted. The man, whom Kit recognised from earlier, smiled uneasily.

'Yes, I can have the photographs ready for tomorrow morning. I'm afraid I can do no earlier as another man asked me this morning if he could have a number of photographs from the same luncheon.'

Kit was curious and asked if he knew the man or could, at the very least, describe him. Sagnier shrugged his shoulders.

'He was English, but I remember little about him.'

Kit thanked him and departed. Outside a light rain was falling. He saw a cab nearby and hailed it and ordered the driver to take him back to the hotel.

Jack Murray

12

Much later that evening, Kit sat with Miller and the off-duty Ida for supper. This was an opportunity to hear more of what they had learned. They chose the same restaurant where Ida had met Miller as it was close to the hospital. Kit listened intently as Ida answered questions. He liked the way she provided sufficient detail as well as a view on the credibility of the individuals they had spoken to. Her clear, concise answers reaffirmed his good impression of her.

Beatrice and Bernie were the principal sources of information; however, one of the doormen remembered Miss Malcolm arriving at the hotel on the morning of the meeting. It suggested she had stayed elsewhere the previous evening. Another piece of information Kit was interested in threw up an answer which appeared to confirm one of his hypotheses.

'The police have not spoken to either the chambermaids or the doormen, but apparently an Englishman did speak to them an hour or two before us,' revealed Ida.

'Interesting. I wonder what's going on with the police. Very strange reaction. I wouldn't worry too much about the Englishman. I've a feeling I know who it was. Let's just say, he's not a material part of this investigation, but it's useful to know. Crafty devil. Anyway, excellent work you two. I knew I could trust you,' said Kit with a smile.

Ida beamed at the praise, but Miller remained expressionless.

'We just need to ascertain who is staying in Room 1012, although I can hazard a guess.'

'It's Sir Jonathan Monk,' announced Miller.

Ida looked askance at Miller and Kit's face registered a mixture of surprise and delight.

'How on earth did you find out, Harry? I would've thought the hotel might be a bit security conscious.'

'I just told reception I was to collect messages for Room 1012. The man at the told me there were no messages for Sir Jonathan Monk.'

Ida smile widened as Miller related his ruse and Kit laughed. It seemed to Kit there was pride in Ida's smile.

'Excellent initiative, Harry. Now I'll need your help tomorrow morning, Harry.'

Kit explained what was required

'Can I help in any way?' asked Ida.

Both men looked at her confused, so she continued hopefully, 'It's my day off. I've nothing else planned.'

'Welcome on board,' said Kit.

The conversation turned away from the activities of the day and on to Ida, who told the men more about her life. Both men were happy to listen, and Ida was an entertaining dinner partner.

'I must compliment your choice of restaurant,' said Kit as the evening drew to a close, 'I wouldn't normally go to a place around here.'

'A lot of the nurses and doctors come here. It's quite cheap,' admitted Ida, 'But we like it.'

As she said this her eyes widened with fear. Miller noted the change in her expression.

'What's wrong Ida?'

'It's that man again,' said Ida, her voice betrayed the anxiety she was feeling.

Miller turned around and caught the eye of the big American from the other evening. Hart was wearing a tuxedo that did little to hide neither the epic nature of his size nor its impressive distribution. The two men looked at each other. Both noted with satisfaction that the other man sported signs of their recent engagement.

The American walked over to the table. Ida held her breath. She hated the idea of another fight taking place particularly as she felt partly responsible for the first one. Another thought struck her. She was worried for Harry. The man walking towards them seemed a different proposition from the drunken buffoon of the other night. Free of the alcohol, his movement was athletic, not ungainly. She guessed Miller was no more than five eight. This man was well over six feet three and built to scale. He looked like he meant business.

'Lord Aston, good to meet you again,' said Hart, looking away from Miller towards Kit.

'Mr Hart,' said Kit warily, not getting up. 'May I present my manservant, Harry Miller and Nurse Roberts, I don't believe you've been formally introduced.'

Hart stared down at Miller, then his face broke into a big smile, 'You handle yourself pretty well, Mr Miller. I think I owe you and Miss Roberts an apology for my behaviour the other evening.'

Miller shook his hand and grinned, 'Think nothing of it. I'm just glad you didn't land that punch, Mr Hart, I'd still be unconscious now.'

Ida breathed a sigh of relief. She looked at Miller. Throughout he'd seemed unperturbed by the prospect of taking on the big American.

'I'm glad I didn't. Call me Howie, by the way. Mind if I join you for a few minutes?'

'Please do,' said Kit.

'How is your investigation going, Lord Aston?'

'It's a challenge. We haven't been able to speak to everyone we would like nor in the way we would like,' said Kit pointedly but not in too unfriendly a tone.

Hart smiled ruefully at this, 'Yes Colonel Terrell was never going to allow his team to be cross-examined. Whoever killed Mantoux, it wasn't one of us, though.'

'You don't think it was Miss Malcolm?'

'Open-minded. She's an interesting lady.'

Kit smiled at this, 'I've been wondering exactly what your role is, Mr Hart. You don't strike me as a diplomat.'

Hart touched his eye and laughed, 'Yes, not my strong point. What's your view on my role?'

'You work for American Intelligence would be my assessment.'

Hart laughed at this but did not confirm or deny the truth of Kit's view, 'I don't think your friend Mr Stevens, is a diplomat either by the way. I think he's going to be disappointed soon regarding his lady friend.'

Hart looked intently at Kit and guessed this was not new news.

'Perhaps we can compare notes, Mr Hart. We believe that Miss Malcolm is conducting at least two affairs besides Mr Stevens.'

'I know of one,' replied Hart looking more serious, 'two is news to me. Shall we reveal our cards?'

Kit nodded and said, 'One is an Englishman, the other is not. We know who the Englishman is but, I hope you'll forgive me, it wouldn't be appropriate to say who.'

Hart nodded shrewdly, 'In that case, I think I can guess, Lord Aston. We weren't sure about this, so thanks for confirming. You don't know the other man?'

'No, just that he's not English and that she spent the night with him before the murder of Mantoux,' responded Kit.

This was also new for Hart, 'We weren't aware of her movements the night before, but it fits.

Kit looked at Hart, 'What fits?'

'Well, Lord Aston, I might be able to fill you in on who she was with the night before. It was the dear departed Monsieur Mantoux.'

'Can you expand on this?'

'No, I think you may draw your own conclusions, Lord Aston.'

'As you say, Mr Hart, an interesting lady but it doesn't make her a murderer.'

'True, but it suggests she's many other things which won't be happy news for you Brits, never mind your friend Mr Stevens.'

Hart left soon after leaving Kit, Miller, and Ida to finish their drinks. Ida looked at Miller and Kit with a smile.

'I was worried there would be more trouble when he arrived. He's very big.'

Both Kit and Miller laughed at this.

'He's a strange cove,' replied Kit, 'But all in all, I think he's on our side.'

-

When Kit returned to his hotel, there was a note from Spunky asking him to come up to his room upon his return. Kit made his way up to the first floor and knocked on the door. It was less than a surprise to find Spunky moderately sozzled. Kit had been with Spunky on numerous occasions when his erstwhile friend, in fact they both, had enjoyed one too many glasses of cheerfulness for even the sturdiest of constitutions to withstand. Kit judged his old friend to be somewhere past the first bottle of champagne, possibly even nearing completion of the second.

Spunky's room was larger than Kit's and it had large French windows that led out to a generous terrace. Kit followed Spunky out to the terrace and sat down at the table. The terrace overlooked a street along the side of the hotel, Rue La Perouse.

'Lovely terrace. Do you sit out here much of an evening?'

'Absolutely old boy, every evening if I can. It's a very peaceful way to begin or end an evening. Treat myself to a nip or two before zedd-ing the night away.'

Kit glanced over the balcony; the street was deserted.

'I see what you mean. Very quiet. Anyway, why did you want me up here?'

'I think you're losing it, bloodhound,' smiled Spunky, 'Didn't you see it?'

'In point of fact, I did. I just feared to mention anything.'

Kit turned his head and looked at an item sitting atop Spunky's bed.

'Duchamp?' suggested Kit shaking his head in disbelief at the sight sitting before him.

Spunky grinned proudly, 'Correct. Apparently, this is a replica. The original one was lost. It's a men's...'

'Urinal, Spunky. Unless I miss my guess, you've just purchased a urinal.'

13

Hotel Majestic, Paris: 17th February 1919

It was six o'clock in the morning when Percy Pendlebury was rudely awoken by the sound of banging on his door. Pendlebury sat bolt upright in his bed and ordered a dry martini. It was then it dawned on him that it was dawn. However, he smiled with some pride that his instinctive reaction to order alcohol had not failed him. The banging persisted.

'Alright, alright I'm coming,' shouted Pendlebury angrily.

More banging on the door.

'I said I'm coming, you blithering idiot.'

Pendlebury reached the door as the banging stopped. He opened the door. The corridor was empty. Few would have called Pendlebury an unreasonable man. In fact, he was sure, if quizzed, his chums would support to the hilt the proposition that he was as patient as the next chap. But this was the absolute pip in his book. No one should be able to force a free Englishman to awaken from a particularly peaceful slumber and then not hang around to deal with the consequence. As he considered the unjustness of life, of people and the malevolent nature of the French in particular, Pendlebury noticed an envelope at his feet. On the front was written one word: *Pendlebury.*

He opened the envelope. A glance at the bottom of the letter confirmed it was anonymous. It was handwritten but quite legible. When he had finished reading the letter, he closed the door quickly and rushed to get dressed.

-

Angela Malcolm lit a cigarette, inhaled, and then blew smoke in the direction of Inspector Briant as she walked past him out of the police station. The sun was invisible behind a thick blanket of cloud. She didn't care. It felt wonderful to feel the fresh air lick her face again. A man accosted her as she was leaving.

'Hello, Miss Malcolm, my name is Pendlebury.'

Angela Malcolm stopped and looked at the man who had stopped her.

'Yes?' she asked, half amused by the man's Wildean appearance, the dark cape with red silk lining and soft-brimmed hat.

'I'm a journalist. I'd love to hear more about this shameful arrest.'

Miss Malcolm smiled at Pendlebury and walked past him down the steps, ignoring his pleas to stop. In the street in front of the police station was a waiting car. She climbed in gracefully.

Both Pendlebury and Briant tried to look inside. Moments later the car drove away, Briant's gaze followed it all the way along the street until it was out of view. He turned and looked at Pendlebury, who returned his look.

'*Parlez-vous Anglais?*' asked Pendlebury hopefully.

Briant turned and walked back into the station. It was just after seven o'clock and he suspected this was not going to be a good day.

-

As usual, Kit heard Spunky before he saw him. His friend breezed into the hotel restaurant, waving at Kit but attracting the attention of virtually every other diner. Even by Spunky's standards, he seemed excited. Or agitated. Sometimes it was difficult to tell them apart where Spunky was concerned.

'It's incredible, Kit. They've released Angela, I've just heard from Briant.'

'Wonderful! When will she be here?'

'That's the problem, Kit. They released her two hours ago. She was picked up by a waiting car. No one knows where she is. Apparently that damned fool Pendlebury was there, but she ignored him.'

'Pendlebury? How on earth did he get news of this?' responded Kit, amazed at this development.

Spunky sat down and related all he knew, which was very little. It was clear he was delighted that no charges would be made, but somewhat miffed that she had not rushed into her lover's arms at the first flash of freedom.

'I gather from Sir Jonathan that they heard last night she was to be released in the morning,' finished Spunky.

Kit decided it was time to broach a subject that lay heavy on his mind.

'Spunky, have you been thinking about asking Miss Malcolm to marry you?'

Spunky's monocle fell onto the table as his eyes widened.

'That's a no, I take it,' continued Kit.

'Good lord, Kit. I mean to say. Do you take me for a gentleman?' spluttered Spunky.'

'Yes, silly mistake, Spunky old chap. I won't repeat it. Promise.'

'I mean I like her and all that. It's been jolly good fun. But Angela knows the score with someone like me.'

'You can't tame a tiger,' said Kit, smiling with relief.

'I don't think you're treating this with the high level of seriousness it merits, bloodhound.'

'Sorry. Look what do you know about Miss Malcolm, her background? Has anything come back yet?' pressed Kit.

'I know what she told me. Expecting a phone call later this afternoon from a chum on the background checks on all our team.'

'I suppose what I'm driving at is if Miss Malcolm or any other person in the meeting on our side was with British Intelligence, would you necessarily know?'

'You can't expect an architect to know every hod carrier on the building site, old boy,' replied Spunky.

Kit laughed, 'Thanks for that, Spunky.'

'Don't mention it, Kit,' said Spunky airily, 'But I must say, old bean, you were a particularly good hod carrier in your day.'

'I need your help this morning, Spunky, hence the slightly early start. And given this news about Miss Malcolm's release and Pendlebury, it's even more important.'

Kit explained his plan to him and Spunky readily agreed.

-

The police station was as busy as usual when Kit entered it for the third time in as many days. After introducing himself at the reception he was shown through to the back. He went up to the second floor. There were a few offices each occupied by one or two people. At the end of the corridor was his destination. Inspector Briant rose to greet him as Kit entered.

'Lord Aston, *bonjour.*'

'*Bonjour* Inspector,' replied Kit shaking his hand.

Both men sat down and Briant went straight to business.

'Doubtless, Lord Aston, you wish to know why Mademoiselle Malcolm was released without charge.'

'Anything to do with the fact she was clearly innocent?' said Kit unable to disguise a note of irony in his voice.

Briant smiled and replied, 'We had no proof. *D'accord.* But you will agree this is a different thing.'

Kit smiled also in acknowledgement, 'True, but it does not explain why she was arrested in the first place.'

'This I can explain,' said Briant. 'I was told to arrest her.'

'By whom?'

'That I cannot say.'

'I understand. May I inquire if this same person asked you to release her?'

Briant nodded but did not reply. Kit took this to be a yes.

'Where is she now?' persisted Kit.

'I believe she is with friends, but I cannot say.'

'You mean you won't say.'

Briant smiled ruefully, 'This is something resolved at a much higher level, Lord Aston. I think your enquiries should end now; don't you think?'

This was mystifying to Kit. The attitude of Briant was explicable if pressure was being exerted from above but what of Mantoux?

'And the murdered diplomat?'

'This is a police matter, Lord Aston. Perhaps you should use your remaining time here to start sightseeing,' said Briant with a finality that told Kit the meeting was over and possibly his reason to remain in Paris.

-

Spunky sat in the reception of the Hotel Majestic, one eye on yesterday's Times. The other eye would have been used for looking at the comings and goings of people in the foyer, but he only had one good eye following the War. Every so often he looked up from the paper. People arriving or leaving invariably looked at him because of his rather piratical eye patch and the fact that he was positioned so close to the door. He spotted his man leaving the escalator. He moved first to the reception to hand in his keys and then headed out of the hotel.

'Hello, Stevens, what are you doing lazing around here?' asked Geddes as he headed out the front entrance.

'What ho, Geddes, just catching up, don't you know, cheerio,' said Spunky holding up The Times.

Geddes gave a salute and was out the door. Spunky waited until he had walked another fifty yards down the street and then he rose from his seat and began to follow him. As a precaution he wore a hat, removed his familiar eye patch to be replaced with a bandage and an old overcoat purchased at a flea market on his behalf by Miller. The sight of a man in Paris wearing facial bandages looking like he'd fallen on harder times was far from rare in the city. He would blend in with depressing ease.

Spunky followed Geddes all the way along Avenue Kleber towards the Arc de Triomphe. Geddes switched right and headed in the direction of Avenue Marceau. There he went to a small café and sat down with another man who was occupying a pavement table. Spunky edged forward to get a closer look at his companion. When Spunky saw him, he exhaled loudly.

'Wasn't expecting that. What are you up to old boy?'

-

Harry Miller was enjoying wearing his new suit very much. He looked every bit a well-to-do Parisian strolling along the boulevard. He was even wearing sunglasses, which he'd never done before. This was useful as the February sun was bright and it helped disguise the effects of his *contretemps* with Hart.

In reality he was performing a task for Kit. Up ahead, Howie Hart was making his way along the Champs Elysees. Halfway along, the big American skipped across the road and cut along Rue de Presbourg and walked into a café on the corner.

Miller had a clear view of him sitting down at a table outside on the pavement. He waited for a few minutes, reading a paper. He was on his second coffee when another man arrived at the café and immediately went to the same table as Hart. Neither man seemed particularly pleased to see the other. The man was almost as tall as Hart, less bulky but well made. He was dressed impeccably in a dark suit.

Within a few minutes, it was apparent they were engaged in a sharp exchange. Miller cursed his inability to get closer and to hear what was being said or even the accent of the other man.

Suddenly, Miller felt a hand grasp his shoulder. Miller spun around to defend himself. He stopped immediately, so confused was he by the sight before him.

Julian Fink-Nottle usually skipped breakfast in the hotel on a Saturday morning, choosing instead to have a long leisurely breakfast at a café on the Left Bank He strolled happily along the bank of the Seine, observing the birds searching for food.

Unnoticed by him, strolling along the Seine was a young lady. Ida Roberts had been entrusted with the task of observing Fink-Nottle's movements for the morning. The long route taken by Fink-Nottle was also highly welcome for Ida. Her life seemed to be a treadmill which took her from her bedroom to the hospital, to dinner before sinking exhausted into bed. Day after day. Meeting Harry Miller and Lord Aston had added a bit of badly needed excitement to her life.

The walk also gave her time to think about Harry Miller. She liked him, and it seemed he liked her. But marriage was the last thing on her mind. Nursing was tough, it was tiring and more often than not, she would fall into bed sleeping, crying or both. It was also exhilarating. It gave her purpose. She was doing something that was making a difference to lives. Although she didn't think of this explicitly, it lay beneath everything she did. Her parents had both worked. Her mum had been a nurse and her father had worked on the docks. They had given her values that would stay with her for the rest of her life.

She had youth, energy, and freedom. And she was in Paris. The idea of romance appealed to her no less than to anyone else of her age. With Harry Miller, she sensed it would be different. He was authentic and likeable. Not only that, but he'd also served his country and had stood up for her without hesitation, without a moment's concern for his own safety. The last thing she wanted to do was hurt him. She wondered if he really did feel something towards her.

Up ahead, Fink-Nottle seemed to have settled on a café. Ida followed him in. Frustratingly she could not sit near him. Ida ordered breakfast. Kit had insisted on giving her expenses. She made sure she would provide him with a receipt and change. It didn't matter to her how rich he was. This was how she had been brought up.

Fink-Nottle had settled down to read a French newspaper and enjoy his breakfast. Ida was beginning to think it a wasted morning when she saw Fink-Nottle rise to greet a young man with dark hair and one of the most beautiful girls Ida had ever seen. Her hair was blonde, she was around Ida's age, and she had beautiful clear blue eyes. She seemed Scandinavian rather than French. After a few minutes, the group was joined by another woman. She was a lot older than the other three. It was difficult to see her face beneath a pair of spectacles and a black beret.

As Ida had suspected, she was too far away to hear what was being said. The throbbing noise of the café patrons and waiters put paid to any hopes of catching any of the conversation. The new arrivals might well be a couple, thought Ida, but it was hard to be certain. Neither took anything to eat or drink. Instead they seemed to be conversing but not in a way that seemed social. The young woman seemed to be doing most of the talking but her features were serious, business-like almost rather than social.

The young couple departed after twenty minutes leaving Fink-Nottle and the older woman. They chatted for a few minutes longer and then she rose from her seat and went to pay the bill. Both left in opposite directions. Ida had already taken the precaution of paying her bill ten minutes previously to make a swift exit. She gave Fink-Nottle a generous start, but as he looked to be retracing his footsteps back to the hotel, she was able to maintain a safe distance behind. More time to think. Life was never straightforward, maybe that's why God gave people the capacity to think. Or maybe because people could think, life could not be straightforward. As she walked along a road, she had walked many times before, Ida knew she was lost.

-

Kit departed from the police station convinced the Inspector knew more than he was prepared to admit. As Kit had nothing to offer in return, there was little he could trade. Kit sensed Briant's hands were tied, or it was possible the investigation was really being conducted by someone else, with Briant the public face, or scapegoat. It was impossible to tell.

Jack Murray

Acting on an impulse, Kit hailed a taxi. As they drove through the crowded streets of Paris, Kit spotted a bookshop. On a whim, he asked the taxi to stop and wait for him. A few minutes browsing failed to help find what he was looking for. On the point of giving up, he noticed an assistant looking at him. He called the young woman over and said in French.

'Good morning, mademoiselle. I'm looking for a book on a very unusual subject.'

The young woman smiled and replied in perfect English with a gesture to the extensive range of books in the shop, 'I am sure we can help, monsieur. What are you looking for?'

Kit told her. She raised her eyebrows and laughed. Then she said, 'Follow me, sir.'

-

Miller stared at the man who had grabbed him by the shoulder. The man had a grin on his face and a bandage around one of his eyes. The extraordinary look of the man, aside from his injury, stopped Miller from reacting more belligerently.

'You're Lord Aston's man, aren't you? He told me you'd be following Hart. I'm Stevens.'

Miller nodded in recognition. Kit had mentioned his friend would also be tailing someone but had not said who. Spunky nodded towards the two men.

'Hart is meeting the man I'm tailing, Geddes,' explained Spunky.

'They don't seem to be the best of friends,' observed Miller.

'No, they don't. I'd love to know what the spat was about. In fact, I'd love to know why they're even meeting in the first place. I wonder if Monk is aware of what Geddes is up to. Or Terrell for that matter. Very curious indeed.'

'Look, they're leaving,' noted Miller. Spunky turned his back to the café door. He and Miller made as if they were in conversation. Hart and Geddes parted, walking in different directions. With a brief nod farewell, Miller and Spunky also parted company to continue tailing each of their men.

Hart looked to be heading back down the Champs Elysees in the direction of the Hotel Crillon. The weather looked to be turning and Miller regretted the lack of an umbrella or overcoat. Unexpectedly, Hart continued past the Crillon and onto Place de la

Concorde. He passed through the enormous square and on to Rue du Mont Thabor. Midway down the street he disappeared into a doorway. Miller guessed this was his office.

Miller waited outside the office for ten minutes before walking up to the front to look at the front door. To the right of the door was a brass plate with the names of who occupied the offices. All of them had French names except one which was blank. Miller pressed the buzzer. A few moments later there was an answer.

'Yes, who is it?' said a woman's voice in a distinct American accent.

'*Pardon, je m'excuse,*' said Miller in, what he hoped, was a passable French accent. At least to American ears. Miller guessed the office to be on the top floor. Mission accomplished, he returned to Hotel Majestic.

-

On his way back to the hotel, Kit returned to the photographer's studio. Sagnier seemed as pleased to see him as before, which is to say not. Sagnier went into another room to retrieve Kit's picture. As he was looking for the photographs, Kit used the opportunity to peek at some of the other prints. It was clear that Sagnier had been very busy because there were dozens sitting in neat piles on a table. Each batch was labelled with a scrap of paper at the top with the date and location. From what Kit could see, Sagnier had been to a couple of the hotels occupied by the Americans, including Hotel Crillon.

Sagnier returned with Kit's photographs. Kit took a quick look through them and picked out the photo of Miller with Ida. He held it up for Sagnier to see.

'Can you make me another one of these,' asked Kit, smiling.

This was greeted with mild irritation from Sagnier, 'No, monsieur, I am much too busy.'

'No problem. In that case, can I buy the negative from you?' replied Kit. Sagnier thought for a moment before agreeing.

The photographer went into his darkroom to look for the negative. This gave Kit the opportunity to look at some of the pictures taken at the Hotel Crillon. The first group of photographs revealed nothing of interest, nor did the second. However, it was clear to Kit that Sagnier was focusing on tables where there was a man and a woman present. This made Kit wonder further about

Sagnier's motives. The noise from the dark room suggested Sagnier was returning.

Kit quickly arranged each stack and started to sort through the batch of photographs he'd purchased. One in particular made him smile. Sagnier returned and handed Kit the negative of Miller and Ida.

'Thank you, monsieur,' said Kit taking the negative and putting it in his wallet, 'One more thing. Perhaps the man you mentioned is in one of the photographs you've printed for me.'

Kit removed one photograph and handed it to the Frenchman. He pointed at the man in the photograph.

'Was this him?'

'*Oui, monsieur,*' confirmed Sagnier.

It was Pendlebury.

-

Kit had arranged with Miller and Ida to meet back at the Majestic for lunch. As Miller walked into the restaurant, he saw Kit sitting alone reading a book. Miller looked at the cover and then at Kit.

'Don't ask, Harry. Suffice to say this book is testing my French and my boredom threshold in equal measure.'

A few minutes later, Ida returned. Over lunch the two reported, in detail, what they had observed during the morning. The news that Geddes and Hart had met up did not surprise Kit unduly, but he did not explain why. Ida's report was, as ever, concise but detailed enough to give Kit a good picture of Fink-Nottle's companions.

'It was impossible to hear what they were saying but from what I could hear, they were speaking French.'

'I see. Was there anything else, Ida?'

'Well two things. As Mr Fink-Nottle and the lady were leaving, I had the impression, remember it was noisy, that the older lady was an American. I'd assumed she was French initially because, well, she had a certain style about her.'

'Very interesting,' replied Kit. He wasn't sure if this was material but perhaps something he could ask Fink-Nottle about if he saw him again. 'You said two things?'

Ida looked uncomfortable and glanced at Miller before answering, 'This will seem odd, but I had the feeling I was being followed. There was a man who had been behind me when I was following Mr Fink-Nottle. He also came into the café.'

'What happened after you left?' asked Kit.

'He stayed, so in the end I wasn't sure what to think, but I wanted to mention it anyway. Sometimes, well, as a nurse you get attentions. I wasn't sure if it was something like this.'

Kit smiled sympathetically, 'Yes, I'm sure you get a lot of unwanted attention, Ida. Can you describe the man?'

Ida's had excellent observational skills. She described Pendlebury to within an inch of his silk-lined cloak. As she did so, the sound of jazz music erupted from the nearby ballroom. It took Ida by surprise, and she spun around.

'Good lord. I thought this was a peace conference, not a dance hall.'

Both Kit and Miller broke out onto broad smiles.

'Well I'm not sure there's a lot of peace between the British and the Europeans now. However, it doesn't seem to be getting in the way of the serious business of partying. Do you like dancing, Miss Roberts?' asked Kit.

'Yes, I do, not that I have much opportunity these days, Lord Aston.'

Kit smiled and said to Miller, 'Harry, why not take the afternoon off and entertain Miss Roberts.'

Miller needed no second invitation and led the delighted Ida off to the ballroom. Meanwhile, Kit went in search of Spunky. He went in the direction of the hotel bar. Sure enough, Spunky was there with the first gin and tonic of the day.

'Hello old man. How did your hod-carrying go?' asked Kit.

'I'll stick to more cerebral activity in the future. I think I must have tramped every foot of Paris. I suppose I should be glad that the British taxpayer doesn't have to fund Geddes's transport but, I mean to say, by midday I'd have even been willing to take the blasted metro.'

To which Spunky added a few other observations on Hart and Geddes which had a Biblical dimension and were delivered through gritted teeth.

'Glad you had so much fun,' said Kit breezily, ignoring Spunky's discontent with fieldwork, 'much to report?'

Spunky updated Kit, covering similar ground to Miller's report earlier. Intriguingly, Geddes had also met up with one of the French officials assisting the deceased diplomat.

'Couldn't get near enough to hear what they were talking about, old bean. Even with my brilliant disguise, that fool Geddes would have cottoned on fairly sharpish, I suspect.'

'He's no fool, Spunky.'

'He's no foreign office official either apparently. You were right, Kit. He's one of ours. I must get closer to this, methinks. He was in Germany feeding back a lot of the information to us. Grandmother was German apparently, so fluent. He spent two years in Switzerland, going back and forth into Germany. I still think he's a fool, or full of himself, but he doesn't lack for spunk, I'll give him that.'

'He could just have been acting as a conduit from Monk to keep lines of communication open,' pointed out Kit.

Spunky looked dubious. 'He has one meeting with an American spy, one meeting with a French official, who knows, maybe a spy also. Meanwhile Angela, who is not a spy, by the way, is still missing. I'd love to know what his game is.'

'Angela's not one of ours then?'

'That suggests you think she is working for someone, not necessarily His Majesty's Government.'

'I'm open-minded on your lady, Spunky, so should you be.'

Kit took Spunky through the activity of the morning. If Kit's plan for the morning had been amusing to Spunky, when he had finished relating his plan for the following evening, Spunky was virtually clapping in delight.

'I say, maybe this spy business is more fun that I thought.'

'Sorry Spunky, you can't come along, strictly for the hod-carriers.'

-

Miller led Ida off the floor as the sounds of the music faded away to be replaced by applause for the band.

'Phew, Harry, I don't think I've danced so much in years.'

'Me neither,' said Miller.

Ida looked up immediately with a look of concern on her face. She took Miller's hand, 'Harry, I'm sorry, that was a terrible thing for me to say'

'Don't be silly, Ida, I know what you meant. I can't tell you how much I enjoyed this afternoon, Ida.'

'Me too, Harry. Doesn't feel real. All of this.'

Ida gestured around her at the grand surroundings of the Hotel Majestic ballroom, the well-dressed people, the perfect diction filling the air. She laughed at the ridiculousness of it all.

'Not bad for a girl from Croydon and a boy from Peckham,' she observed, her face beaming. She knew this was a day she would never forget, a place she would never forget, spent with a person who made her feel happy.

'Not bad at all,' agreed Miller looking around him. Their eyes met. Ida's smile radiated from every pore. It combined sweetness with gratitude. Miller felt overwhelmed. Out of practice. It used to be so easy. A bit of cheek, some chit chat and then sometimes he was a very lucky man. But this was different. She was different. He sensed she felt the same.

'When this is over, maybe we should talk, Ida.'

'Yes, we should, Harry.'

The band leader announced the last dance. Ida and Miller looked at one another. Both smiled and nodded. Miller took her hand and led her onto the floor to dance one more time.

14

After leaving Miller and Ida, Kit went to the reception to retrieve his room key. As he was collecting the key, the receptionist also handed him an envelope. Kit turned away from the desk and looked at the note. It was handwritten and read:

Dear Lord Aston, my sincerest apologies for the late invitation, but are you free this evening to join me for dinner? Would 7pm in the hotel bar be convenient?

Sir Jonathan Monk

Kit turned around immediately and returned to the desk. He wrote a note accepting and asked that the note be conveyed to Monk immediately. Following this, he returned to his room to relax and dress for dinner.

Kit's room was quite a bit smaller than he was used to. Unfortunately demand for rooms in the hotel had been such, he had little option but to accept what was left for himself and Miller. He sat down at the table facing his bed and went through the available evidence in the case. A diplomat had been murdered in a meeting with senior British, American, and French officials. The only suspect had been released without charge due to a lack of evidence and on the instruction of someone more senior than the investigating officer. No obvious investigation of the crime had taken place beyond the arrest of Miss Malcolm. This was inexplicable to Kit unless the police either knew who had killed Mantoux, or had sanctioned the assassination themselves or, and this beggared belief, Mantoux was not really dead.

The most likely option, to Kit, seemed the first. They would wait to reveal the true killer until after any arrest. This left him without any obvious role, and yet too many things remained unexplained. Kit wondered if the surprise meeting with Monk would throw some light on the unease he felt about the situation.

Kit walked through the hotel bar. It was still early, but the bar was beginning to fill up. All the men were dressed in tuxedos. There were a few women also, all dressed in fashionably short cocktail dresses. Monk was at a table on his own. He waved at Kit, who made his way over and joined him.

'Thank you for joining me, Lord Aston. I hope you'll be able to dine with me.'

"Yes, Sir Jonathan. I've no other plans so you've saved me from my own company,' said Kit smiling.

'Excellent, I've arranged to meet up with my American counterpart, Terrell. He and I have had a couple of meetings away from the usual places, just the two of us. We both think it a good idea to maintain momentum while we await news on the Mantoux business. If you'll come with me, I have a taxi waiting for us.'

Both men rose and left the bar. Kit had not brought an overcoat and regretted it immediately as he stepped into the chill of the night. Monk noticed his companion's reaction to the cold.

'I'm frightfully sorry, Lord Aston. That was thoughtless of me, I should have said.'

'Nonsense, my own fault,' said Kit grinning ruefully.

It was a short taxi journey to the restaurant. On the way they talked about commonplace subjects; however, it was clear to Kit that Monk had something on his mind. As they neared their destination, Monk finally broached the subject.

'Lord Aston, I wondered if, in your inquiries, you'd been made aware of certain rumours regarding Miss Malcolm?'

Kit glanced at Monk and replied non-committedly, 'I've focused a lot of my investigation on Miss Malcolm, clearly. When we met, I was impressed.'

Monk nodded, 'She is very impressive, and your diplomacy does you credit. To be specific, were you made aware of rumours relating to myself and Miss Malcolm?'

'I was.'

Monk greeted this news with a smile. He seemed strangely relieved.

Kit continued, 'Do you know what has become of her?'

'No, Lord Aston. This was something I hoped you could shed light on,' admitted Monk.

'I'm afraid not. Her disappearance, rather like Miss Malcolm herself, is something of a mystery. How long have you known her professionally?'

Monk reddened slightly at this question before responding, 'I met her last year, she was working with another department in the Foreign Office. When I knew that I would be involved in the Peace negotiations, I remembered something about her background being half French, so I requested that she join my team.'

Kit wasn't entirely sure what he should ask because he wanted to know so much. It was often this way. Instead he said nothing, keeping his gaze on Monk. Silence, in Kit's experience, wasn't just a response, it was also an effective question. It created a vacuum and people, not just nature, abhor a vacuum. Monk was clearly in a mood to talk.

'Look, Lord Aston, cards on the table. You know, and I suspect half of the delegates at this conference know, that Angela and I were having an affair.'

Kit nodded but remained silent.

'I'm a married man, Lord Aston. I intend staying this way. I have no doubt that Angela had other male friends. We never spoke of this. Anyway, what I am trying to say in a very roundabout way, I suppose, is that I trust your discretion in this regard. This had nothing to do with the murder of poor Mantoux.'

'I understand, and I agree. Your relationship with Miss Malcolm is not material to the investigation. Is this why you invited me to dinner?' asked Kit.

'Partly, Lord Aston, but there were a number of other reasons. Principally, I would like you to find Miss Malcolm. I, sorry we, in the British delegation need to know she is safe. The second reason is Terrell was keen to meet you again and hear more about the investigation,' replied Monk before adding, 'I think we've arrived.'

-

They walked into a restaurant which sat opposite the Casino de Paris. The interior was intimate, the noise levels anything but. It seemed the American delegation had decamped to this restaurant and collectively agreed to get drunk. Kit raised an eyebrow in amusement to Monk, who grinned in return. They passed one table that was engaged, competitively, in drinking shots. Each successfully negotiated shot was greeted with cheers from the table.

At the back of the restaurant they located Colonel Terrell. He was sitting with who Kit took to be Miss Morris. It was hard to tell such was her transformation. Far from being a spinster with a cat, this incarnation of Miss Morris was as an attractive fifty-year-old woman wearing a very fashionable dress, elbow-length opera gloves, bright red lipstick, smoking from a cigarette holder. Monk seemed less than surprised by the black swan-like change in Miss Morris.

'I don't think I need to make any introductions, do I?' asked Monk.

'Of course not. Lord Aston, a pleasure to see you again,' said Terrell rising from his seat and shaking hands with Kit. Miss Morris remained seated, looking quietly pleased by Kit's reaction. They shook hands also, without Kit passing comment on the extraordinary change that had taken place.

The meal passed pleasantly with both Monk and Terrell obviously keen to avoid discussion on the French diplomat's unexpected demise and the even more unexpected arrest, release, and disappearance of Miss Malcolm. As they neared the end of the meal, Terrell invited Kit to join them across the road at the Casino de Paris.

'Are you familiar with jazz, Lord Aston?'

'I can't say I've heard much of it, Colonel. I gather it's rather popular in Paris now,' admitted Kit.

'Some of our boys are playing in the casino. They go by the name of the Scrap Iron Jazzerinos,' said Terrell, 'Come over and give it a listen. It'll make a change from Bach, for you maybe,' suggested Terrell with a friendly grin.

The party made its way over to the casino which turned out to be more of a theatre than a gambling parlour. It was full of noise, people, heat, and smoke. The building seemed to vibrate with the remarkable noise coming from the stage. It was music but not like anything Kit had ever heard before. Half a dozen soldiers were playing a mixture of instruments: brass, drums, a violin, and guitar. The sound was brassy, playful, and joyously untamed by turns. Rules of harmonic structure were laid waste by the music that seemed to leap off the stage and into the bodies of those listening. The musicians appeared to be having the time of their lives and the reaction of the crowd was equally enthusiastic. It seemed to Kit that the music, the people, and the surroundings were one. No other sound made sense in such a place or at this moment. After what Europe had been through, the elemental force of jazz seemed like a catharsis.

During an interval, the group found a semi-circular booth to sit on plush red seats.

'How was your first experience of jazz, Lord Aston?' asked Terrell.

Kit replied truthfully that he had never heard anything quite like it.

'Well I'll take that as a positive view,' laughed Terrell.

'It is, Colonel. Perhaps this is a good moment to ask you about why you wanted to see me.'

Terrell looked at Monk and then smiled widely. At that moment a young man came over to the group. Terrell stood up and shook his hand.

'Lord Aston, may I introduce you to Thierry Simon.'

Kit stood up and shook hands with the young man. This was one of the other men who had been in the room when Mantoux had died.

'My condolences on the death of Monsieur Mantoux.'

'*Merci,*' replied Simon, sitting down at the table with the party.

'Thierry, Lord Aston was asked by the British delegation to look into the death of Mantoux.'

'I see,' said Simon looking grim, 'And what do you make of this unfortunate episode?' His English was excellent.

'A murder with no body, no suspects and, apparently, no investigation. Is this the standard approach to criminal investigation in France?'

Simon laughed bitterly, 'No Lord Aston, it most assuredly is not. Colonel Terrell asked me here tonight to meet you. All of us who were with Monsieur Mantoux in the French delegation are as mystified as you. We have been told not to ask any questions.'

'Really? By whom?' pressed Kit.

'I cannot say. I will not say, to be more precise. What I will say, though, is that I think you should consider finishing your investigation, Lord Aston.'

Kit smiled at this suggestion, and thinking of Briant's advice earlier replied, 'Twice in one day. I must be losing my touch.'

He caught Monk's eye as he said this. Monk returned this look with a nod of approval for his answer.

'I hope that you will take the advice being offered. This is a matter for the authorities,' before continuing with emphasis, 'The French authorities. To be blunt, you have no jurisdiction here.'

At this point Monk intervened, 'Thierry, I would be happy to ask Lord Aston to discontinue, but the French authorities will have to be more transparent on what is happening. And don't forget, Miss Malcolm is still missing.'

'I understand Miss Malcolm refused the police offer of being returned to her hotel and went voluntarily into the waiting car. This is not a police matter, but a matter of choice. Her choice,' replied Simon firmly. However, realising his tone was more aggressive than he had intended, he resumed in a more conciliatory manner, 'But your point about the lack of information is well made. I will convey this to the relevant people, Sir Jonathan.'

'Thank you, Thierry.'

Simon left the table. His departure was followed by silence at the table for a few moments before Terrell filled it with the one thought on everyone's mind.

'They're keeping something back. Something has them spooked. I wish I knew what it was.'

Monk nodded in agreement and then turned his attention to Kit.

'I see no reason for you to stand down, Lord Aston. No reason at all.'

15

Hotel Majestic, Paris: 18th February 1919

Kit finished his breakfast. As he sipped his tea, Percy Pendlebury entered the dining room or, to be more accurate, made an entrance. Ever the consummate actor, Pendlebury's technique, for so it must be called, was a three-part process, refined diligently over the years at countless social engagements.

Firstly, and of critical importance, be not the first to arrive. Lateness was not just fashionable; it was a mark of respect. It recognised the particular roles of host and special guest. Also, and more prosaically, it was easier to be noticed in a crowded room than one devoid of people. Secondly, upon arrival, stop in the doorway long enough to be observed, affecting a striking silhouette. Finally, stride forward confidently with a smile. Look around you and acknowledge people. Whether those people wanted to be acknowledged was not of any trifling concern.

Kit looked on with amusement as Pendlebury weaved his way through the tables, choosing the route least designed to avoid high ranking officials. At one point he caught Kit's eye and gave him an admonishing look. Kit grinned sheepishly and indicated the empty seat opposite him.

'Naughty boy, Lord Aston, naughty boy,' said Pendlebury. It was a point in Pendlebury's favour that he never bore a grudge when he had been misled although he was not beyond using such transgressions as future leverage.

Kit held his hands up in *mea culpa*, 'Look Percy I was telling you the truth, just not all of it. How on earth did you find out?'

'A gentleman of the press never reveals his sources, old boy,' responded Pendlebury while attracting the attention of a waiter.

'Do you know where Miss Malcolm is now?' asked Kit.

'I was rather hoping you could make up for your misbehaviour and give me the scoop.'

Kit looked disappointed and it was clear to Pendlebury he didn't know.

'So, she's flown the coop,' added Pendlebury shrewdly.

A waiter set down a pot of coffee and a plate of croissants in front of the journalist.

'I've taken rather a fancy to these continental breakfasts, I must say. Beats kippers and runny eggs into a cocked hat if you ask me,' said Pendlebury tucking into the breakfast.

'Did you get much material from the photographs for your column?' asked Kit with a smile.

Pendlebury barked in laughter, 'I wondered who the other English gentleman was. Strange chap, that photographer. He didn't seem very happy about selling his pictures.'

'Yes, I noticed. He goes around a few of the hotels where the delegates are staying taking his pictures, but he didn't even have a business card. What do you make of it?'

'He's either in the same game as me or he's Intelligence, which is to say, the same game as me.'

This made Kit laugh, 'I was thinking along similar lines. One more thing, Percy. Why are you following Ida Roberts?'

'Your nurse friend?' smiled Pendlebury.

'There's no story there, Percy. I would consider it a favour if you left her alone. You're barking up the wrong tree if you think she and I are an item.

'I guessed it must your man, not you, who was the object of her affection. Nice looking girl though.'

'She's a very nice girl.'

'Message received, old chap,' nodded Pendlebury with a more serious look. Kit nodded to him also. He knew this was the end of the matter.

Pendlebury consumed the rest of his breakfast. Looking up from his plate, he caught sight of Spunky arriving in the dining room. Objectively, he appreciated Spunky's ability to make an equally impressive entrance. If he didn't know better, it looked as if he were following the same book as Pendlebury. Kit also saw the imminent arrival of his old friend. It never ceased to amuse Kit how Spunky's personality seemed so ill-suited to the career that he had landed in.

'I should probably exit stage left, old boy. I've a feeling your chum will not be best pleased with me now,' announced Pendlebury, rising to his feet.

Before Kit could ask, why, the journalist was off and over to the other side of the large dining room with a speed surprising in so large a man. It demonstrated once again that when someone has an axe to grind, best to get out of the kitchen.

Kit gazed at his friend who was busy weaving his way through the tables and the waiters like a drunken man playing rugby. He sat at the table, looking distinctly Spunky-like. Gone was the hail-chap-well-met. If he wasn't looking dejected, he was far from seeming 'jected. He rested his elbows on the table and covered his face with both.

'You don't seem at full pip, Spunky. What's wrong?' asked Kit lapsing into Spunky-speak.

'Shall we start with everything and work down from there?' suggested Spunky.

'Go on.'

'Well ignoring my titanic hangover for a minute and the disappearance of the finest filly I've been on the gallops with, I've just heard from Chubby in London that Pendlebury has broken the story about the murder of Mantoux. The French diplomat affair is all over the newspapers. Well, we knew it was on the cards, I suppose, after he turned up at the police station.'

Kit nodded, 'Yes, somewhat unfortunate, but can't be helped.'

'Fat-headed poop, that man,' said Spunky rubbing the side of his temples, 'I saw you talking to him. What did he want?'

Kit laughed, 'An apology of sorts. I'd been less than truthful to him previously.'

'Didn't stop him finding out about Angela. Did he say who spilled the proverbials?'

'Sadly, and not surprisingly, silent on that topic,' replied Kit, 'He doesn't know where Miss Malcolm is either. I believe him, incidentally. This is the mystery of the moment. On a separate note, Spunky, are you sure you're not overdoing it a bit with these artist friends of yours? Hardly seems to be an evening when you're not completely stewed to the gills.'

'Nonsense, old bean, I have my eye in now.'

Kit shook his head doubtfully. Rather than dwell on this he turned to a different topic. One that had been bothering him for the last day and of which the conversation with Pendlebury had reminded him.

'Do you know who would have approved that photographer chap's access to the hotel?'

Spunky looked unsure, 'Not a clue. I'll find out.'

As he said this, Kit saw Fink-Nottle approach the table. Spunky looked round at the new arrival and did little to hide his lack of enthusiasm.

'Another newt-nuzzling fat head coming towards us. All roads lead to Aston apparently.'

Fink-Nottle waved towards Kit and finally arrived at the table.

'Fink-Nottle,' said Spunky by way of acknowledgement.

'Stevens,' said Fink-Nottle with arguably even less enthusiasm than Spunky. He then turned his attention to Kit, 'Any news of Miss Malcolm, Lord Aston?'

'No, we were just discussing her mysterious disappearance. What of your work? What will happen now?' asked Kit.

'I think Sir Jonathan is keeping lines of communication open. Hopefully we can resume soon,' replied Fink-Nottle. He seemed nervous as usual. Kit wasn't sure if this was his permanent state or just how he was with relative strangers. It was difficult to reconcile his jumpy demeanour with the impression gained from Ida of a man about town, very much at home in Paris.

Fink-Nottle soon left Kit to join a nearby table. Spunky was unimpressed.

'Useless. Don't know where we pick 'em up.'

-

In fact, Pendlebury's sudden departure wasn't just a consequence of a desire to avoid the ire of Spunky. As he exited the dining room he looked once again at the note in his hand. It was in the same handwriting as the previous note tipping him to the French diplomat affair. It read: *Meet me in Place de la Concorde by the north fountain at 10.30am.*

The note, like the previous communication, was anonymous but this time it seemed like his mysterious informant was willing to reveal his or her identity. This person would clearly have been aware of his breaking the story on the French diplomat. Perhaps he would now be able to break the story on where the mysterious Miss Angela Malcolm had disappeared to. Perhaps even a chance to meet the lady in question.

With no little excitement, Pendlebury hailed a taxicab to take him to the large square. One thought struck him as he took the short cab ride to the square. The Hotel Crillon was nearby. He wondered if his mysterious informant was an American. The journey took less than ten minutes. He was glad he had worn a thick coat rather than his usual cloak as the sunshine belied a briskly cold morning.

He walked over to the fountain. There were a few people, children, couples floating around but no one who seemed likely to provide him with a second scoop in as many days. However, he was a few minutes early. Rather than stare at any passer-by and risk drawing attention to himself, he spent a few moments perusing the fountain. On a large stone basin sat six figures allegorical figures on the prows of ships. These figures supporting the circular vasque upon which were further carving supporting yet another vasque. Water shot up and then cascaded down to the lower vasque and then the basin. A little bit vulgar, thought Pendlebury.

As he finished his inspection, he looked up and saw a man approaching the fountain. He was tall, and well-dressed in a dark pin stripe suit. From the corner of his eye, Pendlebury guessed him to be in his thirties. Pendlebury felt a tingle. He was convinced this was his man.

The man was very near now and clearly approaching him. He risked looking up. As he did so there was a gunshot and then another. As he slumped to the ground, Pendlebury wondered who had been shot. Nearby a young woman screamed and saw the man who had approached Pendlebury run away. Beside Pendlebury's body lay a revolver.

-

Rather than wait for Spunky to come back to him on the source of Sagnier's remarkably free access to the conference hotels, Kit took a taxi to the studio on Rue Jean Giraudoux. Leaving the taxi, he made his way up the stairs. The door was open, so he walked on through. He was greeted by an old man who was not Sagnier.

Kit asked the man, '*Bonjour monsieur, où est Monsieur Sagnier?*'

'I don't know,' replied the man in French, 'he left yesterday. Very strange.'

'How long had he rented this office?'

'Since the beginning of the year. He paid three months in advance.'

Kit saw no value in asking further questions. Bidding the man farewell, he left the office and walked down the stairs. The news about Sagnier bothered him immensely. He disliked coincidences and unaccountable behaviour. Nothing about Sagnier made sense, from his unlimited access to the conference through to the early departure from his rented offices. There was no doubt in Kit's mind that this was connected to his visit the previous day.

Hailing a taxi, he asked to be dropped off at the Hotel Crillon. Entering the hotel, Kit was again struck by the higher levels of security. It made the freedom enjoyed by Sagnier even more perplexing. He went up to the reception and asked them to call Colonel Terrell. There was no response in his room. It was a similar story with Hart. This was inconvenient but not unexpected. He left a message for both men and left the reception area. Taking a chance, Kit went into the dining room to see if either man was there. Once more there was no sign of the men. Giving up he made his way out of the hotel.

On his way out, he ran into Miss Thomas who was just entering through the main doors in the company of a middle-aged man with silver hair and an impressive silver moustache. Kit stopped for a moment and pondered whether he should interrupt their conversation. She had once again transformed from society hostess to personal secretary and seemed unrecognisable from the previous evening.

'Miss Thomas,' called Kit as he exited the hotel.

She looked very surprised to see Kit, but this was soon replaced by a warm smile, and she walked over to Kit with her companion.

'Lord Aston, what a pleasant surprise. May I introduce Doc Holliday.'

It was now Kit's turn to look surprised.

'Not the original one, Lord Aston, if that's what you're wondering,' said Holliday, extending his hand.

Kit laughed, 'I must confess it did cross my mind, Doctor Holliday.'

'Call me Doc, everyone else does,' said Holliday with a grin. Standing near him, he looked to be closer to sixty than fifty, but his face had a light tan and exuded vitality. It made him seem a great advertisement for his profession.

Miss Thomas smiled up at Kit and said, 'If you're looking for Colonel Terrell or Mr Hart, they're in a meeting with the President.'

Kit returned her smile, 'I'm impressed. As it happens, I've just left a message at reception but perhaps you could convey it to the Colonel or Mr Hart. I was interested to find out if they knew, or perhaps you do even, who might have given permission to a photographer called Sagnier to have access to this hotel.'

'Photographer?' said Miss Thomas looking confused, 'I can't say I've seen one around the hotel. It seems a bit strange.'

'That was my thought also, but he's definitely been here. I saw some his photographs when I was in his studio,' replied Kit.

'I think I've seen him,' said Holliday, 'tallish guy, wore a beret.'

'That's him,' nodded Kit.

'I can find out, Lord Aston. I'll send a message to your hotel,' smiled Miss Thomas. This was welcome news for Kit. They parted soon after with Kit hailing a nearby cab. He was keen to avoid walking as his leg was beginning to ache once more.

-

The cab journey lasted around ten minutes, arriving at an office near the Louvre. Kit saw Spunky waiting for him on the street. Spunky waved to Kit and immediately he strode over.

'Good timing. Shall we go in and look at Missus del Gioconda?' suggested Spunky.

'Splendid idea. I haven't been to see the old girl in at least ten years.'

The two men walked into the Louvre and found their way to the room containing the Mona Lisa. There was a large crowd around the painting. After several minutes, they were close enough to have a relatively unobscured view.

'Don't know what he saw in her,' said Spunky as they looked at the painting.

'Leonardo?' asked Kit, surprised.

'No, the husband. I've been to Italy several times and I can tell you; those dark-haired beauties take some beating.'

Kit laughed, 'Only you, Spunky, could stand in front of the most famous portrait on the planet and assess its merit based on how willingly you would make love to the subject.'

'I wouldn't expect you to understand aesthetics, dear boy.'

They stayed on the Louvre to have lunch. Kit related his activities in the morning. To Kit's surprise, there was no official confirmation of Sagnier's right to walk freely in writing. Spunky confirmed he'd spoken with the hotel manager and the head security for the British delegation.

'This somewhat begs the question how he managed to go around the lobby and dining rooms unimpeded,' acknowledged Spunky.

'Unless he was accompanied by someone from the British delegation, of course,' suggested Kit. As he said this his eyes had a faraway look which Spunky recognised.

'Do you know, Kit, you positively glow with intelligence when you're thinking. I normally scratch my backside when I need to kick start those brain cells of yours,' said Spunky before eating a mouthful of a delicate truffle-flavoured poulet.

After finishing the meal, they left the museum and walked through the *Cour Carrée* towards the road. At the edge of the grand courtyard near the road, they saw a soldier propped on a board with wheels, drawing on the pavement. The two friends walked over to see his work. He was young, certainly younger than them. Both legs were stumps below the knees. The soldier looked up at them. There was no sorrow or pity in his eyes. Only anger. Kit nodded to him and looked at the chalk drawing on the pavement. It showed Prime Minister Clemenceau made to look like the Mona Lisa. It made both men smile.

Kit and Spunky both knelt. Each put a handful of francs into the man's bowl. Kit looked once again at the young soldier. There was no mistaking the sorrow in Kit's eyes, the pain of a man who could not do more to help. The soldier looked back at Kit and shrugged. He couldn't bear, but was used to, the polite sympathy in people's eyes. Sometimes he wanted to scream at those who showed him pity when what he needed was money. He looked down at the amount of money in the bowl. He would eat for another month, maybe more. The soldier looked back up his two benefactors and nodded.

'*Merci*,' said Kit.

They walked along the road looking to find a cab. After a few minutes they were in a taxi on their way back to the hotel.

'If you've nothing else to do on that afternoon, Kit, how about meeting Duchamp?'

Kit smiled and said, 'I'm not sure my liver can take a night out with you.'

'It'll just be Duchamp,' explained Spunky.

'He of the urinal,' said Kit, sceptically.

'You'll like him. He loves chess. I told him you were one of the finest players in the country. That piqued his interest. I've invited him to the hotel. He wants to play you.'

'He's played you already, old boy,' laughed Kit.

-

Kit sat facing Marcel Duchamp on the small terrace in Spunky's hotel room. Duchamp was a similar age to Kit and Spunky, slightly built with a mop of dark hair combed back off his forehead. His face was dominated by a prominent nose and a mouth that seemed to turn down in a frown. However, his eyes twinkled with good humour and intelligence. After a few initial pleasantries, Kit decided that he liked Duchamp very much.

The Frenchman's first action upon arrival in the room had been to set the urinal, which he called, 'Fontaine', on its back, turning it upside down in effect, rather than in the traditional upright arrangement.

'Sorry, old chap,' said Spunky sheepishly.

'Do not worry, but it is good to display correctly, *non*?' His English was impeccable and occasionally betrayed hints of an American accent, a legacy of where he had spent the last few years.

Kit looked at Duchamp as they decided on white and black.

'Did you make '*Fontaine*' yourself?'

Duchamp smiled and said, 'Is it important if I did not?'

'It would subvert the idea of art, I suppose, but then again many of the Renaissance masters had studios produce work for them,' replied Kit.

'Precisely, Lord Aston. My only action was to choose this readymade object.'

'Because it appealed to you?' asked Kit.

'*Non*, because I was completely indifferent to it. It is for others to decide how they feel towards this piece.'

'This is art as philosophy,' pointed out Kit, making the first move on the chess board.

Duchamp made his first move and then smiled back at Kit, 'Chess can be war, *non*? So why should art not be philosophy?'

Jack Murray

16

Harry Miller took a taxi back to Rue du Mont Thabor. It was nearly nine o'clock in the evening. The pavements were deserted thanks to the incessant rain beating down. He was carrying a bunch of flowers. Arriving at the building he'd seen Hart entering earlier, he paid the driver and climbed out. He hopped up the steps trying hard to protect the flowers from the rain.

The rain made it difficult to read the name plates on the building. Thankfully, there appeared to be some residents in the building, not just offices. He pressed the first buzzer. No response. Then a second. Still no response. The third proved lucky.

'*Oui?*'

'Flowers,' said Miller in French.

The buzzer sounded to allow Miller to enter. Miller took a lift to the second floor and knocked on the door of the apartment. An old woman answered. Miller judged her to be around eighty. She looked rather taken aback to receive a bouquet of flowers. The last time she had received flowers from her husband was 1897. She looked at the card Kit had written. It read: *From an admirer.*

She thanked Miller and fished in her pocket for a tip. Miller earned five centimes for his commission. In the background he heard her husband yelling from another room. By the tone of his voice he was probably wondering who the hell it was. His wife was thinking along similar lines but for entirely different reasons. Her husband was about to get a shock in the floral form of his wife's mysterious lover. The look on the old woman's face was clearly saying - how am I going to explain this?

Miller continued foot up the stairs to the fifth floor. The first door had an empty name plate. He guessed this was his target. He removed from his pocket two nail files and set to work opening the door. Unlike British doors, the French door proved to be better made to withstand forced entry. He would have to enter from the outside. This was something he'd done many times before, unenthusiastically. Apart from the physical risk, there was greater chance of exposure.

The stairs led up to one more floor. At the end of the corridor was a door. Miller walked towards it. Fortunately, it was open. He found himself in a dark stairwell, with concrete steps leading up to another door. Moments later Miller was on top of the building. It provided a wonderful view of Paris. In the distance he could see the Eiffel Tower lit up like a Christmas tree. Below, he could see the street. Cars splashed along the road, but the pavements were deserted. He returned to the stairwell. It was too wet, and he had all night for this job. Sitting down, he made himself comfortable and used his backpack as a pillow.

Miller woke up three hours later, his head propped up against the naked brick of the stairwell. His neck felt stiff. He spent the next ten minutes trying to recover the feeling in his arms and legs. Finally, some blood appeared to find its way to his extremities.

Outside the rain had, for the moment, stopped. Offering a silent 'thank you' he went straight to the side of the of the building. The street was deserted. He looked in his bag and fished out a rope. Securing it to a colonnade, he swung the rope over the edge and tugged on it several times with all his might. He took a deep breath, hopped onto the edge of the building, and began to abseil slowly down the side of the building.

His minute's descent felt like a year of his life. But he had landed on the small balcony of the target office. He tried the window. It was shut. However, it was unlikely to be locked. From his bag he retrieved a thin metal lever and slipped it into the gap between the two windows. A little pressure and he felt it give. He was inside seconds later.

The office was small. Three desks, a filing cabinet, a picture of Woodrow Wilson and the Stars and Stripes flag comprised the total furnishings. He went straight to the cabinet and opened the first of the four drawers. Inside were several folders. He inspected them but saw nothing related to the murder of the French diplomat.

The second drawer was full of newspapers. He disregarded it and moved on to the next drawer. Several minutes fruitless searching through the papers suggested Hart and his colleagues were capturing material related solely to the conference. He hit gold in the final drawer.

A folder marked Mantoux lay within. He opened it up and looked inside. There were a dozen postcards with neat handwriting. All the key individuals related to the murder were described in the post cards. He read each one with increasing interest and finally incredulity. Time passed more quickly than he had bargained. His curiosity was piqued by shouts coming from outside on the street. Miller ran to the window. A group of people were staring up at him.

The rope.

They'd seen the rope hanging from the colonnade and made the correct assumption. He cursed himself but realised there had been no choice. Rushing back to the folder he quickly replaced the cards and set them carefully back in the bottom drawer. On an impulse he opened the third drawer and took out the files related to the conference and threw them on a nearby table.

The way out was likely to be blocked so he went back to the window. The only way was up. He grabbed the rope and heard the volume of shouts increase. Whistles were blowing. Miller prayed that the French police were not armed as he used the rope to pull himself back up the side of the building. He felt his arms burning as he strained every sinew to reach the top quickly.

As he reached the top he glanced down at the street. There were people looking at up at him from windows on the same floor as the office. It would take them no time to reach the roof. He was trapped.

Miller sprinted to the stairwell door, twisted the handle to lock it from the outside. Seconds later he could hear banging from inside. He ran to the other side of the building to see if there was an escape route. Trying to jump to another building was impossible. He didn't have time to untie his rope. On the side of the building was a drainpipe. He saw no choice but to take his chances with it. The pipe felt solid. He gripped it tightly and hopped over the edge of the building. Slowly he began to make his way down, trying to block out the sound of the stairwell door crashing open.

As Miller inched his way down the drainpipe, the sound of voices overhead grew louder. Moments later he realised he'd been spotted. Ignoring the shouts, he continued down the side of the building until he reached a window. He was now on the third floor. It was at least fifty feet to the street below. No chance he could jump uninjured.

Keeping one hand gripping the drainpipe, he swung his foot onto the window ledge. Balanced thus, he used his other hand to gain a grip of the edge of the wall nearest the window. With something approaching a prayer he pushed his way from the drainpipe and fell forward towards the window. He was now balanced on the window ledge. Turning around slowly, he used his heel to break the window. A few more kicks and he had enough space to get inside.

It was a department store. Women's dresses were all around him hanging on racks. He ran towards the exit. Along the way he saw a dress folded neatly in a shelf marked, petite. It occurred to him the colour would suit Ida, so he grabbed it and tore down the stairs.

At the entrance of the shop, he tried the doors. They were locked. He looked around and spotted a chair presumably used by a security guard. With a silent apology he threw the chair against the door window. The crash of chair against glass felt like it would wake up half of Paris. He jumped through the opening onto the street, startling a young couple walking hand in hand. They stopped and stared at him. He stopped also and looked at them. Their clothes looked very worn. He was on a crutch. There was no need to ask why. With a salute to the man, he handed the young woman the dress. It looked the right size.

Shouts behind the couple told him his pursuers were close at hand. The woman stuffed the dress onside her coat while Miller escaped into the night pursued by three policemen.

Jack Murray

17

Hotel Majestic, Paris: 19th February 1919

Kit sat at the breakfast table reading *Le Monde*. Anyone observing him would have been curious as to what was amusing Kit, because much of the news seemed devoted solely to the lack of progress at the Peace Conference. He looked up at the arrival of Miller. Folding his newspaper, he smiled up at his manservant.

'How did it go last night, Harry? Any trouble?'

'Nothing I couldn't handle, sir,' said Miller with a smile.

'I'm glad to hear it,' replied Kit, also smiling. He unfolded his newspaper and showed Miller the headline in one of the inside pages of *Le Monde*. Even Harry's basic French could translate the story of a mysterious break in at a noted department store in Paris.

'Shocking, sir.'

'Indeed,' grinned Kit, 'but at least the mysterious intruder escaped. Anyway, let's wait until my friend Mr Stevens arrives before you report. I have a feeling he'll enjoy the story as much as I will. Have some breakfast while you're waiting. It's rather good.'

Harry happily assented. He rose and strolled over to the enormous layout of breakfast items laid out on the tables. The buffet included classic Parisian brioche, hams, melons, as well as the unmistakeable British influence of eggs and bacon but thankfully no black pudding. Miller had never understood the appeal of this northern delicacy. Sticking with British, he enjoyed a large, cooked breakfast while they waited for Spunky's arrival.

-

They didn't have long to wait. Spunky's arrival, as ever, was a cause for much looking up from the breakfast tables of the great and the good. It was clear he had been on an epic bender the previous evening owing to a combination of a certain greenness around the gills and an uncertainty around some of the basic principles involved in putting one foot in front of the other.

Finally making it to the table, he sat with a heavy thump on the seat and groaned. However, if nothing else, Spunky always took a certain pride in his powers of recovery. After a moment or two, Spunky's eyes found their range and focused on Miller. As much as his head throbbed with the aftereffects of being with such cheerful companions in Montparnasse, he was immensely curious to find out what Kit's man had found out. Kit had shared with Spunky Miller's unusual qualifications for the task the previous day.

'Another day, another hangover. This must be some kind of record for you?'

'In point of fact, I once went on a run of nine days getting sozzled each evening. Never learnt. You should've come out with us last night, Kit. Duchamp was desperate to get a return match with you. Well done by the way, I had a few bob on you from a couple of the chaps in the café. Not sure what time I returned, but I was asleep as soon as my feet hit the pillow.'

'Glad to hear it. I'm sorry I couldn't stay but it was pretty obvious you and Duchamp were out for more than a quiet snort.'

'Don't remind me,' said Spunky mournfully, 'anyway, enough of my woes. What news from Mr Miller here?'

Miller related what had happened in a hushed voice to Kit and Spunky. The story of the break in seemed to put Spunky in a finer fettle.

'I managed to locate a folder related to the meeting. There was no report on the murder but there was a bunch of post cards related to the individuals in the meeting including yourselves.'

Kit and Spunky looked at one another in surprise.

'We're honoured,' was Spunky's response, 'Complimentary, were they?'

'Neither flattering nor complimentary, sir. They believe that you're working for British Intelligence but there is a question mark on the exact nature of the role. They have a little on your War record, your injury, when and where it was sustained.'

At this point Miller looked a little uncomfortable and looked at Kit.

'Go on,' smiled Spunky, picking up on the discomfort of Miller, 'What else?'

'A little about your family background, sir.'

'Ahh, I understand. Well, nothing to be ashamed of. And what of Lord Aston?'

'They know Lord Aston also works or used to work for British Intelligence. They know he was in Russia and that he helped Prime Minister Kerensky escape the Bolsheviks in 1917,' said Miller, unable to contain his incredulity. "Did you really steal the ambassador's car, sir?'

Kit laughed, 'Nonsense, they gave it to us. Well, sort of.' Noticing Miller's look of surprise, 'I hope you won't think too ill of me, Harry.'

'It's not that, sir, it's the dates. How did you come to be in the middle of No Man's Land a month later?'

'Hod-carrying, Harry, if you believe some. It's a long story and for another time. Anything else?'

'Not much. A little on your War record and family background. They didn't seem so interested in this.'

'Don't blame them, nor am I,' laughed Kit.

'And the key players from the meeting?' asked Spunky.

'Not much on the French. They seem to be straightforward members of their foreign office. On Mantoux more in a second.'

This raised the eyebrows of both Kit and Spunky. Miller had obviously found something.

'What else?' pressed Spunky.

'On the British side, they believe Mr Geddes is part of the British Intelligence. They said he'd spent a lot of time in Germany and Switzerland during the War. Mr Fink-Nottle they had little on apart from his educational background, Cambridge, and the fact he is at the Foreign Office.

'And Angela?' asked Spunky, sitting forward.

Once again, Miller glanced at Kit, who merely nodded, relieved he would not have to deliver the bad news.

'Most of the card contained what we already know, sir. But there was something new,' said Miller, clearly uncomfortable. 'The Americans believe she is part of French Intelligence.

Spunky sat back in his chair and exhaled. But Miller had not finished.

'She is also known as Angelique Mantoux. The murdered man was her...'

'Uncle?' said Kit.

'Yes, sir. It seems she lied about her name to the Foreign Office. It's not Delaroche.' replied Miller.

Miller paused for a few moments to let the news sink in. Kit looked at Spunky. It was difficult to tell if he was not taking the news well or if it was merely the legacy of the previous night, but Kit's friend was looking distinctly ashen faced.

'How are you, old man?'

'Fine, Kit,' said Spunky, regaining his vim, 'I'm more worried about what Monk might have revealed to her when he was in the saddle.' Kit looked stunned.

'You knew about Monk?' exclaimed Kit.

'Come on, old bean. Every dog on the street knew apparently. I only found out afterwards, but I wouldn't be much of a spy if I hadn't guessed, would I?'

Kit laughed in relief and confessed how much he had been dreading this revelation to Spunky. Then he turned to Miller to ask if there were any other things in the file.

'Only one other thing, sir. They kept referring to something called ORCA. Everyone in the card system was labelled either ORCA or possible ORCA or not ORCA. There was nothing else to explain what they meant by it.'

'Spunky? Any ideas?

'Harry, you've done a sterling job. A lot of things falling into place. I think we can guess what Geddes and Hart were arguing about now. I suspect our man knew nothing of Mademoiselle Mantoux, bit like myself, alas, until Hart told him. On the one hand it's good that they've shared some of their intel, but they kept it from us for a long time which doesn't bode well for levels of trust.'

'And ORCA? What's this?' prompted Kit.

'Ah yes, ORCA. I have to confess; this is a bit of a concern. ORCA is an acronym for *Organisation des Révolutionnaires, des Communistes et des Anarchistes.* Neither we nor our American cousins know a great deal about this group alas, but I can tell you, there's a lot of concern in London, Washington, and Paris about them. They provide financial support and weapons to groups around the world, from Europe to South America and Asia. They are amorphous, working in small cells, but we have no idea as to their command structure or their objectives beyond causing a dashed lot of trouble.'

When Spunky had finished, Kit looked astonished.

'I had no idea such an organisation existed. Are they connected to the Bolsheviks?'

'We don't believe so. They've not been around for long or at least within our knowledge, but they've had quite an impact. You remember the assassination attempt on Lenin?'

'I thought that was Sidney Reilly and his Russian chums.'

'No, that's what the Bolsheviks wanted everyone to think. Not that Reilly was up to any good as usual, but we've had some intelligence that it may have been orchestrated by ORCA.'

'But surely they'd be in league with the Bolsheviks?' asked Kit.

'Not necessarily, but as I say, we know so little of their aims. However, the strategy is beginning to emerge from the gloom,' explained Spunky

'How do we know even this?' pressed Kit.

'We caught one of their men in London when he tried to recruit one of our boys. I gather he's been persuaded to talk if you catch my drift. They all have a tattoo on their arm, I gather. It's of a killer whale, hence the ORCA acronym.'

As Kit and Miller listened to Spunky speak about ORCA, the level of noise in the restaurant suddenly seemed to increase significantly. One moment there had been the hum of conversation and the clink and clatter of plates and cutlery, now there were raised voices and shouting. Spunky rose immediately and went over to a group of men to inquire what was happening. He returned moments later, his face now looking positively sick, only this time it wasn't the effects of champagne. Behind him, Kit could see the arrival of some policemen.

In a voice trembling with shock, Spunky said, 'You're not going to believe what's happened.'

18

Paris: 19th February 1919

Émile Cottin brushed his thick sandy brown hair one last time. He had spent many minutes looking at his reflection in the mirror. There was an unmistakable sign of fear. He felt a faint tick in his right eye, barely noticeable except by him. However, all things considered he wasn't as afraid as he'd thought might be the case. Rather, he had a feeling of elation.

All because of her.

The reflection staring back at him was not exceptional. He was not especially handsome or tall. Certainly not wealthy. He looked more closely at his wispy moustache. It was fairer than his hair. She'd told him to keep it. So, he had. He did everything she told him. Everything.

He recalled the night they'd met. Perhaps it was the absinthe. He closed his eyes and offered a silent thanks to a God he did not believe in for the miracle of absinthe. It was banned, of course, but you could still find it if you wanted. Yet strangely he'd never really drunk it before. Not until that night in the café in Montmartre.

The whole group was there that night, Pierre, Louis, Emile, Sebastien, and a new girl, recently arrived in Paris. She was Russian and quite simply the most beautiful girl he had ever seen. Passions ran high that night as the group discussed the best way to fight against the government. How they could bring the revolution to the people. She had spoken also. He had listened to her, entranced, talk of the transformation in Russia. They all had. They all wanted to be with her. But she had chosen him.

Perhaps it was the absinthe.

He had talked in a way he'd never done before. He spoke of what he believed. Of what they needed to do. His friends had heard his story before, how he had watched in horror as the state troops opened fire on the striking workers at the aviation factory. Her presence in the group emboldened him. Yes, the absinthe, but also her. He felt a clarity of thought, an eloquence in expression, a passion in delivery he scarcely believed himself capable of. The way she had listened was different. It was not just in her ears; it was in her eyes and later through her body that she showed him how much she believed in him and his destiny.

He left the bathroom and returned to the bedroom. She lay sleeping on the bed. Her blond hair covering her face, an arm draped lazily over where he had lain. On the back of a chair was an old, brown corduroy jacket. He took it off the chair and slipped it on.

They had met less than three weeks ago. She'd moved in after a week. His friends looked at him with incredulity. How had he managed to capture such a woman? In fact, it sometimes felt like he had been the one captured. Some days they did not leave the apartment. Some days she didn't bother dressing. He was lost. He scratched the inside of his arm. The rash had not disappeared. It felt uncomfortable, but he kept this to himself. She'd asked him to get the tattoo. One just like hers. Of course he'd said yes. Anything for her.

Outside the sky looked grey, but there was no rain. No point in taking chances. He looked for his fedora. Reaching over he took it from the hook and placed it carefully on his head. It would be time to go soon. He looked down at her and wondered if he should let her sleep. As so often before, she answered the question for him.

She rolled over and sat up on the bed. He looked at her and wondered if he could stay a little longer. She seemed to read his mind and shook her head slowly but with a smile.

'No, Emile. Now it's time to work, my love,' she said, brushing a strand of hair of blonde hair from her face.

Emile Cottin looked at her and nodded his head reluctantly. This was what the last few weeks had been building towards. Instinctively he checked the pocket to make sure it was there. The metal felt cold to the touch.

The other thing she'd asked him to do. Or had he suggested it? Yes, that was it. He'd talked of it and the enthusiasm in her eyes had made him talk of it more. It seemed to excite her. So, he talked of it more. And now it was time.

He yearned to stay.
'*Au revoir*, Emile.'
'*Au revoir,* Kristina.'

-

Georges Clemenceau brushed the silver hair above his ears one last time. He liked the feeling of the bristles tickling the skin above his ears. He patted down the very few remaining strands on the top of his head and looked in the mirror. His reflection could not hide the deep feeling of fatigue. He was seventy-seven years old. The Prime Minister of France. The *Père de la Victoire*, the father of France's great victory. The years were etched on the lines of his face, or was it the worry? The worry of leading France to victory in the most brutal, dehumanising war in the history of mankind. The worry of securing his country for the future against Germany. Against the Bolsheviks. The British? The Japanese? The Americans? Who could know? All he knew was that his country was on its knees economically, physically, and spiritually. A prayer for its dead.

'Who is it today?' he asked his aide, Henri Mordacq. So many meetings, it was difficult to keep track. How could he be expected to read the unceasing stream of communications generated by the Peace Conference? How could he be expected to know what meeting was next? Which country would come to him with their demands for land, recognition, aid? All he could hope to do was be lifted to these meetings and use his experience, his guile, and his principles to guide him. For the moment it was all he could give. And he had given everything for France. He always would.

Behind closed doors he allowed himself to feel fatigue. Mordacq could see him like this also; feel the lash of his impatience. But out there. *Non.* Not in front of Wilson. Not in front of Lloyd George. Not in front of France. For them he was and must remain *Le Tigre*. The light in his eyes was barely a flicker; soon it would be a flame. In a few minutes he would go outside and face the outside world. He knew his people were outside the front door ready to cheer him. To support him. To tell him, *we believe in you.*

He wiped a speck from his magnificent silver moustache, turned and walked towards his stairs. At the bottom, Mordacq helped him on with his coat, patting his shoulders for any dust.

Jack Murray

'Hotel Crillon. You're meeting House and Balfour,' said Mordacq.

'I remember,' he lied, 'do you think I'm an idiot?'.

Mordacq rolled his eyes then looked at him sceptically, 'Indeed.'

Clemenceau smiled sheepishly and shrugged his shoulders. Few could question the great man, but Mordacq had long since earned that right. He had fought for his country on the frontline as a general during the War. He had been wounded twice on the battlefield. When France had made the call, like Clemenceau, he had always answered. And Clemenceau, in Mordacq's opinion, was France. He looked at his Prime Minister. Clemenceau's mouth twitched into something of a smile and a twinkle appeared in his eye. The lethargy began to leave him. In its place energy began to build, fuelled by the anger. He was ready to face France and the world. In that order. And fight for what was theirs.

He stepped out the front door. Despite the grey sky, Clemenceau squinted a little as he left his dark corridor and stepped into the light. As ever, *his* people were there to greet him. The volume and intensity of the cheers increased. He stopped and waved briefly at the waiting crowd then walked forward to the waiting car.

-

Cottin hurried along Rue Benjamin-Franklin. Up ahead he saw a small crowd waiting outside a residence. A car was driving towards the waiting assembly. There were only a few policemen. None of them seemed very interested. Why would this morning be any different from the other mornings? The policemen moved the small groups back to let the car park in front of the building. The engine was running. He would be out soon.

The light brown doors of the building opened. Moments later he appeared. He was wearing a dark morning suit and a top hat. His eyes were barely visible, and his moustache seemed to hide the rest of his face. He seemed to be smiling as the volume of cheers increased. He waved.

Cottin stepped forward attempting to get in front of the crowd. His hand was on a revolver. No one could see what he was about to do, but they were angered by his efforts to barge to the front. It was difficult to keep his arm steady.

He fired.

Screams and shouts. Cottin kept firing. Seconds later he felt the first punch. Then the next. And then the punches were raining down on him. His body was getting tossed around and battered like a boat in a storm. He was thinking of Kristina waiting for him in the bed as he lost consciousness.

-

The French Prime Minister was rushed back inside his residence. Mordacq had heard the shots and ran immediately to the door as the policemen brought Clemenceau in from the street.

'He's been hit,' said one of the policemen, somewhat stating the obvious.

Another of the policemen ran to the telephone to phone for an ambulance.

Tears of rage formed in Mordacq's eyes as he gazed down at the pale face of the impossible man who had made his life and the lives of so many bureaucrats and politicians hell, yet who had carried France through to the bitter end and victory in the war with Germany. Was this how it would end? The bullet of a coward.

Clemenceau looked at Mordacq and something of the old sparkle returned to him. Mordacq saw the change in the old man, and hope returned.

'They shot me in the back,' said Clemenceau with contempt, 'They didn't even dare attack me from the front.'

19

Kit spent the morning in the hotel while the police made security checks in and around the building following the news about Clemenceau.

'I can't say I've ever had much time for the old boy,' confessed Spunky, 'but what a vile act. I wouldn't like to be in that man's shoes tonight. If the French have anything in them, they'll be adding injury to the insult of missing at such short range. I mean to say, to take seven pot shots at a seventy-seven-year-old target that was hardly moving very fast and miss six of them. No wonder they nearly lost a war.'

Kit raised his eyebrows at Spunky in disapproval. But Spunky was unapologetic.

'Needs to be said, old boy, damned poor show on the assassin's part.'

Despite himself, Kit laughed and shook his head in a belated attempt at censure. As they were chatting, Sir Jonathan Monk came over to their table and asked to join them. He was clearly agitated.

'Have you heard the news? It's terrible.'

'Yes, we were just discussing it, Sir Jonathan. How on earth did this madman get so close to Clemenceau?' said Kit.

'Not Clemenceau. Pendlebury. He's been shot

'Good lord! Is he dead?' asked Kit.

'Thankfully no, but they've arrested Geddes. He was beside the body. Pendlebury was operated on last night. Shot twice but neither hit any vital organ.

'Sounds like a French assassin to me; Geddes wouldn't have missed,' said Spunky sourly. This brought a frown from Kit but managed to raise a smile with Monk.

'Who's investigating?' asked Kit.

-

Inspector Briant smiled as Kit sat down in front of him. The assassination attempt on Clemenceau was being handled elsewhere and had diverted the attention of his superiors from his own investigation on the French Diplomat.

'Lord Aston, what a pleasure to see you again,' said Briant, not without some sincerity.

'I hope you'll still think so when we've finished, Inspector,' responded Kit.

Briant seemed shaken by the morning's events and Kit expressed his sympathies for the country. The formal cordialities out of the way, the Inspector got on with the business of the visit.

'Now, Lord Aston, I presume your visit is more than a social call to convey your condolences for this morning. What is on your mind?'

Kit smiled and nodded to the Inspector.

'A number of things, Inspector. Perhaps we should start with Pendlebury.'

'Ahh yes, the attempt on Monsieur Pendlebury. Thankfully it also failed.'

'You've arrested Gerald Geddes, I understand.'

'*Non*, you are misinformed, Lord Aston. We brought him in for questions. He is a witness, not an assassin,' replied Briant, smiling at the look of surprise on Kit's face.

'You're right. I was misinformed. May I ask what happened?'

'Apparently Mr Geddes was sent a note by Pendlebury to meet him at the north *fontaine* in Place de la Concorde. Pendlebury had a similar note, which was anonymous.'

'Both men were set up,' finished Kit, 'Pendlebury to be murdered and Geddes to be seen by witnesses as an assassin.'

'Correct, but the plan failed. They did not kill Pendlebury, and a witness saw a gun thrown from a car. Geddes tried to chase after the car but as you may imagine, this was a race he could not win. He was able to describe the car. We are looking for it of course. This is all I can say for the moment.'

'Of course, Inspector, I understand. Then, if we may, I'd like to return to the murder of Mantoux.

Briant smiled and nodded. It looked as if he knew what Kit was about to say. In this, as with so many things to do with Briant, Kit found himself growing in admiration for the Frenchman.

'Please forgive my directness, Inspector, but throughout this unfortunate episode I've had the feeling that you've been aware of key pieces of information which you have not shared. I accept this is inevitable, but in this case, there's one key piece of information which I think it would have been an act of great kindness on your part to share.'

Briant reddened a little and then a smile broke out on his face, like a naughty child caught with his hand in the biscuit tin.

'By which you mean?' asked Briant in a tone of voice that suggested innocence but was accompanied by a look of unabashed guilt.

'The fact that Mantoux wasn't actually murdered by his niece or probably anybody else for that matter.'

This revelation made Briant silent for a moment. He looked at Kit in admiration. While he had previously found himself liking the Englishman, he did so in a way you might like a cute child: a mixture of amusement and tolerance. For the first time he understood why Kit had been brought over to investigate the crime.

'Lord Aston, the attempt on the life of our leader has been a shock for our country, as you may imagine. What I'm going to tell you now is highly confidential. Monsieur Mantoux survived the assassination attempt principally, as you have said, because no attempt was actually made on his life. Miss Malcolm faked a murder attempt by drugging him, with his permission I might add. She's been on the trail of a group dedicated to anarchy for some time now.'

'ORCA by any chance?' interjected Kit.

Briant looked surprised by this and then the smile reappeared.

'Yes, Lord Aston. ORCA. We received intelligence that they were going to attempt an assassination of a senior politician connected to the Peace Conference. We didn't know the target, when it would happen or who was likely to be the assassin. By faking the death of Monsieur Mantoux, we hoped to shake things up a little. There are several men we have our eye on. As this morning will have shown, we sadly failed.'

Kit looked at the policeman with some sympathy. The police faced an impossible task trying to protect the many senior politicians and diplomats clustered in Paris over the many months the conference was likely to take.

'May I ask how you reached your conclusions, Lord Aston? The information you have given me is classified.'

'I have my sources, Inspector.'

Briant smiled ruefully. It was clear that the meeting was at an end.

'It would be a kindness, Lord Aston, if you do not speak of this further. We would prefer that ORCA do not know we create this illusion to uncover their true intent.'

'Of course, Inspector.'

'I think there is nothing else to say, Lord Aston. Although one thing is bothering me. I don't suppose you heard about the break in last night at the American government offices?' asked Briant.

'Yes, shocking wasn't it. I wonder what they were after,' said Kit trying to look as innocent as possible.

'I wonder what they found,' replied Briant, the smile still on his face.

-

Kit took a cab back to the hotel. The police presence was undoubtedly greater following the assassination attempt. This made sense and Kit was surprised it had taken such an appalling incident to make security more comprehensive. As he entered the hotel, he saw Geddes.

'Lord Aston, may I have word with you?'

'Glad to see you're not banged up in jail. Any news on Pendlebury?'

'He'll live, I gather. Don't know how they failed to kill him. They were close enough and it's not as if he's a small target. Anyway, can you come with me?'

Kit didn't much like the tone of voice from Geddes but complied with his request. The two men walked into the hotel bar and found a quiet table away from the window. A waiter came to the table, but Geddes made a brusque gesture towards the waiter which irritated Kit further.

'What do you want?' asked Kit, getting straight to the point.

'This has been a fun twenty-four hours; I can tell you, what with the shootings of Clemenceau and Pendlebury. The last thing I needed was this.

'There's something else?'

'Yes,' scowled Geddes, clearly angry, 'the Americans are up in arms about the break in at their offices last night. They think I orchestrated it.'

'So? Did you?' asked Kit innocently.

Geddes glared at Kit. The lord's manner, the disinterestedness, the superiority of the man was more than just annoying to Geddes, it was symptomatic of everything that was wrong with Britain. The old school tie still mattered, despite the Somme, Passchendaele, Gallipoli, and the countless other strips of land where the graves bore testimony to the failure of this elite. The future would be for men like him. Men who had reached their position in life through competence not class.

'Don't take me for a fool, Aston. I know it was you,' snarled Geddes.

Kit didn't reply. Instead he tapped his walking stick against his prosthetic limb. Geddes face registered the gesture, but the intense loathing remained.

'So, it's true. I'd heard rumours.'

'Makes it rather difficult to have been me, don't you think?' pointed out Kit, with a smile.

'It doesn't rule out your manservant, Miller. I gather he has form in this area,' responded Geddes.

'So back to my original question. What do you want?' said Kit affecting boredom. The conversation was veering in a direction which could put Miller at risk. Kit realised he did not have to confirm Miller's activities, but it made sense to admit nothing either.

'I want to know what you know,' his manner seemed to change. It was less aggressive.

Kit looked at Geddes, and then a thought occurred to him.

'I'm certain Mr Hart updated you on everything you needed to know.'

Geddes nodded. This deftly confirmed that Kit had authorised the break in. It still left unanswered how much Kit knew, or how much more Kit knew than he.

'If that's how you want to play it, Aston, very well. There's one other person who wishes to see you. Would you mind coming with me?'

This presented a dilemma for Kit. He didn't like or trust Geddes. There was no question he was a dangerous individual. Just because he had not shot Pendlebury did not mean that he hadn't been involved in some way and used his presence at the scene to ensure he was not suspected. However, as far as Kit could tell, they were batting for the same side. And Kit accepted one of his great weaknesses was an innate curiosity. It never did the cat much good, thought Kit ruefully as he rose and accompanied Geddes out of the bar.

-

The two men made the short walk to an alleyway, Rue Nicot, a few hundred yards from the hotel entrance. Geddes knocked on the door of an apartment building. A security guard admitted them, and they walked down a short corridor to a staircase. They took the first flight of stairs to the second floor of the building. The security man made what seemed to Kit a pre-arranged knock. Moments later, the door opened, and they were inside a flat that matched Kit's in terms of size and splendour of the furnishing. Kit noted at least one Gainsborough on the wall. They were led into a smaller drawing room. English genre paintings adorned the wall. Kit wasn't sure if the owner was an anglophile, or they had been brought over by the British delegation.

'Make yourself comfortable; we may be a while,' suggested Geddes.

This prophesy proved accurate, and they waited, mostly in silence, for half an hour. Finally, the door opened and a familiar man of around seventy ambled serenely into the room. Kit rose but the man immediately waved to him to sit down.

'Kit, so glad you could join us. Sorry for keeping you waiting, I was with Lloyd downstairs. Bad business with poor Clemenceau,' said the Right Honourable Arthur Balfour, Foreign Secretary and former Prime Minister.

'How is the Prime Minister, Foreign Secretary?' asked Kit.

'The French one is doing fine by all accounts. I gather he's complaining about the marksmanship of the assassin. Our own Prime Minister is up to high doh about the threat of Bolsheviks, and I, as I'm sure you were about to inquire, feel in dire need of my bed,' said Balfour, rubbing his eyes.

'You don't seem yourself, Foreign Secretary if I may say,' smiled Kit.

'Very kind of you, Kit, I think we both know you mean that I seem all too like myself, only an extreme version,' responded Balfour.

'Too many meetings?' inquired Kit.

'Generally, yes. Specifically, no. Elsa Maxwell, I don't know if you know her, insisted on dragging me out to a nightclub last night,' said the evidently exhausted Foreign Secretary.

'A nightclub? Not like you, Foreign Secretary,' laughed Kit before adding, 'How was it?'

'One of the most delightful and degrading evenings I have ever spent, if you must know,' said Balfour before pausing for a moment as the memory of the previous evening seemed to pass, happily, before his eyes. Looking at Kit directly, he continued in a new tone of voice, 'But we digress. Tell me about the French diplomat affair. Has one of our staff killed someone or not?'

'Categorically not, Foreign Secretary.'

'Oh,' said Balfour. He seemed almost let down.

'Mantoux was drugged by our Miss Malcolm who, it transpires, is also known as Angelique Mantoux. She's a member of French Intelligence and, coincidentally, the niece of Monsieur Mantoux,' continued Kit. He looked at the reaction on the face of Balfour, which by the merest twitch of an eyebrow, registered some surprise. Balfour glanced momentarily at Geddes. This needed little translation and was clearly an admonishment.

'Extraordinary. Why would they do all this?'

'I understand they uncovered a plot by anarchists to disrupt the Peace conference. I believe French Intelligence have a few potential suspects under surveillance. By staging an assassination on a minor, but important, official in the conference, they hoped to shake matters up a little. It was convenient to use Mantoux.'

'It would appear to have failed,' suggested Balfour.

Kit didn't answer for a few moments. Both Balfour and Geddes looked at him, waiting to hear what was on his mind.

'Yes, they failed. That much is certain. But there are some things that remain unexplained. I'd love to meet Miss Malcolm or Mantoux to find out more about who they were following. Are you familiar with ORCA, Foreign Secretary?'

'Sadly I've had their activities drawn to my attention. Are they involved?'

'We can't discount the possibility that they have infiltrated the conference, perhaps via one of the delegations of the principal countries.'

'Well if Mademoiselle Mantoux can so easily infiltrate our delegation,' said Balfour wearily, once more addressing a look towards the unfortunate Geddes, 'then I agree, Kit, it's not just possible but entirely probable. Is any of this connected to that fool Pendlebury's shooting?'

'I believe so, Foreign Secretary, but I need to check further into a few matters,' responded Kit.

Balfour looked even more crestfallen and glanced at Geddes.

'I hope you won't mind me saying, Kit, but I was rather hoping we could have concluded matters as far as you're concerned. Is there really much more you can do that can't be handled by the police?'

This was the key question. Kit had no real authority to continue. Unexplained issues remained for him, but without Miss Malcolm, and now Pendlebury. He realised he couldn't fit all the pieces of the jigsaw together without speaking to both. He took a deep breath as a wave of frustration coursed through his body. It was always this way when the solution lay so close at hand yet remained out of reach. Balfour gazed at him with a half-smile, recognising the conflict in his young friend.

'I don't know if Geddes has mentioned, but I've had, shall we say, some angry addresses emanating from our American friends on an incident last night. Perhaps, Kit, it would be best if you and your resourceful manservant retire gracefully from the scene. Your presence may be construed as, how can I put it, inflammatory.'

Kit grinned sheepishly but another feeling was strong within him: how did everyone know? Balfour looked at Kit and the smile seemed to grow wider, as if he had read his mind.

'I think I'm right in saying there are probably more spies at this conference than genuine delegates. We're all under surveillance one way or another,' said Balfour, rising slowly to his feet. The meeting was over.

20

Ida Roberts sat at the bedside of a yet another new arrival. Thankfully the young man was asleep, or better still, unconscious. The nightmare would only begin when he awoke. For Ida, the key was to focus on the person, not the pain. She knew her discomfort would be momentary. The patient's pain would last a lifetime. No amount of time exposed to the horror of war could inure her to this.

The groans in the ward were a background hum. Her attention was always on the person she was with. They deserved this at least. She rose from her seat and walked to the next bed, then the next. There were fifty beds in the ward, she spent time with everyone. Much of this was spent listening to them talk. When they did so, it seemed to help them take their minds off the pain or worse, the future. It reminded them of their humanity and, for Ida, their dignity.

The only breaks she took were for a cup of tea. Whatever the question, tea provided if not an answer, then solace. She always tried to meet up with Ethel for a chat, but today had been different. There was a lot of activity as rumours of an assassination attempt on Clemenceau filtered through. This had been a shock. It seemed incredible that a man who had led the country through the most horrible war in history, could be so vulnerable to an assassin's bullet. And outside his own home, too.

The strange atmosphere continued throughout the day. It seemed unreal. For Ida, the end of the day couldn't come soon enough. A sense of displacement stayed with her throughout the day. At first, she thought she may be coming down with an illness, then she realised what it was.

It was fear. A sense that things were not over. The job hadn't been finished. More was to come. The news that the assassin was a Frenchman, an anarchist if anything, made things seem worse. An enemy within.

After leaving the hospital, she looked for a newspaper seller, but all the afternoon papers were sold out. It was dark now. A light breeze blew in her face as she walked through the early evening crowd. Outside her small apartment she noticed a newspaper seller. She crossed the road and bought a paper. Her French was sufficiently developed to read confidently these days. She hurried back to her rooms. Indoors, she didn't bother removing her coat, falling instead, onto the sofa, clutching the newspaper. When she opened the inside page of the paper to read the story of the assassination attempt, her eyes widened in shock at the photograph of Emile Cottin. She stared at his face. The hair, the clear eyes, the wispy moustache. Her breathing became shallower, and her heart began beating quickly. She had to get to the Majestic to warn Kit and Harry.

-

Geddes and Kit left the meeting with Balfour and walked along the corridor. Kit wasn't sure how he felt towards Geddes at that moment. His high-handed manner was unquestionably annoying, yet he had clearly been an important, if unheralded, part of the War effort. It was apparent Geddes had no love for Kit, or more likely, Kit's class. But Geddes had given Kit a freer run than he might otherwise have enjoyed in investigating the apparent murder. The only conclusion he could draw was that Geddes had more respect for his abilities than he cared to admit.

'I sense you don't think this is over,' said Geddes, as they stood at the door.

Kit looked at Geddes and nodded, 'No, I can't explain why but it doesn't feel finished. The shooting of Pendlebury is key. Why would anyone take such a risk unless Pendlebury knew or was a witness to something?' Kit stopped for a moment and Geddes could see his mind turning something over. 'Tell me, do you have a list of the meetings the Prime Minister has coming up over the next few days and the attendees?'

'No, but I can get it from his secretary. Wait here. I'll go and get it.'

Geddes turned and walked back up the stairs. As Kit waited, he tried to pin down what was concerning him. It all came back to Angela Malcolm. From an Intelligence point of view, he could understand why she would be in the meeting involving the reparations. If the French and the British disagreed over the size and distribution of the monies from Germany, the more inside information the French had on this, the better for them. This much was obvious. But it may also have been subsidiary to the real reason why she was in the meeting: security. If the French had concerns, fully realised as it turned out, that there was a security risk to senior delegates at the conference, then why did French Intelligence stage the fake murder? And why this meeting? Was it merely a stroke of good fortune because they had an insider in this meeting or was there another reason?

A few minutes later Geddes returned clutching an envelope. He smiled, 'You're in luck. They had a spare copy. It only covers tomorrow and the next day, but we can worry about the other meetings later. 'The two men sat down on two seats in the corridor outside Lloyd George's rooms. Kit smiled to himself and wondered if the Prime Minister might make an appearance. Kit tore open the envelope.

'Do you know what you're looking for?' quizzed Geddes. The tone was more conciliarity.

'No, but hopefully I'll know it when I see it,' replied Kit enigmatically. He stared at the list of delegates in the meetings earmarked for Lloyd George to attend. On the second page, he found what he was looking for. He pointed to a name on the list and looked at Geddes.

'Don't ask me why. It's just a feeling,' admitted Kit.

'You don't seriously think he intends to kill Lloyd George?' said Geddes in shock.

-

Harry Miller tried on the black overcoat. It was far from a perfect fit.

'I'll take it,' he said in French and handed the man the correct sum in francs. He then handed the shopkeeper his old coat and hat. Miller walked out leaving the shopkeeper mystified by the Englishman's actions, especially as the other coat was clearly new and still had a sales label on it. He shook his head.

'*Les Anglais.*'

With a shrug of his shoulders, the shop keeper brushed the new coat down a bit and put it on the sales rail. He looked at Harry's old hat and tried it on himself for size. It was too small. He placed it on a shelf with other men's hats and went to look for a sales label.

Miller strode out of the shop and back towards the café. His man was still there drinking coffee alone. He remained across the road from the café, out of the way, but able to monitor his target's movements. Half an hour later the man rose from his seat. He was on the move again. The new coat felt uncomfortable on Miller, but it was necessary. This was his third coat of the day. Kit had suggested he employ this ruse if it transpired the man, he was following spent longer than usual outside the hotel. He had.

It had been a long day. Miller was hungry, his feet were sore, and he was aching to get back to the hotel, take a bath and eat. His target seemed to be heading in the direction of the hotel. Miller gave a silent sigh of relief. The chill was also beginning to creep through the material of the coat. The warmth of the hotel could not come a moment too soon.

They arrived back in the Majestic in the late afternoon. It was getting darker, certainly colder and there was a hint of rain in the air. Rather than go to his room, his target chose instead to sit in the lobby, reading a newspaper. The assassination attempt on Clemenceau dominated the headlines. For the next hour, Miller sat and watched his target remain seated, clearly waiting for someone to arrive. The only excitement came when he called over a hotel porter and handed him some money. The porter went outside the hotel, returning a few minutes later with the same afternoon newspaper. Miller suspected this was a later edition. Although this explained nothing to him.

The arrival of the new newspaper seemed finally to cause a reaction. Miller recognised the look all too well. He'd seen it before on other men. Probably other men had seen it on him. It was fear.

-

Ida arrived at the Hotel Majestic after seven. It was dark, and she was trembling. She couldn't decide if it was the cold or perhaps trepidation. She gripped the newspaper as she walked through the hotel entrance. She wasn't sure if what she had seen was important, but she knew instinctively Kit had to know. There was an initial inspection inside the hotel, and she sensed the increased level of security with the number of army men she saw milling around reception.

She ran over to the reception desk and asked for the room numbers of Kit and Miller. The receptionist looked at her suspiciously. It did not take him long to make up his mind that Ida was not 'in the trade'. He wrote down the room numbers and handed them to her with a smile.

'*Merci*,' said Ida with a grateful smile.

The receptionist pointed Ida towards the lifts. She took the piece of paper and walked in their direction. It took a few moments before the lift arrived. She walked into the lift, vaguely aware that someone had joined her. Ida turned around to press the floor button. Just then she thought she heard someone shouting her name. The din was too much to be sure. She pressed for the third floor. The other person in the lift reached over and pressed number five. Turning around, she glanced at the person she was sharing with.

An icy hand seemed to grip her. She wanted to scream but the gun pointing at her suggested that it might be the last thing she would ever do.

-

Miller had sat several tables behind his surveillance target for over an hour. There had been no movement. He looked at the time. It was just after seven. Finally, he noticed some activity. The newspaper was put down. It was difficult to see what had caused this change in behaviour.

A minute passed. Then another. Suddenly Miller rose to his feet, it was clear what was happening. He cursed himself for sitting so far away. Had he been too cautious? There were too many tables, chairs, and people in front of him. He rudely barged through groups of people, but up ahead he could see the lift doors opening. Ida was going in. He wouldn't make it in time.

'Ida!' he shouted. But it was too late.

He looked at where the lift would stop. The third floor. Then it continued to the fourth. But Miller was already on the move towards the staircase. He bound up the stairs, knocking people to one side.

-

Kit left Geddes at the apartments on Rue Nicot and returned on foot to the hotel. Although it was a short distance, he could feel a dull pain in his leg. Upon arrival at the hotel he fell into the nearest seat he could find in the lobby. He had hardly been sitting a minute when he sensed someone standing over him. He looked up and gazed in shock at the woman before him.

'Lord Aston, you must come with me.' It was Angela Malcolm.

'Miss Malcolm, or do you prefer Miss Mantoux?' asked Kit, recovering his poise. However, his unease returned as he looked up at the worried face of Miss Malcolm.

'There's no time for this. Your manservant and Miss Roberts are in danger, we must find them,' said Angela Malcolm.

'Good lord!' exclaimed Kit, 'Do you know where they are?'

'No, Miss Roberts is either on the third or the fifth floor. That's where he's taken her.'

'The fifth floor, that's where the meeting room is,' said Kit, 'Would he have a key?'

'Yes, I think so.'

'Is it Fink-Nottle?' asked Kit, looking at Miss Malcolm. She nodded in reply and began moving towards the lift.

-

The lift doors closed at the third floor and continued up. Ida's eyes never left Fink-Nottle. He stared back at her but said nothing. When the lift doors opened at the fifth floor, he motioned with his gun to leave. Both walked out of the lift. Fink-Nottle kept his gun hidden under his overcoat as he pushed Ida along the corridor. They arrived at the meeting room. Reaching inside his pocket, Fink-Nottle took out a key and threw it towards Ida.

'Open it,' he said. His voice seemed curiously high-pitched to Ida, like he was nervous. This was ridiculous; he was the one with the gun. What right had he to be scared, thought Ida angrily.

They entered the meeting room. Ida saw a meeting table with a dozen chairs around it. Fink-Nottle closed the door and took the keys.

'Sit down,' ordered Fink-Nottle.

Ida did as she was told. Her initial fear had dissipated a little. The man before her did not look like a killer but she knew looks, voices and words were the disguises we all wear to hide from the world our true selves. If anything, he seemed unsure of exactly what to do himself.

'I trust I don't need to tell you any attempt to escape or warn people outside will result in your immediate death. I'll take my chances after that.'

Ida nodded, maintaining a steady gaze at Fink-Nottle. Unquestionably he was disconcerted by her spirit. Ida warned herself not to push this too far.

Fink-Nottle walked over to the meeting room phone. He called to reception and gave them a number he wished to be connected with. He put the phone down and the gun also. Patting his pockets, he located a cigarette case and lit himself a cigarette.

'Forgetting my manners,' said Fink-Nottle. He reached over to Ida with the cigarette case. Ida declined.

A minute later the phone rang.

'Hello, it's me. We have another problem. I've been recognised. Can you come for me?'

Fink-Nottle nodded for the next minute as he received instructions.

'Rue la Perouse. Fine I'll see you there in a few minutes.'

As he put the phone down, he heard the lift bell ring. Nervously he glanced at the door. He picked up his gun and walked to the door. He opened the door slowly and glanced through the narrow crack. He could hear running down the corridor. Fink-Nottle drew back and waited.

-

Kit pressed for the fourth floor and then the fifth floor. Miss Malcolm looked at him strangely

'If he's in the room, he'll be on the lookout for the lift, particularly if he's seen us. We'll get out at the fourth floor and take the stairs.'

Angela Malcolm nodded, and they left the lift at the fourth floor. Pain shot up Kit's leg as they rushed to the stairs. He wasn't used to moving at speed, especially up flights of stairs. Each step caused a further stab in his leg.

-

The lift doors opened on the fifth floor and Harry Miller ran out of the lift towards the meeting room. He saw the door was ajar and then it opened fully. Standing in the doorway was his quarry for the afternoon, Fink-Nottle, and sitting behind him, Ida.

'Ida,' said Miller, walking forward, ignoring Fink-Nottle's gun, 'Thank God you're alright.'

'I'm fine, Harry,' said Ida glancing uncertainly at Fink-Nottle.

Miller turned to Fink-Nottle, 'She has nothing to do with this. Don't harm her.'

Fink-Nottle shook his head, 'I must disagree with you. Sit down over there.' He indicated seats at the other side of the table. He pointed his gun slowly at Miller's head to emphasise he meant what he said. Realising there was no choice, Miller reluctantly complied.

Moments later, the sound of the lift bell sounded again. Fink-Nottle glanced out of the room. The lift doors opened but nobody left the lift. Fink Nottle stepped outside the room to get a better look. The lift was empty. Confused he walked back into the room again. He motioned to Ida to stand up. She did so, and he took her arm and led her outside the room. He walked behind her with his gun pressed against the base of her spine. They walked over by the stairs, quietly.

Below, there was the faint sound of steps. Of people climbing the stairs not wanting to be heard. Fink-Nottle smiled. He glanced down to see who was coming, then pushed Ida back into the room and closed the door. Turning to Miller and Ida he said, 'One word from either of you or I will use this.'

The gun was pointed at Ida.

-

Angela Malcolm reached the top of the stairs first. She was holding a revolver. Kit was unarmed and followed her to the office.

'I'll go first,' she whispered. 'If he's there, he won't be expecting you. Take the gun.'

Kit nodded and watched her open the door quietly. She walked in slowly. In front of her she saw Miller and Ida, sitting beside one another. It wasn't until she was further into the room that she realised Fink-Nottle was there also, and his gun was trained on her. He jerked his hand in the direction of Miller and Ida.

'You too, Lord Aston,' said Fink-Nottle. 'Throw the gun in first.'

Silence.

'I said throw the gun in now, Aston. I won't hesitate to shoot.'

There was no response. Miller looked at Miss Malcolm. It was clear she was mystified. Fink-Nottle was in a quandary. Any shooting would cause any security to come running. On the other hand, there was always the possibility Aston had gone for help. He pointed to Ida and motioned for him to join her.

Ida glanced at Miller and stood up. Miller grabbed her arm and shook his head. The click of the revolver caused both Ida and Miller to look at Fink-Nottle. Miller released his grip allowing Ida to join Fink-Nottle. With his gun jammed against the base of her spine, Ida walked through the door as a human shield.

The corridor was empty.

21

'You stay here. If you make any noise or try to escape, remember, I'll kill her,' growled Fink-Nottle. This was a very different man to the one that Angela Malcolm had known in the conference. His eyes betrayed fear mixed with mania. Not the most attractive combination at the best of times but in the pasty features of this man, it resolved itself in the manner of a pig facing a smiling abattoir worker holding a stick.

Miller was on his feet instantly. He was moments away from leaping over the table when he felt Angela Malcolm's hand on his arm.

'Take me, she's nothing to do with this.'

Fink-Nottle ignored him and closed the door. Miller heard the key locking them in. He was on his feet immediately and over to the door.

'Wait,' commanded Miss Malcolm, 'He'll hear you.'

Miller froze and stood by the door, listening intently for any noise outside. There was none. He balled his fingers into a fist, his fingernails digging into the palm of his hand. Rage mixed with nausea.

'If he does anything to her, I'll kill him,' snarled Miller. He started to root around his pockets, but they were empty. He turned to Miss Malcolm, 'Do you have a nail file?'

He was greeted with a look that suggested his question was not just redundant but also patronising. However, she understood immediately what he was going to do. She took a pin from her hair and raced over to Miller.

'Will this do?'

'It'll have to,' said Miller, kneeling to the lock.

-

Kit's gamble had failed, and he knew it.

He stood inside the lift listening. The exchange at the door of the office had been audible. If they came towards the lift, he would be ready. He moved to the side of the lift so that he would not be visible when the doors opened. After waiting a few seconds, enough time for Fink-Nottle and his hostage to have arrived, he released the lift from its hold. He waited. The seconds passed.

Silence.

After a few moments the lift began to move down. He put the gun in his pocket and waited for the doors to open. The lift stopped at the first floor. Kit rushed out as the doors opened and made for the stairs. He could see Fink-Nottle and Ida at the bottom of the stairs, his arm around her like they were lovers. They were moving quickly. Kit raced after them, trying to ignore the spearing pain in his leg. Looking left and right there was no one Kit could alert to the hostage situation right in front. There was no choice. He had to follow.

-

Fink-Nottle reached the bottom of the stairs and looked around. Aston and the others had clearly not warned anyone else of their suspicions. Using his free hand, he pushed Ida forward.

'To the door.'

Ida did as she was told. Strangely, she felt no fear at this point. For some reason she did not think Fink-Nottle would harm her. She wasn't sure if this was because she thought a professional killer would only kill specific targets or because, fundamentally, she did not take this little man seriously. He was so unlike Harry Miller or Lord Aston. But what did that mean? As she found herself driven forward towards the hotel doors, she realised her lack of fear was based essentially on disbelief that this was really happening. There wasn't time to think or be afraid. They reached the doors. She sensed Fink-Nottle looking around him wildly, and then they were through to the cold air. It was evening and the night was lit by lamps, lights in windows and the passing cars. The pavement was deserted.

'This way,' ordered Fink-Nottle.

-

The door clicked open.

'You're good,' complimented Angela Malcolm, somewhat amazed at the rapidity with which Miller had unpicked the lock. Miller didn't hear her; he was already tearing down the stairs.

'And in love,' she added throwing off her shoes and sprinting after him.

Miller leapt down the stairs several at a time. He arrived at the bottom in time to see Kit rushing out the front doors. No one else, from what he could see, was aware of the drama. Behind him he was aware of Miss Malcolm following his exceptionally direct route down the stairs, much to the annoyance of a couple of guests. Miller turned to her.

'Find help! They've gone out onto Portugais.'

'Yes,' replied Miss Malcolm and went in the opposite direction to Miller, who sprinted to the doors fuelled by a fear and anger. He burst through the doors, looking right then left. He saw Kit up ahead hobbling along Avenue des Portugais before turning right onto Rue la Perouse.

-

Fink-Nottle and Ida were forty yards ahead of Kit, walking quickly. Kit's leg felt like someone was stabbing it repeatedly with scissors as he struggled to keep pace. He cursed his injury as Fink-Nottle seemed to increase the gap between them. Outside the hotel, he no longer held onto Ida's waist, choosing instead to run ahead, and clutching her hand and effectively dragging her along with him. This meant Kit could not get a shot off from Angela Malcolm's revolver. Thankfully it meant that Fink-Nottle's view Kit's pursuit was obscured. The couple headed around the corner. Kit hurried in pursuit, an idea forming in his mind. And a prayer.

-

In a matter of seconds, Miller had reached Kit.

Miller spied the gun in Kit's hand. 'Give me the gun, sir, I can reach them quickly,' whispered Miller urgently.

Kit handed Miller the gun, 'Run along the other side of the street, try and hide behind one of those cars. Don't shoot unless I tell you.'

Grabbing the gun, Miller bounded across the road and found a car parked twenty yards behind Fink-Nottle and Ida. He crouched behind the bonnet and waited for Kit to make his signal. Kit looked at Fink-Nottle and then upwards to the floor above. He moved forward slowly and then, choosing his moment, shouted.

-

Fink-Nottle and Ida slowed down. Ida could see he was in a panic.

'Where are they?' he snarled, gripping Ida's hand even harder.

'You're hurting me,' cried Ida.

'Shut up.'

They continued to move forward, more slowly, when they heard a shout from behind.

'Stop!'

Fink-Nottle spun around. He saw Kit standing twenty yards away, his hands in the air, palms facing towards him.

'I'm unarmed, Fink-Nottle. Take me. Leave Ida alone.'

Fink-Nottle pulled Ida closer, one arm around her neck and kept her in front between him and Kit. He raised his other hand holding the gun and aimed at Kit.

'Stay where you are, Aston. I'll kill you both.' And then he looked down at Kit's leg in amazement. Kit had rolled up his trouser leg. Fink-Nottle could make out clearly that he had a prosthetic limb.

'Look,' said Kit, his voice calm, 'I'm half crippled. Take me. Leave her alone.'

Fink-Nottle looked around as a car came past behind him. It wasn't his car. Kit saw the movement and realised he was waiting for someone.

'You're waiting for someone. Take me with you, Fink-Nottle, I'm a better guarantee of safety than some nurse.'

Fink-Nottle stared at Kit. What he was saying was true. Capturing Aston would be a personal coup. They would look at him differently. In a moment he would be transformed from some lackey, an instrument for the higher-ranking men, into a leader. Into one of them.

'Come forward. Slowly,' said Fink-Nottle, continuing to hold Ida closely.

Keeping his hands held high, Kit limped forward. He didn't have to act. He was in agony, and it was etched over his face. He noticed the look on Fink-Nottle's face and smiled ruefully.

'The old leg isn't up to this nonsense anymore,' said Kit with a smile, hoping his demeanour would calm the obviously rattled Fink-Nottle, but hoping also that he would drop his guard.

Kit was only a few yards away when he stopped. He looked at Ida. She returned his gaze, afraid but in control. At any other time, Kit would have dwelt on what an amazing lady this was and wished

Miller the best of luck for the future. Thought of Miller focused his thoughts.

'Don't shoot,' said Kit looking at Fink-Nottle but hoping Miller understood.

-

Miller watched Kit move forward slowly. It was a surreal sight, Kit with a trouser leg rolled up, hands raised in the air. It was clear that Kit was trying to calm the situation. He kept a constant dialogue going in a neutral voice. Miller was impressed by the calmness of Kit in such a situation. He hoped that he would be as steady when his moment came. There would only be one chance. One shot. Ida's life depended on it. From the moment he had threatened Ida, Miller's only thought was how to stop Fink-Nottle in whatever manner he could. He would not hesitate to kill Fink-Nottle, he knew.

He heard Kit say, 'Don't shoot.' He knew the message was meant for him and he felt himself tensing from behind the car.

Fink Nottle slowly released Ida from his grip. He moved slightly so that as she walked forward towards Kit, he remained partially obscured.

And then Miller saw a movement from above. His mouth fell open at what he was seeing.

-

Angela Malcolm ran into the dining room in the hotel, dodging one surprised sommelier and an irate head waiter. She pushed him away and strode forward looking around at the diners. There wasn't time to find out who was running security at the hotel. She was after men with guns.

Soldiers.

There were none in the dining room. She turned and sprinted to the bar, ignoring the stunned looks of the delegates in the lobby. Arriving at the bar she found what she was looking for, three soldiers were standing with a couple of unfamiliar men in suits. Just as she was moving towards them, she felt a trap on her shoulder. She turned around. It was a familiar face.

'Kit Aston needs your help,' she said urgently.

-

Ida walked forward nervously, aware of Fink-Nottle's outstretched arm nervously holding the gun. She could not see if it was trained on her or on Kit. Ahead of her Kit's hands remained in the air.

'That's it Ida. Slowly does it,' said Kit. He seemed utterly unruffled. This gave her a surge of hope.

Kit could see that Ida's body was probably obscuring Miller's view of Fink-Nottle. He moved forward also. The macabre minuet with Ida, was taking place little by little. Both keen to avoid a misstep or a sudden movement. The street was silent as they inched forward.

And then there was an almighty crash. Fink-Nottle was flung to the ground, screaming in agony. Ida also screamed at the unexpected noise and spun around. On the ground lay Fink-Nottle clutching his arm. All around him lay what looked like white earthenware. Lord Aston bent down and calmly took the gun lying by Fink-Nottle's side.

From behind, Ida felt a pair of arms enfold her. She turned around. It was Harry Miller.

'Ida, are you alright?'

'Harry! Yes, yes, I'm fine. What happened?'

They both turned to look at Kit, who was gazing upwards at the balcony.

Spunky waved down at the assembly below him. Beside him was a man that neither Miller nor Ida recognised

'Thanks, old boy, I'm sorry Marcel for all of this,' said Kit gesturing to the street.

'Think nothing of it,' said Spunky, 'Jolly good shooting, don't you think, Marcel?'

As he said this a car drove past. It slowed momentarily. Kit turned towards it but before he could get a good view, it drove off. He caught sight of a woman's blonde hair in the passenger seat.

Behind the group, Angela Malcolm arrived with three soldiers and Sir Jonathan Monk. She looked down at the prostrate, and groaning Fink-Nottle, then up to Spunky, who smiled and waved down.

'Hello, Angela, nice evening, isn't it?' said Spunky like it was a chance meeting in the park with an old school friend.

'Hello, Aldric,' replied Miss Malcom, for want of anything better to say to her former lover. She looked down again at the chaotic scene on the ground and the agonised figure of Fink-Nottle.

Without averting her gaze she asked the question that was on almost everyone's mind.

'Was that a....?'

'Men's urinal?' replied Kit, 'No. It was a work of art.' From above they all heard clapping. Everyone looked up. It was Marcel Duchamp.

'*Merci Monsieur.*'

22

Paris: 21ˢᵗ February 1919

It was with some difficulty that Percy Pendlebury propped himself up in the bed. This was not unusual as he was no longer the athlete of yesteryear insofar as he could have been considered one in any year. His shoulder was heavily strapped from the bullet wound but, he reflected optimistically, it was on the other side from his writing hand, and he had a story to tell. For once he was not only a part of the story as an observer, but he was also a participant. This was a thrilling distinction and Pendlebury was just the man to turn a tale of poor shooting into one of derring-do, featuring he, Pendlebury as an ordinary man caught up in the madness of a continent on the brink of war, or some such nonsense.

It was in this buoyed spirit that he greeted the arrival of Kit clutching what looked suspiciously like a Dom Perignon.

'Lord Aston, you know how to treat a man lying mortally wounded in his death bed.'

'I may have a cure,' said Kit handing over the bottle. 'It was either this or a bunch of grapes.'

'I'm glad you waited until later in the fermentation process.'

'How are you feeling?' asked Kit.

'I think I've escaped death by the skin of my teeth. However, I am dying to know why I was a target for an assassin's bullet and is this likely to happen again?'

As he asked this question, another visitor entered the room.

'Inspector Briant,' said Kit with a smile, 'You've met Pendlebury.'

'The Inspector and I are old friends, now,' said Pendlebury generously.

This was neither confirmed nor denied by Briant, who chose, instead, merely to raise his eyebrows.

'Inspector Briant and I decided it would be best to meet here, Percy, to agree the story, you'll no doubt be itching to break to your adoring public.'

'They are waiting, Lord Aston, have no doubt of that. I shall call it the French Diplomat Affair.'

'Which brings us to the French diplomat in question. Inspector?'

Inspector Briant and looked amiably at Pendlebury, 'We would appreciate if your story suggested that it was, in fact, an attempted murder and that the diplomat in question, who cannot be named for security reasons, was saved by the extraordinary efforts of the French health system.'

'I see,' said Pendlebury, unable to disguise the fact that the story was losing its newsworthiness with every new syllable uttered by the Frenchman.

Kit smiled as he saw Pendlebury's obvious disappointment.

'Fear not, Percy, old chap, we have better news. The assassin, who also cannot be named, was an anarchist friend of Emile Cottin, the madman who tried to kill Clemenceau, and he is implicated in the attempted murder of one Percival Pendlebury.'

'I say,' said Pendlebury cheering up, 'this is rather rum. Is it true? Not that it matters.'

Kit looked at Briant and then replied, 'You're going to like this even more, Percy. The reason why there was an attempt on your life was that you sat in the same café as your killer, so to speak, and Emile Cottin. They saw you, but you were not to know who they were. We believe he was also the author of the anonymous notes to you. It seems he wanted to create as much embarrassment for the peace process as possible. I'm afraid they were using you in this regard.'

'You don't say. So they recognised me, how wonderful,' exclaimed Pendlebury delightedly before the realisation dawned on him that it was far from good news, 'I say, are you sure they won't try again?'

'They have no reason, Percy. We've caught the two men. Both will spend a long time in prison.'

Pendlebury looked at Briant, who nodded confirmation.

'That's spectacularly good news. But tell me, how did you catch my would-be assassin?' asked Pendlebury, already writing the story in his mind.

The Inspector took over the narrative, 'You have Lord Aston to thank for that, *Monsieur*. He made a connection between the French diplomat case and the assassin. I believe you were following Miss Ida Roberts who, in turn, had been following a man under suspicion by Lord Aston. By chance, this man was meeting Emile Cottin. It was because you could link the two together that they attempted to kill you, as Lord Aston says.'

'I say, Kit, well done. Definitely forgive you for the earlier misdirection.'

'Thank you, Percy, that's been weighing heavily on my mind,' said Kit.

'So it should,' admonished Pendlebury before asking, 'And what of Miss Malcolm?'

'She's entirely innocent, *monsieur*.'

'Whatever Miss Malcolm is,' replied Pendlebury, 'I certainly wouldn't accuse her of being innocent.'

-

At that moment, Angela Malcolm was strolling arm in arm by the bank of the Seine with her good friend and former lover, Spunky Stevens. Up ahead Notre Dame rose imposingly against the steel grey sky. Along the bank, other couples walked hand in hand, some old, many young, all attracted to the river like thieves returning to the scene of the crime.

'You'll forgive me, Aldric?'

Spunky laughed and looked at her, 'Nothing to forgive my dear. We both play the game a bit. You're a girl after my own heart in truth.'

He looked at her and knew it was the truth. He liked her a lot, more than any girl he could remember. Angela Malcolm understood this. She was trained in deception. Whether it was as an agent of deception or uncovering it, this was her world. She knew the best form of deception was when it lay close to the truth. It had been easy to deceive Spunky into believing she loved him because she probably did.

'I'm glad there'll be no hard feelings, Aldric. And I'm sorry about all the things you found out about me.'

'Well if I'm going to be used then I have to say it was jolly good fun.'

Angela Malcolm stopped. She looked up at Spunky. There was hurt in her eyes.

'I didn't use you. Monk yes, but not you. I liked you. I never meant it to become what it did. It was never in the plan.'

This perked Spunky up no end, 'Enough of this. Let me treat you to a nice lunch, then you can give a gentle, lingering kiss so that I will remember you always and to say goodbye.'

'Can we say *au revoir* instead?'

-

'Not the nicest of days,' said Ida looking up at the grey sky. She was walking in the Champ de Mars hand in hand with Harry Miller.

'Still not a bad view,' replied Miller, laughing.

'Yes, Croydon doesn't have anything like this, even in summer.'

They were approaching the Eiffel Tower. Its dark skeleton stabbed the sky. A long queue of people snaked from its base. Nearby a musician played a melancholy violin. The music cut through the air, caught Miller's breath in its grasp and carried it away along with his heart. He didn't know if he wanted to laugh or cry. This was possibly the happiest day of his life, but it would have to end at some point and within its conclusion would come another ending that he couldn't bear to think about.

'Shall we?' asked Ida with a grin.

Yes, thought Miller, I'll go with you anywhere you want me to. He nodded, and they joined the queue.

The journey up the tower was too short. Miller felt like screaming for the lift to slow down. Around them, the crowded lift was filled with tourists. American voices mixed with English reserve and Italian exuberance. Ida excitedly pointed out buildings below in the rapidly ascending lift. Miller gazed down at Ida, her face radiating happiness, animated by a vitality that Miller had fallen in love with.

The higher they ascended, the colder it seemed to become. Ida wrapped the coat around her and giggled.

'We'll catch our death out there, are you sure you want to go out?'

'We've come this far, Ida,' said Miller raising his eyebrows.

'We've come a long way, Harry Miller, and no mistake,' laughed Ida.

They walked out, and the cold air seemed to slap them. The top deck was crowded, and Miller looked around for a quiet spot where they could stand together, alone. Ida seemed to be of a similar mind and Miller felt his hand being pulled. They found a spot less disturbed by the human traffic because the view was obscured. Miller looked at Ida and he could see the tears in her eyes, or maybe his.

'I've been dreading this, Harry,' said Ida.

'Me too,' admitted Miller.

They were silent for a moment, gazing at one another instead. Ida knew Miller was waiting for her to say something. This was typical of him. He knew what she would say, perhaps, in fact probably, he felt the same. Finally, she found her courage, she found the words and she gripped Miller's hand even harder.

'This last week or so, Harry. It's been a dream. I've never met anyone like you before. I'm not sure I will again. I'm not sure I want to.'

Miller nodded. He felt the same, but the words didn't come to him. But they were unnecessary. Ida knew.

'There's so much I want to do, Harry. So much I want to see. But I don't want to lose you.'

'I don't want to lose you, Ida.'

'Well then, we're agreed, Harry Miller,' said Ida laughing and crying. Them a thought seemed to strike her, 'What time is it, Harry?'

Miller was confused, this was an unexpected question. He looked at a clock on the side of the tower.

'It's nearly eleven,' answered Miller, returning his gaze to Ida.

'If I were to stand here on this spot, at this time, five years from now, do you think I might meet someone who'll ask me a question? The only question I'll want to hear at that moment.'

'What will your answer be?'

'Yes.'

-

Kit returned early evening to the hotel. He was surprised to find Miller in his room packing clothes.

'I thought you'd be out with Ida.'

'No sir, she's on duty tonight. We've said our goodbyes.'

Kit looked at Miller silently putting clothes into the bag. Gone was the cheerfulness, the stream of humorous chatter. Kit knew there was little he could say that would lift Miller, so he didn't try. Instead he reached into his coat pocket and withdrew a photograph on a card. He handed it to his manservant. It was of Miller and Ida, taken by the mysterious Sagnier.

Miller smiled when he saw the picture, but a shadow passed over his eyes.

'I thought you might like this, Harry. I hope I haven't done something wrong.'

Miller looked up from the picture and smiled, 'No, sir. Far from it. This means so much. I'd forgotten about it. Thank you, sir.'

'You're welcome, Harry. I liked her very much. I hope you'll stay in touch with her.'

'I will, sir. Be sure of that,' said Miller. There was no mistaking the look in Miller's eyes and Kit's heart swelled in hope for his friend.

'Inspector Briant and I saw Pendlebury earlier. He's on the mend.'

'What did you tell him of his would-be assassin, sir?'

'I'm afraid we had to mislead him again. It couldn't have been Fink-Nottle. I was his alibi. So, I fear we may never know, but I suspect it was the same person, or people, Fink-Nottle was trying to escape with the other night. Anyway, I'll leave you to it, Harry, I'll only be in the way. I might pop down to see Spunky.'

Kit left the room and walked down the stairs to the first floor. He walked along the corridor coming to Spunky's room. Just as he was about to knock on the door, he heard voices inside. It was too difficult to hear who was there, so he went ahead and knocked. A minute passed without response. He knocked again. Just as he did so, the door opened slightly.

'Hullo, Kit,' said Spunky brightly.

'Hullo, Spunky, just popped down to see what you were up to.'

'Oh this and that,' replied Spunky enigmatically.

'I thought I heard voices.'

As Kit said this, he heard the voice of a young French woman followed by a giggle.

'*Dépêchez-toi,* Aldreek.'

'Coming, my darling,' replied Spunky to his companion in the room.

Another voice, this time a different French lady said, 'Who is it, Aldreek?'

'No one, darling,' responded Spunky, before turning to Kit, 'Duty calls, old boy.'

Kit smiled and nodded, trying to get a glimpse into the room.

'Need any help?' asked Kit hopefully.

'No all under control,' smiled Spunky as he shut the door.

8 Months later:

Belgravia, London: 1st October 1919

The door to Kit's apartment opened. First through the door was Sam, barking happily at returning home. Following him through the door, Harry Miller stooped down and picked up some mail that had been slipped through the bottom of the door. Kit walked in after Miller, coat over his arm. He threw it over the back of the sofa and sat down. Sam leapt up onto the sofa and then onto Kit's knee, wagging his tail. Kit stroked him behind the ears and spoke to Miller.

'Leave the bags, I have the feeling his highness here wants to be fed. Can you give me the post?'

Miller handed a stack of mail to Kit and went to find some food for Sam. There seemed to be dozens of items in the post, which was not a surprise. He and Miller had been away from the apartment for nearly six months. Kit threw many of the envelopes onto the sofa and extracted one small envelope. The stamp was French, and it was addressed to Harry Miller. Kit smiled when he saw the feminine handwriting, both careful and pleasing to the eye compared to his own lazy scrawl.

There were several other small envelopes that required his attention. His heart sank as he saw them. Christmas invitations. As much as he loved Christmas, the invitations meant only one thing. Miller walked holding a small bowl with food for Sam as Kit went through the invitations one by one saying, 'No, no, no.'

'What's that, sir?' asked Miller putting the bowl on the floor.

'All of the Christmas parties I'm not going too. Sorry, we're not going to.'

Miller laughed, 'You're very popular, sir.'

'Very single more like. All of these invites are made with the express purpose of marrying a daughter off to me.'

Kit opened the last of the invites and raised his eyebrows. Miller noted the shadow passing over Kit's expression. Kit looked up at Miller's concerned face.

'Lord Arthur Cavendish,' said Kit holding the invitation up.

'I don't believe I've visited him,' smiled Miller, 'but it's difficult to remember all my clients.'

Kit laughed out loud. Then he added, 'I might think about this one.' He seemed more serious as he said this. Miller's curiosity overcame his decorum.

'Why sir? Is this because there are no daughters?'

Kit smiled absently, 'No daughters but he has two nieces, or granddaughters more likely. Esther Cavendish is reputed to be one of the most beautiful women in the country.'

To Miller's eyes, the prospect of meeting her did not seem to make Kit happy. Quite the opposite, in fact. Miller wondered about the life Lord Kit Aston was expected to lead. Part leisure, but also part duty. As the eldest son of a Lord, Miller guessed there would always be a pressure on Kit to marry and produce a male heir. It was the natural order of things for people like him. It seemed to offer him no pleasure. After a few moments, Kit seemed to snap out of his reverie and handed Miller an envelope.

'This came for you from Paris. From the postmark it's about a month old. You'd better go read it and get a reply in the post as soon as you can.'

I will, sir, thanks.'

Miller walked into his room and sat on the edge of the bed. He glanced at his bedside table. On it was a framed picture of him and Ida. He tore open the envelope and began to read.

Kit stared at the invitation without reading it. He thought about Cavendish. They'd met on several occasions, and he liked the old boy. Unlike the usual array of old generals and majors who were still fighting the last war, Cavendish had impressed Kit both as a soldier and as a man. Fear gripped him as he thought about Cavendish the father. What could he say? How could he tell him? His eyes misted over, and he found breathing more difficult. For months he'd felt free from the guilt and now it was back, attacking his weakness. He stood up and walked over to Miller's room to tell him he would accept the invitation.

Kit knocked on the door. There was no answer initially then he heard Miller say to come in. He walked in and saw Miller sat crumpled on the bed, the letter from Ida in his hand. His spirit seemed not to have left his body so much as evacuated it.

'What's wrong, Harry? Is Ida alright?'

Miller looked up; despair etched into the pores of his skin.

'She's getting married, sir. Tomorrow.'

-

Paris" 2nd October 1919

Ida looked at her reflection in the mirror. She hoped the signs of her tears had gone. Stuck on the mirror was a photograph of a man and a woman. She took it off the mirror and looked at the message on the back. It read: *Memory of a happy day. I hope to see you again someday soon. Your friend Harry.*

She quickly put the photograph into the top drawer of her dresser and made one last check of her make up. There was a knock at her bedroom door.

'Ready?' asked a familiar voice.

Ida opened the door and saw Ethel standing with a sympathetic smile, holding a bouquet.

'Yes ready,' replied Ida.

The two women walked down the stairs and out of the front door. A car was waiting for them and a small crowd of well-wishers. Ida smiled to them but did not stay to chat. Ethel shut the car door. Both women waved to their neighbour as the car sped off.

'How are you feeling, my love?' asked Ethel.

Ida could not speak. She smiled and shrugged her shoulders.

'It's for the best, Ida.'

'I know,' said Ida, unsure of what she was doing or why.

-

Washington: 2nd October 1919

Dr Hubert "Doc" Holliday walked along Pennsylvania Avenue away from the White House. He removed his coat and threw it over his arm. His face glistened with sweat although it was not especially warm. His lungs laboured to breathe, although he was not walking especially fast. And he wanted to walk fast. He wanted to sprint as far away from the building behind him as he could. Tears formed in his eyes, and he didn't try to stop them. Over and over he heard his friend, Cary Grayson, the President's physician saying, 'Doc, he's paralysed. He's had a stroke. How could this happen?'

But Doc Holliday knew how the stroke had happened.

Resisting the urge to run, Holliday stopped and raised his arm as a taxicab approached. It slowed down and pulled over beside him, and he climbed in. He told the man where to take him.

A few minutes later Holliday could see his destination ahead.

'Stop here please, I'll walk across the road.'

Holliday climbed out of the cab. In front of him was a man begging for change. He reached into his pocket and threw a nickel into the pork pie hat. Across the road was a diner. He waved towards a woman sat by the window. She looked up and registered his arrival. The expression on his face told her everything she needed to know. Moments later he was sat opposite.

'It hasn't gone to plan,' said Holliday.

'Meaning?' replied the woman.

'Wilson's had a stroke. He's paralysed.'

The woman shook her head in frustration.

'We've failed again in other words. They won't pay us now, Doc. Mark my words. You've gone to all this trouble drip feeding whatever the hell you were giving him for the headaches and all we get is a cripple? They won't be happy.'

She ran her hand through her blonde hair. Holliday looked at her as she did this. He saw, perhaps for the first time, it was turning grey. Or perhaps it already had, and she was using these new colours.

'I won't get near him now, Evelyn, that's for damn sure.'

'What'll they do?'

'Lock him away probably. Can't have our enemies knowing the President is a cabbage, or as near as damn one.'

She stubbed out her cigarette on the plate.

'What a mess. What a mess.' She stood up and put on her coat. "Watch your back, Doc.'

Evelyn Morris picked her handbag off the seat and left Holliday alone in the diner. He looked down and saw she'd left him the bill.

The Kit Aston Novellas

The End

Jack Murray

Research Notes

I have made every effort to ensure historical authenticity within the context of a piece of fiction. Similarly, every effort has been made to ensure that the book has been edited and carefully proofread. Given that the US Constitution contained around 65 punctuation errors until 1847, I hope you will forgive any errors of grammar, spelling and continuity. Regarding spelling, please note I have followed the convention of using English, as opposed to US, spellings. This means, in practice, the use of 's' rather than a 'z', for example in words such as 'realised'.

This is a work of fiction. However, it references events that happened and real-life individuals. Gore Vidal, in his introduction to Lincoln, writes that placing history in fiction or fiction in history has been unfashionable since Tolstoy and that the result can be accused of being neither. He defends the practice, pointing out that writers from Aeschylus to Shakespeare to Tolstoy have done so with not inconsiderable success and merit.

I have mentioned a number of key real-life individuals and events in this novel. My intention, in the following section, is to explain a little more about their connection to this period and this story.

The Paris Peace Conference 1919

Paris was the capital of the world in 1919, according to historian Margaret MacMillan. During the first six months of 1919, the great post First World War powers assembled not just to create a peace settlement with Germany and its allies but to reshape the world, creating new nations in Europe, the Middle East and Asia. The leaders attending included President Woodrow Wilson, Prime Ministers Lloyd George, and Georges Clemenceau. Each spent close to six months in expensive Paris hotels, arguing over the details that would result in the Treaty of Versailles and the formation of the League of Nations. The supporting cast to these men were no less extraordinary: Ho Chi Minh, Herbert Hoover, Arthur Balfour, Lawrence of Arabia, and Ignace Paderewski.

Britain found itself at odds with many countries, including former allies, in Europe during the conference as the future of Europe was hammered out. I hope this book has given a flavour of Paris during this extraordinary period; a city recovering from an appalling war, overrun with politicians, conference delegates and soldiers returning from the conflict. It was also a Paris that would soon reassert itself as the artistic centre of the world with new strains of modern art developing in Montparnasse and the arrival of jazz music.

Prime Minister Georges Clemenceau (1841 - 1929)

Clemenceau was a French politician, physician and journalist who was Prime Minister of France during the First World War and chief negotiator at the Paris Peace Conference in 1919. Clemenceau survived an assassination attempt by an anarchist named Emile Cottin.

President Woodrow Wilson (1856 - 1924)

Wilson was a two term US President (1913 -21). Initially opposed to bringing the US into the War, he was finally forced to throw in with the Britain, France and Russia following Germany's submarine warfare on US shipping and the notorious Zimmerman telegram. He suffered a stroke on October 2nd, 1919, following a long period of overwork and stress brought on not just by the Conference but by the desire to gain support for the League as well. This may not have been his first stroke, but it was certainly the most debilitating. Many suspect that his wife, Edith, played a major role in running the country as news of his illness was withheld from the wider public.

Arthur Balfour (1848 - 1930)

The 1st Earl of Balfour was Prime Minister of Britain between 1902 and 1905. He was very much an elder statesman at the Paris Peace Conference, supporting Lloyd George as his Foreign Secretary. Famously brilliant in debate, he lacked interest in the detail of management, preferring abstract thought to concrete action. However, his famous letter, which came to be known as the "Balfour Declaration" was a pivotal moment in the formation of Israel.

Marcel Duchamp (1887 – 1968) and "Fountain" (1917 & 1964)

Duchamp was a French artist, chess player and writer. He was at the forefront of art movements such as Dada and Surrealism. His piece "Fountain", a porcelain urinal, signed R Mott, was first exhibited in 1917 to the shock of the art world. It is considered one of the most iconic works of art from the 20th century. It was lost soon after it was exhibited before being made again in 1964. There were no other known versions. It is certainly the most famous of the various readymade objects Duchamp exhibited in this period before he abandoned art for a short time in favour of chess.

Emile Cottin (1896 – 1936)

Cottin was a French militant anarchist responsible for the attempted assassination of French Prime Minister Georges Clemenceau in 1919. Clemenceau often joked about Cottin's bad marksmanship – "We have just won the most terrible war in history, yet here is a Frenchman who misses his target 6 out of 7 times at point-blank range. Of course this fellow must be punished for the careless use of a dangerous weapon and for poor marksmanship. I suggest that he be locked up for eight years, with intensive training in a shooting gallery." He was initially sentenced to death before it was commuted to ten years. Following his release he published a pamphlet '*Why I shot Clemenceau*'. He was killed during the Spanish Civil War.

The Kit Aston Novellas

HAYMAKER'S LAST FIGHT

The SECOND Kit Aston NOVELLA

Jack Murray

Jack Murray

Copyright © 2020 by Jack Murray

All rights reserved. No part of this publication may be reproduced, distributed, or transmitted in any form or by any means, including photocopying, recording, or other electronic or mechanical methods, without the prior written permission of the publisher, except in the case of brief quotations embodied in critical reviews and certain other non-commercial uses permitted by copyright law. For permission requests, write to the publisher, addressed 'Attention: Permissions Coordinator,' at the address below.

Jackmurray99@hotmail.com

This is a work of fiction. Names, characters, businesses, places, events, locales, and incidents are either the products of the author's imagination or used in a fictitious manner. Any resemblance to actual persons, living or dead, or actual events is either purely coincidental or used in a fictitious manner.

The Kit Aston Novellas

1

National Sporting Club, London: 16th December 1909

Kit Aston strolled along King Street in London's Covent Garden. It was after seven o'clock in the evening and his dinner suit was proving somewhat inadequate cover against the force of a British winter. Snow was in the air. The exposed parts of Kit's face were stinging. Up ahead he could see a crowd milling outside his destination.

'Full house,' suggested Olly Lake, walking alongside Kit. He lit a cheroot and put it in his mouth.

'Good. It'll be warm inside,' said Aldric 'Spunky' Stevens. 'I don't mind telling you, boys, that another minute out in this weather and the world may be denied any future little Stevens running around getting under everyone's feet.'

'I'm sure there are plenty as it is,' replied the fourth and tallest member of the group, Charles 'Chubby' Chadderton. His lean frame belied his school nickname. Olly Lake handed him a cheroot and the four young men strode ahead purposefully through the thronged streets of Covent Garden.

Despite the cold, market stalls were still doing business. Competition for attention among the street hawkers was intense and seemed entirely based on the volume of noise that they could generate. The men and women shopping confronted the four friends like a gale force headwind. Every step closer to their destination was fought for with the intensity of a war of attrition. As they walked along the crowded street, one young man smacked into Olly Lake.

'Watch it,' said a cockney voice. A moment later the voice's owner was lying on the ground holding a cut mouth.

'Olly,' exclaimed Kit, 'what on earth are you doing?'

The young man on the ground was making the same enquiry in language that was as robust as it was passionate. Lake dragged him to his feet, none too gently. He reached into the young man's pocket and extracted a wallet that he'd ghosted away from Lake seconds earlier.

A look of fear surfaced on the young man's face. He was probably twenty, around the same age as the four men surrounding him. Olly Lake brandished his wallet and looked like he was about to dispense a severe form of justice there and then.

'What should I do with you?'

'I'm sorry, guv,' said the terrified young man. He wanted to say more but the tears came first.

Kit reached into his pocket and found a half crown. He put it in the young man's hand and motioned with his head for him to go. The young man looked at the money and the look of desolation was replaced by relief. He turned and ran into the crowd.

'You're too soft, Kit,' drawled Lake. Then he clapped his friend on the back and added with a grin, 'That's why I like you.'

'We're here,' said Chubby.

The four young men looked up at the sign over the entrance. It read: 'The National Sporting Club'. It was a redbrick building with white quoins at the corners and around the entrance. The four young men made their way through the crowd and the hubbub towards the white pillars of the entrance. The doorman nodded to the four toffs walking past him. Class, he thought, you can almost smell it.

Just behind the four men another two men appeared. The doorman eyed them warily. Cedric Grimshaw had been doorman at the club since it had opened in 1891. He'd seen all types come into the club over the previous eighteen years. He could read 'em like a book, he boasted. Often.

The two men who followed were of a different stripe to the four men who'd just walked in. They resembled one another. One was short the other a little taller. Well made. Well dressed, too. But not toffs. The doorman was about to stop them but the shorter man, sensing the mood of the doorman, looked directly into his eyes. The doorman was no fool. He turned away as if he'd lost interest. His knees were shaking though, and it wasn't just the cold. The

National Sporting Club was an odd place. He knew these men were part of a very different world to many of the members of this private club.

He was right.

Charles 'Wag' McDonald and his brother Bert were the leaders of the 'Elephant Boys' a criminal gang which was beginning to achieve a dominant position in south London. Wag McDonald liked to dress well. He liked to associate with toffs, but opportunities were limited for a man such as he: a businessman. The National Sporting Club was a notable exception. Here he was like the nobility around him. A fight fan.

The entrance hall was crowded. The bar was mobbed. The noise, ear splitting. McDonald loved it. The braying sound of the upper classes at play, away from the civilising influence of their wives, was a sight to behold. One young man was busily downing a series of short drinks, set up in sequence on a table. Each drink was of a different colour. Around him men, young and old, were cheering him on. This sporting effort, so vocally enjoyed by his friends, represented the other end of a spectrum from the violent nobility they would bear witness to later in the ring. They would do so, at the club's request, in complete silence.

Just above the heads of this group was a poster advertising the fights that would take place later. Top of the bill was the man that had brought around thirteen hundred men out on a cold December night to the centre of London: 'the Boston Tar Baby'.

The nick name was geographically inaccurate. Sam Langford was from Nova Scotia, in Canada. He was five feet six inches of raw power and athleticism. He'd fought at every weight from lightweight to heavy. Top fighters of the day avoided him. He should have been a world champion. One thing held him back: his colour. Even when Jack Johnson broke the colour bar in defeating Tommy Burns for the World Heavyweight Championship, the door remained firmly closed for Langford. He was simply too dangerous.

Langford's opponent this evening was the British Heavyweight Champion, William Hague.

'What do you think?' asked Wag McDonald of his brother.

'Our boy's no mug. Could be a good fight.'

Wag McDonald nodded but offered no opinion on this. Privately he thought Hague would be lucky not to end up in hospital. Langford was a step too far for the tough Yorkshireman.

Bert heard his brother say that he was off to get the drinks at the bar a few feet away.

He scanned the rest of the poster. The fights had already started from the undercard. There was a lightweight contest on that that moment. The main supporting fight was between an English light heavyweight, Gunner Joe Farrell, and a man whose name had been crossed out.

'That's a pity,' said Bert McDonald. 'I was looking forward to that one. Bloody hell, look who they've brought in. That's a mismatch.'

Wag McDonald was ordering two drinks for them. He turned around and said, 'Who did you say the replacement was?'

-

Dan 'Haymaker' Harris stood at the door of the house he shared with his mother in Lambeth. Dixie Harris looked up at her son. She was less than five feet, so she looked up at most everyone. Dan was only a little taller, but his shoulders seemed to fill the doorway. He was wearing a suit whose seams could barely contain his muscular frame. It was his best suit. His Sunday suit. His only suit.

Dan was thirty-three years old. He looked ten years older. He'd always lived at home. There were times when Dixie thought he'd leave. Temptation was everywhere. But he'd stayed. He'd found no one that deserved him. And he deserved the very best. He was a good boy. Too good.

Dixie studied the face of her beloved and only son. It was a face that had been on the wrong end of thousands of blows. One of his ears could, kindly, be described as cauliflowered. His nose was a flattened, boneless protuberance. Heavy scar-tissue around his eyes made them slant downwards. It was a face to love but, perhaps, not to fall in love with. And Haymaker was loved by everyone who knew him. What he lacked in pugilistic potency he more than made up for in more substantive character traits: an unyielding integrity, a humility that came from a deep religious conviction and a compassion that was all his own. None of these qualities had proved remotely helpful in the brutally violent profession in which he traded.

Nature had bestowed upon Haymaker a knockout punch. But nature is capricious. The concussive power that lay in fists sat atop unusually short arms. To detonate his sense-depriving power on opponents, Haymaker had to withstand several blows coming from the opposite direction. As a result, Haymaker's face betrayed how bad a bargain this was. His fight record confirmed what was evident on his face. No titles had come his way. He'd never been close.

'Are you sure, my love?' asked Dixie for the hundredth time.

Haymaker wasn't sure. He was out of his depth. A younger, bigger, stronger opponent. He, a last-minute replacement, was only there to be knocked out; to be a stepping-stone for someone whose career would go higher and further than he'd ever gone. But it was Christmas. The house was cold. His mother's old overcoat was threadbare.

'Yes, mum, I'm sure.'

They walked out of the door together into the cold night. Dixie craned her neck upwards and pronounced with certainty that it was going to snow. Haymaker glanced at his mother. A snowflake must have fallen on her cheek. He could see it roll down slowly. He looked away.

2

The four young men walked into the bar of the National Sporting Club. It was crowded but some were leaving to watch the first fight from the undercard. Kit, Olly and Spunky immediately rushed towards some seats that had been vacated.

'Usual, Chubby,' said Spunky cheerily to the one man still standing.

Chubby cast a cynical eye over his friends and nodded. He trooped over to the bar and stood beside a short man who was asking someone who the replacement was. He heard a name that he didn't recognise. The barman looked towards Chubby.

A couple of minutes later, clutching four half pints of beer in hands with impossibly long fingers, Chubby arrived at the table.

'Took your time about it,' drawled Olly.

'No tip, then,' said Chubby, drolly.

'I say, Kit, isn't that your...' Spunky's observation went unfinished.

'Uncle Eustace,' exclaimed Kit.

As Kit said this, an elderly man, sitting at the bar chatting with another man of a similar vintage, looked around. A big smile erupted on a face that was already cheerful to begin with. He waved at his nephew. Kit stood up and walked over to join the two men.

'Kit, my boy, how good to see you,' said Eustace Frost. He was a man in his mid-sixties with a mane of grey hair and a friendly-flushed countenance that suggested a convivial nature. 'Have you met Lonsdale?'

The gentleman facing Eustace turned around. He was younger than Kit's uncle but not by much. Hugh Lowther was the fifth Earl of Lonsdale and one of the co-founders of the National Sporting Club. He would later give his name to a belt worn by British boxing champions at each weight.

'Hello, sir,' said Kit shaking hands with Lonsdale. Nearby a man was offering wagers on the outcome of the Langford, Hague fight. An American. Kit glanced towards him and said, 'Has our man any chance tonight, do you think?'

Lonsdale smiled and held his hands out.

'William is good, there's no question about it but I fear he may find this a step too far in class. What do you think, Kit?'

'I agree, sir. I saw Langford two years ago here against Tiger Smith. Nipped off from school to do it. My teachers weren't best pleased.'

'I'm sure they weren't, Kit. But you're not still at school?' asked Lonsdale. The American in the background was now taking all manner of bets from the optimistic, the patriotic and the blind drunk.

'No, sir. I'm at Cambridge now reading mathematics and modern languages.'

The three men turned towards the American who was surrounded by very well-dressed men. He was noting down the value of the wagers. The odds were evens which struck Kit as being remarkably ungenerous given the reputation of Langford. At a certain point the American held his hand up to silence the crowd. Then he said, 'Right, I think that's enough for now. Thanks, gents.'

Kit turned to Lonsdale and his uncle grinning.

'I have a feeling that Mr Langford has just wagered his purse with all of these gentlemen.'

'I have a feeling you are right, Kit. Furthermore, I suspect he will be considerably richer by the end of the evening.'

Uncle Eustace pointed to Lonsdale's drink and asked, 'Another?' It was clear that Kit's uncle was going to enjoy his evening away from Aunt Agatha to the hilt.

'No, Frost. I must dash. I must meet the fighters. Poor form not to, really.'

Lonsdale made his farewells and Kit suggested that Uncle Eustace come over and join the rest of his friends. This idea was met with evident delight. He ordered a few shorts for the boys to help chase down their beers.

-

'Did you put a bet down?' asked Wag McDonald when Bert returned with their beers.

'You kidding? It was some Yank, and he was only taking bets on Iron Hague beating Langford.'

McDonald looked around at the men offering up their money. He shook his head and grinned. His racecourse racket was a good earner, but he could earn so much more at this kind of affair. Here the great and good and well-oiled of London congregated. There was money to be made here and no mistake. But they would never allow it.

'He's probably with Langford. I don't know how else he'd be allowed to run a book.'

'That's what I thought,' agreed Bert. They drank their pints in companionable silence, looking around at their betters braying like sheep and shadow boxing as they explained how their boy could overcome the Boston Tar Baby.

Yes, he could make lots of money with people like this, thought the head of the Elephant Boys. Just then he felt a touch on his arm. He turned to Bert who used his eyes to indicate where he should be looking.

'Well I'll be,' said Wag. 'What's he doing here?'

The man in question was looking at Wag and Bert thinking something similar.

-

Phil Herbert saw Haymaker and Dixie walking towards the club and waved. Haymaker waved while Dixie smiled and nodded. The greetings were warmer than the weather. However, there was concern etched on the face of Haymaker's cornerman. Phil Herbert was, by any standards, a veteran of the fight game. Once upon a time he'd fought bare knuckle bouts before the sport was legal. He'd been training fighters for over twenty years. He only trained fighters he liked.

'You sure about this, Dan?' asked Phil. 'Farrell is big. He's fought against the best.'

Haymaker waved off the objections with his large paw. It was too late now. he'd committed. It was a six round catchweight contest against a heavyweight, Joe Farrell. Haymaker was giving away around twenty pounds in weight and six inches in reach.

Herbert looked to Dixie Harris. He could see she was torn about the night ahead. Each knew that Haymaker's chances were poor at best and there was the risk of injury.

'I've tried, Phil. He won't listen.'

'Fine, but the first sign of trouble, Dan, I'm pulling you out of there.'

'You can't, Phil,' said Haymaker. 'If I stay the six rounds then Peggy said he'd double my purse.'

Peggy, in this case, wasn't a woman but Arthur Bettinson, the co-founder with the Earl of Lonsdale of the National Sporting Club. A former amateur champion himself, he was widely respected by all connected with the sport for having brought legitimacy and respect where before it had been illegal and dangerous for those participating.

Herbert's face fell. He knew that the extra money would help all of them. Yet he feared the worst for Haymaker. He'd been with him for over twelve years and a hundred fights. Haymaker had won more often than he'd lost but those victories often came at a cost. The payment was written all over the face of man he looked upon as a son.

They trooped into the club via a side entrance and made their way to the changing room shared by several fighters. The corridor was crowded with people connected to the fighters. The noise was deafening.

They reached the door and the group of three stopped and looked at one another awkwardly for a moment. Then Phil grinned and pointed to the changing room.

'I'll see you inside,' said Phil. He left them.

Dixie put her hand up to Haymaker's cheek. She was trying desperately not to cry. Feelings of guilt meshed with the love she felt for her boy.

'Daniel don't do anything stupid. Keep moving. Change to southpaw when you must and keep your gloves up. Go down if you must. Take a breather. Break his flow, Daniel.'

Haymaker nodded throughout this. He could have given the speech himself by this stage, he'd heard it so often. But this time, unusually, he could not reply. Something was tightening his vocal cords. It wasn't nerves. It was something else and he felt like crying. This wasn't his way, however. He drew his mother close to him and they hugged. Then Dixie spun around and ran off into the crowd. Haymaker watched her go before turning to go into the changing room.

Phil was standing beside two men. One was young, dapper, and well-made, the other, older, taller, and made to hurt people. The look on his trainer's face was grim. No, it was anger, realised Haymaker with a start. He walked forward and, with a sinking heart, said, 'Hello, Mr Kimber.

Billy Kimber smiled and regarded his near neighbour in Lambeth. Their paths had crossed over recent years. Kimber headed up one of many racecourse gangs who ran protection for bookmakers amongst their other money-spinning rackets.

'Dan, it's good to see you, my friend. I mean it.'

His accent was from the Midlands although much of his time was spent in the capital. The smile on his face was genuine but the look in the eyes was hard. It meant business. Haymaker knew what this business was likely to be. Kimber didn't waste time beating about the bush.

'Dan, I've just put a wedge on our boy 'Iron' to beat the Yank. Now, I'm not that confident about the result. William has a good punch so there's always a chance against a smaller man like Langford. I thought it might be an idea if I laid off some of the money on one of the other fights. You know, when I saw it was my neighbour fighting, I said to Archie here, didn't I, Archie, that Dan was the man. He'd look after his neighbour. I said that, Archie?'

Haymaker looked up at the man he guessed was Archie. He knew him from years ago. A heavyweight fighter who'd never amounted to much. Archie nodded and grinned. The remaining teeth were a reminder that his relatively unsuccessful career as a boxer had merely been a stepping-stone to his true calling. As chief thug in Kimber's gang, Archie found his level which involved putting the frighteners on bookies who were half his size.

'Anyway, Dan,' continued Kimber. 'I need you to fall in the third. Now we both know you can't win. Why make it hard on yourself? Six rounds are a long time in the ring with someone who is at least a stone or two heavier. Why spend Christmas in hospital? Farrell says he'll go easy on you in the first three rounds, then, well you know what to do.'

Kimber patted the cheeks of Haymaker just hard enough to for him to notice and be irritated by it. But what could he say? Somehow, he'd managed to avoid this throughout his career. They'd left him alone. Until now. Of all times.

Haymaker stared back into the implacable, cold face of fight fixing. He felt sick. The bile rose within him, and it was all he could do to avoid giving physical vent his fear and loathing. He couldn't speak.

'Well, Dan?' asked Kimber softly.

'Yes, Mr Kimber,' replied Haymaker.

3

Uncle Eustace was greeted like a long-lost conquering hero by the four young men. He was clearly adored by all. And why not? He'd been married to Kit's Aunt Agatha for thirty years or more. This was a testimony to the purity of his heart, the strength of his constitution and the thickness of his skin. All these qualities, and more, were needed to withstand the withering sarcasm that the aforementioned good lady was capable of when the mood took her.

'When did you get back from wherever you where?' asked Spunky, thereby confusing himself and all present with the exact nature of his inquiry.

Uncle Eustace was already three and half sheets to the wind by this point and took a few moments to process the question asked by the young man who, coincidentally, was just as far gone.

'Well, we sailed into Southampton a few days ago. We were out visiting Alastair in San Francisco. He's well before you ask and was keen to know how you were, Kit.'

A few minutes passed by as further inquiries were made as to the health, happiness and whatnot of Uncle Alastair before Kit turned to the thought that was uppermost in his mind at that moment.

'So, Uncle Eustace, is Aunt Agatha on her own tonight?'

The face of Kit's uncle fell slightly causing a smile from the nephew.

'Betty's over.'

'Ahh,' said all present. Nothing more needed to be said. However, Kit, emboldened by a few glasses of cheerfulness earlier, asked anyway.

'Are we to assume by your presence tonight that you are, once again, in the doghouse?'

'Your aunt is a wonderful woman Kit.'

The four young men nodded. Genuinely. None better said Spunky and Chubby in unison.

'Truly a wonderful woman,' continued Uncle Eustace. 'I have loved her from the moment I set eyes on her. I will love her until the day I die, Kit. However,' Uncle Eustace leaned forward, causing the others to lean forward also. 'However, as wonderful as she is, and as much as I love her, she is possessed of a tongue that could shave a rhino's hide.'

This was greeted with sage nods around the table. All had been at the receiving end, at one time or another, of a surgically precise verbal slashing from Kit's diminutive aunt. All treated these moments as badges of honour earned in the harshest of combat zones.

'What did you do wrong?' asked Kit, grinning. Good manners and a sense of loyalty to his aunt prevented him from adding, this time.

'Gather round,' ordered Uncle Eustace. 'You are about to learn a life lesson from someone who has suffered stab wounds in the ghetto of marriage. Chiefly this: whenever a woman asks you a question, be on your guard.' These last four words were said with utmost emphasis.

There were a few heads nodding in agreement at this. Spunky exclaimed, 'Yes, I've often wondered why they ask us anything when they clearly aren't the least bit interested in the answer.'

'There you have it, Spunky, old chap. For example, if Kit asked you, Olly, do you think a nine will reach the green? You say yes, or no. Or try an eight to be safe. It's a simple exchange of information. One question followed by one answer. Both parties satisfied. This is not so with women. This has nothing to do with advice or help or guidance. What women want to know is do you love them unconditionally. Every question, every comment you make is superfluous and irrelevant in their eyes. They are not interested in your opinion on anything. Your answer must further consolidate in her mind the thought that you are blindly and stupidly in love.'

'What did you do, Uncle Eustace?' asked Kit.

'She asked me if her new dress made her look big.'

There was an inhalation of breath around the table. This was a beginner's mistake. How could an old warhorse like Uncle Eustace fall so quickly at the first fence?

'I know what you're thinking,' said Uncle Eustace, recognising the look of shock on the eyes of his disciples. 'But in my defence, I will say three things. Firstly, I began the evening back at the house if you take my meaning.' To ensure the young men took his meaning, he bent his elbow back and forward several times in a drinking motion.

'I wasn't quite at the top of my game. Secondly, I recognised the trap immediately. Oh yes, I'm not completely useless, no matter what Agatha says. Anyway, I thought that I could stay on the fairway by saying that she perfectly suited the extra inches. All men want someone they can hold onto.'

Olly and Spunky shook their heads at this before the latter put his head in his hands. Both were expert practitioners in the art of seduction. In truth, Olly was an expert, Spunky's success came at the price of a high number of rejections.

'Now listen closely, this is the part that you can learn from. Agatha, of course, went quiet at this point. So, I knew I was in trouble. She thanked me for my honesty.'

Whistles of shock followed this revelation and another few shakes of the head. The danger signals were all too apparent.

'I knew I was in deep trouble by now. You see, boys, when a woman asks you a question like this, you must never, under any circumstance, answer it. Instead, you simply reject the premise of the question. Dismiss it out of hand. Then follow it up with the usual fat-headed nonsense our betters like to hear.'

This was greeted by nods from everyone around the table. It made complete sense. However, Kit could see a wicked gleam in the eye of his uncle.

'Go on,' said Kit. 'You've something else, haven't you? You said there were three things at the start. What was the third thing?'

A smile erupted over the face of Uncle Eustace. A smile that resembled that of a schoolboy emerging from a shop clutching a handful toffees that not two minutes previously he'd been dared to steal.

'Ah Kit, you would make a wonderful detective. Well,' said Uncle Eustace, picking up his gin and swirling the contents around for a moment. 'You see, I'd always intended coming to see the fight tonight.'

Five glasses clinked amidst the laughter and Kit knew, once again, why Agatha had married this man. Outside on the street, a Salvation Army band began to play 'Deck the Halls'.

4

'You're on now.'

The referee walked into the changing room and pointed at Haymaker. Then he went off in search of Gunner Joe Farrell. Haymaker and Phil Herbert exchanged glances. It would be fair to say there was little confidence or bravado evident in their demeanour. In another part of the changing room, they could hear a man roaring himself into a state of psychotic hatred.

Haymaker rose from the ground where he had been stretching and where he firmly believed he would be returning in a matter of minutes. This was confirmed when he saw his opponent for the first time. The ex-army man was over six feet in height and there was barely an excess pound on his heavily muscled frame. He wondered for a brief second about the possibility of running away.

The referee led them out of the changing room, and they walked in silence along a long corridor that led to a large dimly lit room. In the centre was a square raised platform with a post at each corner. Three ropes were attached to the posts and pulled parallel under tension to form the boundary of the competition area. This was the ring.

The referee ordered the two men and their cornerman to opposite corners. Polite applause greeted the arrival of the two fighters. Haymaker looked around him. He'd lost count of the number of fights he'd had at the club. Thirty? Maybe even as many as forty. He felt an emptiness as he looked around at the well-dressed spectators. Many were wearing dinner suits. All here to see the great Sam Langford.

Haymaker climbed through the ropes and tested the surface by bouncing on the balls of his feet. He did this as a matter of habit. In fact, his traditional approach to boxing was somewhat more flat-footed. His strategy was as invariable as it was painfully unsuccessful. Stand in the centre of the ring, make his opponent come close, get inside, and instigate a war of attrition.

On those occasions where his opponent picked up that gauntlet, Haymaker's chances increased considerably. However, should the other fighter decide to stay at a distance and pick him off, shot by shot, then Haymaker was in trouble.

Farrell was prowling on his side of the ring doing everything to imply ownership of the space short of beating his chest and grunting. The heat of the room was already causing perspiration to mat Haymaker's hair. He felt a wave of nausea engulf him as the referee called them into the centre of the ring. Haymaker walked towards Farrell keeping his eyes trained on him. He was met with an implacable stare. There wasn't much sign of fear in those eyes. In fact, Haymaker could see something else. Something beyond confidence.

Certainty.

'Ladies 'n gentleman,' shouted the announcer, 'we have our penultimate fight of the night. A catchweight contest owing to the late withdrawal of Freddie King. In the blue corner, from Bolton, Lancashire, weighing in at one hundred and seventy-five pounds, Gunner Joe Farrell.

'If he's one hundred and seventy-five pounds then I'm Father Christmas,' said Uncle Eustace. This comment was drowned out by the sound of the polite applause rippling around the room.

'You could be right, Santa,' said Spunky. 'He's one hundred and ninety if he's an ounce.'

Kit looked aghast at the disparity in size between the two men. It was clear that the club had matched a middleweight against, at the very least, a light heavyweight or bigger. The ring announcer continued his introduction.

'In the red corner, weighing in at one hundred and sixty-three pounds, from Lambeth in London, Dan 'Haymaker' Harris.'

The applause greeting the hometown fighter was significantly greater than what had been given to his opponent. It was clear that the crowd's sympathies were as much due to the unequal nature of the contest as the fact that he was 'one of theirs'. In truth, Haymaker was not one of them. He was a Christian about to face a rather large lion with a knockout punch in both hands.

'Poor fellow,' said Kit. This fight should never have been sanctioned. He felt an anger at the man he'd met earlier, Lonsdale.

What was he thinking? He hoped that the smaller man would see sense and keep away from the clubbing power of his opponent long enough for decency to allow him a well-earned rest in the second or third round.

-

'Bloody hell,' said Bert McDonald. 'Haymaker's in for it tonight.'

Wag McDonald was thinking the same thing. He felt a twinge of sadness for reasons that he could not explain. He'd met the fighter before, briefly. There was always a certain something about him that he'd liked. In a dishonest trade he seemed to be an exception. If rumours were true, then he was not the man you went to if you wanted to have a fight thrown.

The disparity in size made the result inevitable in Wag's view. Mind you, he'd seen Haymaker lose enough fights to know that defeat wouldn't be solely due to the impressive physicality of the bigger man. Quite simply, Haymaker had never learned how to defend himself against smarter opponents.

'Poor fellow,' said Wag. He wondered what sort of financial straits the boxer must have been in to accept such a fight. It was a hard old world. You had to be tough to survive and thrive in such a world. As he thought this he wondered where Billy Kimber was seated. He looked along his row which was three back from the front and then around the other side of the ring. There was no sign of him. Then, out of the corner of his eye, he saw him, seated in the front row just to the right.

The ring announcer finished the introductions. Wag watched the fighters return to their corners. Haymaker seemed to be looking for someone in the crowd. The boxer nodded at someone. Wag turned around and saw an older woman waving to him. It was too dark for Haymaker to see, but Wag could not fail to notice the tears streaming down the face of the woman.

-

Dixie Harris could not breathe. Her chest had closed in on itself and she wanted to die there and then. The man he was fighting was so much bigger than her boy. It was all she could do to stop herself running down to the front and begging him to walk away. She caught his eye and he nodded to her. There was even the ghost of a smile. He was such a good boy. Then he turned away. His business was to begin.

She wiped her eyes and sat down. All around the room, silence had fallen. It was a strange place. The National Sporting Club required silence during the bouts. To Dixie, it felt unnatural to treat a contest such as this like it was a piece of theatre. It was anything but. It was raw. It was real. The pain displayed on this stage was genuine. The fear, the anger, the hatred, and the love towards your opponent were not simulated. Such emotions and their physical manifestation through violence required noise; excessive noise, to give it context, to give it colour and to pay proper respect to the sacrifice of the two men. She could not contain herself any longer.

-

'Come on, Dan,' shouted a woman's voice in the crowd.

There was swell of good-natured laughter through the crowd before silence. The only noise Haymaker could hear in those final few seconds before the bell was the sound of his heart thumping like timpani played by a gorilla. Phil Herbert was saying something about keeping his hands up and moving. In truth, Haymaker was past listening. It was always like this. He knew the theory. The ear, his eyes, his nose all suggested he'd never followed it.

Clang.

This was it. The referee drew back to the side and Haymaker watched as the enormous form of Farrell approached him. He was smiling like a jackal. Haymaker lurched forward towards his opponent like the Light Brigade at Balaclava. Farrell tried a few lazy jabs which even Haymaker could dodge. It was obvious the man from Bolton was in on the fix. Perhaps he would go easy on him for the three rounds. Pull his punches and...

The next jab was followed by a hook that damn near tore Haymaker's head off. He looked in shock at his opponent. There was a wide grin on Farrell's face. It was a grin full of venom and cruelty. The frightening thing for Haymaker was that he suspected the hook had been pulled. But the weight disparity was just too much. The three rounds were going to hurt and evidently Farrell was intent on enjoying his advantage to the full.

-

Kit grimaced as the hook scattered perspiration all over the front row of the ring. He silently urged the smaller man to cover up. In fact, Haymaker did the opposite. He waded into Farrell and clinched. This was probably the safest place to be in such a situation. Up close, Haymaker could negate the enormous power of his opponent and avoid the clubbing hooks that would quickly disconnect any normal man from his senses.

'I fear Haymaker could be in for a short night,' whispered Uncle Eustace. 'I certainly hope so for his sake.'

'I agree,' said Kit.

They watched the two men lurch across the ring in a drunken caricature of a Tango. Haymaker was holding on for grim life. Keep holding thought Kit just as the referee separated them.

-

Phil Herbert watched the two men with a feeling of impotence. Like Haymaker, he'd never amounted to much as a fighter. As a trainer he'd been a stepping-stone, much as he had been in his fighting days, for young men destined for bigger things. He felt no bitterness. He loved boxing. It had fed him and his family. There were no complaints. It provided an outlet for young men, troubled young men. He'd been one. Boxing had helped him turn his life around. Now he had the chance to do the same for others.

His heart lurched as Haymaker dodged another swinging punch from the big Lancashire boxer. At least Haymaker was moving. Twelve bloody years he'd never moved like that. Maybe things might have been different if he had.

He wanted to shout to his man to keep moving. But for the moment his man was moving; backwards, sideways, anyways.

-

It was nearing the end of the round and Haymaker was blowing hard. At this rate he would not make it under his own steam to round three never mind with the able assistance of Gunner Joe Farrell's massive fists.

Clang.

Haymaker slumped onto the seat and Phil Herbert gave him some water and wiped his face with an old white towel. Haymaker looked at the towel. It was stained already or perhaps it always had been. He hadn't noticed. The room was applauding their efforts which made it difficult to hear what Phil was saying,

It hardly seemed a minute had passed when he was up again and trotting out to meet his nemesis. The pattern for the fight had already been set. Wild swings from an opponent whom Haymaker realised was probably every bit as unskilled as him. But he had size and strength and youth. First, Farrell would swing, Haymaker would evade and then duck inside and cling onto the rock-hard torso of the younger man. Each would pound the sides of the other with impunity but with little effect, at least as far as Haymaker was concerned. The repeated drubbing from Farrell was beginning to tell on Haymaker's ribs.

The round finished much as it had started, with Haymaker clinging on. He sat down and his eyes caught those of Billy Kimber. The Midlands man was staring at him, willing him to understand that this was his moment. The third round was seconds away, and then it wasn't.

Clang. Round three.

Haymaker trooped out to the centre of the ring. The look on the face of Farrell had changed. He was no longer smiling. Now he was intent on finishing the job. Collecting his purse and, no doubt, a little extra from Kimber and off home. The question on Haymaker's mind was how he would do it. A single punch or...

Farrell ripped into Haymaker suddenly, swing punches from every direction. Defence went out of the window. His aim was twofold: hurt his opponent and end the fight. The dedication and resolve he was devoting to the former of those objectives seemed, to Haymaker, a source of great pleasure to his opponent.

A jab momentarily stunned Haymaker and he began to fall backwards. An uppercut glanced off a place just below Haymaker's belt. There was no time to feel the pain or, indeed anger, as the foul punch was followed by a left hook that he never saw. Only the ropes stopped Haymaker from falling.

Haymaker lay stunned on the ropes, hands held out as if on a cross.

# Jack Murray

5

'That must have hurt,' said Wag, wincing at the blow that had sent Haymaker sprawling against the ropes. Bert nodded in agreement.

'It's over now. He should have taken a count at least.'

Wag found that he was gripping the arms of his seat tightly. The plight of the little man in the ring was getting to him in a way that he was genuinely surprised by. What drove him to take the fight? What was driving him to stay on his feet? Stupidity certainly. Pride, too, suspected Wag. You got that with some people. He'd always recognised it when he saw it. Invariably it came wrapped in integrity. This had nothing to do with intelligence or smarts. It wasn't about women or men. It was something you were either born with or had instilled into you when you were a kid.

He turned around and glanced up at the woman who he guessed was the mother of Haymaker. Her hand was covering her mouth as if she was physically trying to stop herself from screaming. Fear and anxiety were etched onto the parts of the face he could see.

-

'Go down,' urged Kit. 'Go down.'

Olly Lake glanced at Kit and smiled.

'Not too loud, old boy. Don't want us thrown out before Mr Langford appears.'

Typical Olly thought Kit. He didn't take anything too seriously. Or perhaps he didn't care. Probably this. Kit did not know Haymaker but at that moment he felt a deep sympathy for him. He was a last-minute replacement, and he was clearly in over his head. It must have been a desperate situation for him to agree to such a one-sided contest. Such courage though. To step into the fire, knowing you would be badly burned. Could he ever have such courage? Would he ever be called upon to demonstrate such character?

Probably not.

His life would take him in a wholly different direction: a title, an estate and marriage to a beautiful, similarly titled young woman. Life had given him immense advantages that he'd not had to lift so much as a finger to acquire. The little man hanging onto the ropes had little inheritance unless you counted raw courage.

'Get on with it,' said Olly.

A man near the front, wearing a red Father Christmas hat, stood up. Kit wondered why he'd not seen him earlier. The man shouted at Haymaker.

'Move.'

The sound of Santa's voice cut through the silence.

-

For a moment Haymaker could not focus. His eyesight seemed to have lost its ability to define shapes. His brain was still trying to make sense of what had happened. His groin felt like a mule had kicked it in anger.

He'd been here before.

The scrambling of the senses, the jumble of shapes and the noise of his own laboured breathing. Then he saw Father Christmas. A bright red speck that his eyes picked up amongst the black and white haze on the other side of the ropes.

The man stood up, he seemed to be shouting something like...

Haymaker moved moments before a lunging swipe from Farrell could separate his head from his body. The force of the blow unbalanced Haymaker's opponent. Haymaker stepped forward and hooked a vicious punch into an area at the bottom of Farrell's ribs.

Even the person in the back row could hear the grunt that greeted this punch from Haymaker. They fell into a clinch which seemed to last until the bell.

Haymaker returned to his seat not daring to look at Billy Kimber. The crowd, meanwhile, applauded ecstatically. They were clearly delighted that the smaller man had given the heavyweight something to think about.

Phil Herbert threw water over Haymaker and wiped him down.

'Go after his ribs. You hurt him, Dan. You hurt him.'

Haymaker knew he'd hurt him, but his mind was on other things. What would happen when the fight ended? Kimber and his gang would think nothing about inflicting all kinds of violence on him and Phil that would make this fight seem like a scuffle on a rugby pitch.

Clang. Round four began.

-

Phil Herbert watched Haymaker trudge forward as if he were wading through quicksand. He knew his boy was tired. The elation at seeing him land an effective blow on the opponent was short-lived. He'd seen this before. As soon as the other fighter realised that Haymaker packed a punch, he would keep his distance and begin, instead, a slow, tortuous demolition of Haymaker's face, body and even the indomitable spirit.

The two men were clinching again, at least. But the stamina sapping effort of keeping hold of the opponent would tell eventually on Haymaker. Another thought had occurred to Phil. Haymaker had not gone down. This would spell trouble. He glanced over at Billy Kimber. His face was a mask. But Phil could sense the anger within him. There would be a price to pay. He saw Kimber rise from his seat and walk up the aisle to an exit.

Right now, they needed a miracle.

-

The protracted, patient, and painful annihilation of Haymaker began from the fifth round. Farrell found his range and that range was well beyond the flailing arms of Haymaker. Jab after jab marked his face as precisely as a dart. The big Lancashire man avoided clinches, punched, and moved; punched and moved. A knockout would be saved until the last moment. This would be his revenge. In the meantime, he would punish the middleweight pug who'd denied him his third round knockout bonus.

Haymaker could do little to avoid the probing punches that stung rather than de-sensitised. His legs were like water and his arms were deadened with pain. He took great gulps of air. At least his body had been spared a beating. He could still breathe, and boy did he need every bit of oxygen he could drink. He knew what was happening and knew, also, that he was now powerless to stop it.

His opponent would play with him like a cat with a captured mouse. He'd bide his time and then, sometime in the final round he would pounce and deliver the knockout blow.

This was the way of things. He'd been beaten like this before. It was part and parcel of the trade. Yet he felt angry. He'd not felt this way since his younger days when hope had still been his. Then the resentment of losing had boiled over and made him lose all sense of shape. Defence went by the wayside as he flailed away in search of a knockout.

Now he was older. Slower. And wiser, after a fashion. He knew this game.

He'd be ready.

He backed into the ropes and invited the big army man to attack him. The invitation was ignored but it often bought him time to rest and slow the fight down. Slow the flow of his opponent.

At least until the sixth and final round.

-

'I can't believe Haymaker made it this far,' said Bert.

Wag was surprised also and wondered if there was a fix in. There was no question that Farrell had slowed down significantly since the third. Wag suspected that Haymaker had inflicted more damage than people realised. Perhaps a rib. If that were the case, then there was no question that Farrell would not want to take any more chances. He was safe at a distance. Haymaker was too small, too ponderous to get close enough to take advantage of what he'd done earlier.

'I think he could take it to a decision. Not that it matters. He needs a knockout now,' said Wag.

'No chance of that,' said Bert.

'None,' agreed Wag. His attention was distracted by the sight of Billy Kimber returning to his seat. He whispered something to his bodyguard and who rose immediately. The two men headed away from the ring. Wag followed their progress as they walked past the woman Wag believed to be Haymaker's mother.

-

A rustle of murmurs rippled round the room. Dixie could hear what people were saying and wished she couldn't. She listened to a rhythmic applause greet the gladiators as they rose for the beginning of the sixth and final round.

Dixie was miserable, proud, and exhausted. She'd felt every blow. She wanted to cry again but this would be to betray the bravery, the awe-inspiring courage she was witnessing from her boy. He was still standing. Still standing against a man two weight classes above him. Absorbing an horrific beating. She could barely bring herself to look.

Clang. The sound of the bell made her wince.

-

It was there on his face.

The malevolence. The desire. The single-minded objective that he would try to take him out in this round. This was it. Haymaker inhaled deeply as his opponent approached. Inhaled and hoped for a second wind to help him sail away from the storm that was about to descend on him.

It did not come.

Farrell started off like he had the last two rounds: peppering jack-hammer jabs onto the rapidly disintegrating features of Haymaker. The blows were stronger, or so it seemed to him. They were coming more rapidly. The pace increasing. Haymaker shifted sideways like a wounded crab. He tried to bob and weave more. It worked up to a point then Farrell would take stock and resume his patient punching action. He had three minutes. He would use all of them if necessary.

He was gasping for air as he moved. There was a noise in his ears, the sound of his heart pumping blood around his body. The fists of his opponent pummelled into his face, yet he continued to lurch forward weaving like a drunken man on the deck of a storm-tossed ship. He willed his aching legs to move to the side and forwards and back. Bitterly, confusedly, madly he refused to crumble.

But he heard another noise also. It was a noise he hadn't heard at the start. The sound of his opponent breathing in the same hot, stinking air as him. The pace of the jabs had slowed. Haymaker threw himself forward into a clinch. The momentum, for the first time, forced the army man to retreat. Only a few feet but it was a victory of sorts. Haymaker pinned his opponent's tired arms to his side until they were wrenched free.

He looked into Farrell's eyes. He was exhausted. Farrell swung a long loping right that he sensed rather than saw. His left eye was rapidly closing. Another lunge by Farrell was sidestepped almost accidently by Haymaker.

Then he saw it.

Farrell's body was wide open. His ribs had a target painted on them. Haymaker unleashed a vicious hook that landed on the same place as his only other noteworthy blow. He followed this up with a right cross that detonated on Farrell's solar plexus.

The whole of the room flinched collectively at the impact of the punch.

Farrell collapsed to the ground so heavily that Kit had to stop himself shouting 'timber'.

Uproar.

Haymaker stared down in disbelief at the prone figure on the ground. His breathing slowed down as he counted with the referee. He was up to four now and Farrell had barely moved.

Five.

Farrell rolled to the side.

Six, seven.

He was on his knees.

Eight. Nine.

He was on his feet, and he staggered towards the nearest rope for support. Haymaker was standing over him throughout the count, ready to pounce. And he did.

Six rounds of torture inflicted by the big army man went into the fusillade of punches launched by Haymaker. The fatigue, the pain, the years of failure evaporated in those moments. This was no scientific precision bombing. It was a Maxim gun, and it was firing shots from all directions.

Farrell collapsed again just as the bell rang.

A cornerman leapt into the ring and helped his stricken fighter up as the referee pulled Haymaker away. Then the referee walked over to Farrell. He glanced sorrowfully at Haymaker. Turning again to the semi-conscious heavyweight, he raised his arm.

6

Dixie Harris burst into tears when the result was announced. Tears of pride. Relief, too. The fight was over, and her boy had lost. There had never been any doubt in her mind that this would be the result. But Dan had not only withstood an enormous amount of punishment he had come within a whisker of stealing the fight. Farrell would not forget her Dan in a hurry.

Unable to stop herself she ran down to the corner where Phil Herbert was towelling the sweat off Dan's head and face. Phil stopped for a moment, and he tapped Haymaker on the shoulder. He turned around and saw his mother through half closed eyes.

He'd taken a fearful beating.

Dixie couldn't say anything. She touched the cheek of her boy and did not try to stop the tears that were falling freely now.

'I'm all right ma,' lied Haymaker. It was such an outrageous fib that Dixie had to deny force of habit in telling him off. Just this once she accepted the lie. It was what she wanted to hear.

'I'm so proud of you, Daniel,' she managed to say at last. The referee was calling the two combatants to the middle to take the final acclaim of the crowd who were still on their feet applauding.

-

The McDonald brothers were on their feet clapping as the two fighters trooped to the middle of the ring. They watched them embrace.

'Have to hand it to old Haymaker,' said Bert.

'That was some fight. I thought he had 'im at the end. I really did,' agreed Wag. He felt unaccountably proud. The performance of a man he barely knew should not have affected him. Yet it had. The courage he'd witnessed was undeniable and from within himself Haymaker had even found something more. This was not just an unwillingness to lie down and simply take a beating but, instead, a desire to challenge the fight gods and mother nature herself. He'd dared to win. In this defeat there was no shame or glory. Only pride and the proof that Haymaker was a man amongst men.

The referee, he noted, seemed to be talking to Haymaker about something. Then he shrugged and said something to the ring announcer. The announcer was a man in his sixties who'd been at the Club since the very beginning. He was a fight man. He nodded and held his hands up in a manner that immediately hushed the crowd.

'Ladies and gentlemen,' said the announcer, 'Haymaker Harris has asked permission to say a few words. Please be silent.'

With that he turned to Haymaker who stepped forward nervously and glanced briefly at the announcer. He received a nod of approval.

'This'll be interesting,' whispered Bert.

-

Haymaker stepped forward and turned to Ed Mackay, the announcer. Mackay nodded and smiled supportively. He liked Haymaker. Always had. Showed respect. A good boy. Haymaker turned again and faced one side of the crowd. He caught the eyes of his mum and Phil Herbert. Both were frowning and shrugging their shoulders in the manner of people wanting to know what the hell you were doing. Boy, did he recognise that expression on his mother.

For reasons he could not explain, a fear gripped him. It was a terror that exceeded anything he'd ever felt in the ring. Tears trickled down his cheeks and he wiped them away.

'I've never spoken before in the ring,' he started nervously. 'Anyway, ladies and gentlemen, I wanted to congratulate my opponent. Well done, Joe. That was a good fight. Thought I had you there at the end, but you were strong. Well done.'

There was silence in the room as the audience listened, transfixed by the sight of the little middleweight speaking.

'I'm glad you liked the fight. It's going to be my last fight. I'm retiring, for good. And I just wanted to say thank you to all of you. You've always been so kind to me. You've always given me such good support. I don't know what to say.'

He stopped himself for a moment. Struggling against the tears he continued.

'That's it, really. So long and I hope you all have a happy Christmas. And thanks, I mean it.'

Silence followed this short speech from the least-likely speechmaker in the room. Haymaker turned back to Mackay and nodded.

Wag McDonald wiped something from his eye. He was more emotional than his enemies would ever realise. When Haymaker finished his speech there was silence in the room. It was unearthly. Uncertainty as to what the Club permitted. But Wag was certain as to the only response possible to the courage and the pronouncement he'd just been witness to. To hell with decorum. To hell with the Club rules.

Wag didn't care.

'Three cheers for Haymaker,' shouted Wag at the top of his voice. 'Hip, hip...'

A few rows away, Kit and his companions gave full vent to the Hoorays that followed at Wag's instigation. When they'd finished there was a prolonged burst of applause for Haymaker who was waving to the crowd, even more dazed than he had been by the fists of Gunner Joe Farrell. The tears flowed freely but he made no attempt to wipe them away.

He walked to the corner where his mother and Phil Herbert were waiting. Ducking under the ropes he climbed down to the floor of the room and hugged them both. Then they let him walk ahead, head held high towards the changing room, the cheers of the crowd echoing in his ears. This was a moment he would never forget.

And his triumph did not end there. As he walked through the doors leading onto the corridor to the changing room, he came eye to eye with a man he recognised all too well.

'Good fight, sir,' said a North American accent.

Haymaker stared at Sam Langford in disbelief. There was a smile on the Canadian's face. He was lost for words. Finally, he managed to mumble a tearful thanks before the pressure of the crowd coming through the door forced him forward towards the changing room.

-

Wag McDonald watched Haymaker make his triumphant exit not only from the room but from boxing itself. There was a lump in his throat. He knew what he had to do. Turning to Bert he said, 'Let's go.'

Bert was confused but went along with his brother, as he usually did. The two men shuffled along the row and headed for the same door that Haymaker had exited through a minute earlier.

The corridor was crowded with newsmen, trainers, and Club officials. Wag spied Haymaker up ahead. He was shaking hands with Farrell who then disappeared through a door.

'Haymaker,' said Wag approaching the boxer. He was standing beside the diminutive woman who he'd seen cheer him earlier and his trainer. Up close he could see all too clearly the evidence of the beating that Haymaker had received from the big Lancashire man. But he could see something else, too.

Dignity.

Haymaker' eyes widened when he saw who it was. Dixie Harris had no idea who had just addressed her son and turned to point out, as mothers often do at the most inopportune moments, that his name was Daniel. The man seemed young, but he was well-dressed, and his accent was not typical of the clientele of the Club. He was from south of the river. It was a resolute face. Hard. Not soft and futile like so many of the men she saw around her.

'Mr McDonald,' said Haymaker, in a voice that was as respectful as it was watchful.

Dixie Harris picked up on the tone and decided to postpone the visitor's earful until she understood who he was and what business he wanted to transact. She confined herself to a look of impatience that both Wag and Bert recognised as they possessed a mother of their own.

'Sorry to interrupt, Haymaker,' said Wag in a friendly manner, he glanced at Haymaker's mum and then back to the boxer. Even Haymaker, whose understanding of social niceties was matched only by his ability at needlework, appreciated that introductions were in order.

'Mr McDonald, this is my mum. And this is my trainer, Phil Herbert.'

Wag and Bert both touched their hats and said hello to 'Mrs Harris'. Dixie Harris was somewhat mollified by their politeness but remained on her guard for any familiarity that exceeded acceptable social intercourse while standing outside a boxing changing room.

'I want to say, Haymaker, that was a wonderful fight. I thought you had it won at the end. Hard luck,' said Wag. 'I was wondering what your plans were now that you are retiring.'

Dixie had a similar question in mind as the news had come as something of a surprise, a welcome surprise, to her. She turned to Haymaker; one eyebrow raised.

'I don't have any plans, Mr McDonald. I just know I can't keep fighting all my life.'

Wag wasn't quite sure he agreed with this but there were ways and means of deploying such naked courage and immutable integrity. He was about to suggest how.

'Would you like to come and work for me, Haymaker? I've heard good things about you. All say the same. You're your own man. You don't take a dive. I like that. More than that, Bert and I could use a man like you. Someone we can trust. What do you say?'

Dixie's eyes widened and she turned to her son. She was about to shout at him to say yes when she saw the look of gratitude on her boy's face.

'Yes, sir. Yes, I'd love to work for you, Mr McDonald.'

Wag held out his hand and shook Haymaker's hand. It still had the bandages on it.

'Then it's a deal, Haymaker. Enjoy your Christmas. You start Boxing Day. You know where to go, don't you?'

Haymaker nodded, unable to speak. He simply nodded as he watched the two McDonald's touch their hats again and wish them all a Happy Christmas.

'Who was that?' asked Dixie, glancing up at her son. Then, moments later she followed his gaze down to his outstretched hand. He was holding a ten-pound note. 'Never mind, son,' continued Dixie, staring in wonder at the money the man had handed her son. It could have been old Nick himself for all she cared. Then, much to her shock, her son called out to Wag McDonald. He hauled his aching body down the corridor and caught the head of the Elephant Boys.

'Mr McDonald. Thank you, sir. There's one thing I meant to ask you. I need a small favour.'

Wag McDonald smiled and winked up at his brother. 'Name it, Haymaker.'

7

An hour later, Kit, in the company of his four young friends and Uncle Eustace, was walking through the foyer of the National Sporting Club. All were in a high state of excitement at the night of fighting they'd witnessed.

'I thought our boy was going to do it,' said Chubby. 'Langford wasn't at the races.'

Spunky wasn't so sure. He shook his head in disagreement.

'I think it was a fix. I think Langford was paid to allow him a few rounds before he sent him to sleep.'

They passed the American gentleman they'd seen in the bar. He was once more surrounded by well-dressed men. The American had a grin wider than the Atlantic and who wouldn't? He was stuffing oodles of cash from the losing punters into his pockets.

'I think he and Mr Langford are going to have a very happy Christmas on the ship back,' laughed Kit. 'I wonder how much he's won.'

'More than enough to buy a bottle of champers or two,' suggested Uncle Eustace with a grin. 'Speaking of which, can I interest you in joining me for a night cap?'

The four young men agreed as one that this was the very thing that they were going to suggest. They marched out of the Club almost arm in arm in their comradeship. The night air hit them like a blast after the hot sweaty atmosphere of the boxing auditorium. It was very welcome indeed.

They turned to walk along King Street which was thronged with men and women. The Sally Army band was still there, bravely playing on despite the cold. Kit separated himself from the group and dropped a few pounds into the collecting tin, then returned to his friends just as the brass band started up, 'God Rest Ye Merry Gentlemen'.

'Where's Uncle Eustace?' asked Kit when he returned.

Olly Lake nodded towards a group stood by the entrance to the changing rooms.

'May I congratulate you, Mr Harris, on a splendid fight,' said Uncle Eustace, shaking the hands of Phil Herbert, Dixie Harris and then Haymaker himself. 'I think if there'd been another round you'd have won.'

Haymaker smiled at the unknown man and thanked him. The man was a toff but a good sort all the same. His ruddy cheeks and ready smile radiated warmth in the cold night air. He tipped his hat to Haymaker and the group before disappearing off into the crowd.

Haymaker looked down at his hand.

'Look at that,' he said to Phil and his mother.

They looked down and saw that Haymaker was clutching two ten-pound notes. This was proving to be some night. Haymaker handed one to Phil.

'I can't,' said Phil.

'You will,' said Dixie thereby ending the discussion as only mothers can. She looked up at her son and saw his eyes were fixed elsewhere. She followed his gaze towards two men. They were a bit like the men they'd met earlier. Young, well-dressed, and hard. Dixie saw the same in them as she'd seen in the man, she now knew led one of the most feared gangs in London. Of course, she'd heard of the Elephant Boys and her son was going to join them. The men walking towards them were cut from the same stone. And they didn't look happy.

Dixie looked from the men and then up to her son. She could see, despite the scar tissue and swelling, the fear in his eyes. His hand gripped hers tighter and then he released it suddenly and stepped forward to meet the two men.

'Stay back, Phil,' said Haymaker. The former bare-knuckle fighter immediately ignored what his fighter had said and stepped up beside him.

Billy Kimber's face was impassive. He watched Haymaker and Phil Herbert approach them. He was, oddly, impressed by this. Haymaker looked like he'd been beaten over the head with a cricket bat. It was not a sight for the faint-hearted. He marched forward until he was only a foot away from the two men he'd come to see.

'You didn't go down, Dan? What happened?'

'Sorry, Mr Kimber. I couldn't. He hit me low. He shouldn't have done that.'

Kimber nodded and looked at the old trainer beside the boxer. What on earth did he think he could do? It was almost funny. A beaten-up pug and an old trainer going to take on his boy. At this point he could probably deal with them on his own. The fighter was in no state to mix it, that much was clear. His movement had been like those of an old man nearing the end. He felt sorry for him. Almost.

Then he saw Haymaker's eyes flick to something just behind him. Kimber turned around and found himself staring into the face of Wag McDonald. Bert was just behind him.

'Wag,' exclaimed Kimber. 'I thought I saw you earlier.'

'Hello, Billy. Enjoy the fights?' asked Wag, reasonably.

'For the most part, yes. I dropped a few quid, however on one of them.'

'So, I gather,' smiled Wag. 'I'm surprised you didn't lay it off.'

'I did, as it happens,' replied Kimber, eyeing Wag closely. 'Found a toff who was feeling a bit certain that our boy here would be leaving the premises by way of a stretcher before the sixth. I offered him fives that it would go the distance.'

'Fives?' laughed Wag. Even Haymaker was surprised by the turn in the conversation. His mind did not work as quickly as the two gang leaders, but it was beginning to dawn on him that Billy Kimber, after losing his initial stake on one bet had made it back on another.

'I'd have gone up to seven if he'd pushed. I mean, anyone mad enough not to dive after I asked them, nicely I might add, was probably more than capable of surviving another couple of rounds against Farrell.'

Wag shot a glance towards Haymaker and then returned his attention to Billy Kimber.

'He's a good boy is Haymaker. If you were wanting to take him on, Billy, it's too late. I've nabbed him for us.'

Kimber turned to Haymaker and studied him for a second before looking back at the McDonalds. He smiled and nodded his head.

'He's a sound bloke all right. You've made a good choice there, Wag. I wish I'd thought of that, I really do. Have a good Christmas, boys,' said Kimber, touching his hat. He turned back to Haymaker and added, 'You, too, champ.'

Then he and his minder walked off into the crowds. Wag and Bert watched them go and then, with a wave, headed off in the opposite direction.

Phil Herbert let out a long sigh. Then he clapped his fighter on the back and said, 'Well, I'm glad I didn't have to beat the hell out of Billy Kimber. Doesn't seem such a bad bloke when you get to know 'im.'

'No. Not so bad.'

The two men walked back to Dixie Harris who'd gone over to a spot near the Sally Army band. They stood either side of her and listened to them start a new carol. Through his half-closed eyes Haymaker saw one snowflake and then another waft gently through the air, falling slowly down and landing on his mother's cheek. Mother and son looked at one another for a moment. Neither spoke. There was nothing to say. It was all contained in the way they looked at one another. Then they both turned their attention to a young woman in a dark navy uniform. She began to sing:

In the bleak mid-winter
Frosty wind made moan.
Earth stood hard as iron,
Water like a stone;
Snow had fallen, snow on snow,
Snow on snow,
In the bleak mid-winter
Long ago

The End

Jack Murray

Research Notes

I have mentioned several key real-life individuals and events in this novel. My intention, in the following section, is to explain a little more about their connection to this period and this story.

Charles 'Wag" McDonald (1885 – 1943)

McDonald was a leader of a south London criminal gang known as the 'Elephant Boys' who were based in the Elephant and Castle area of London. He was assisted by his brother Wal, and they formed an effective partnership with Billy Kimber (who features in the TV series 'Peaky Blinders'). McDonald led an interesting life. He fought in the Boer War before to returning to England to take over the leadership of the Elephant Boys. He then volunteered for active service during the Great War. When he came back from France, he took over leadership of the gang once more before escaping to the US in 1921. He worked in Hollywood for several years, getting to know many of the stars. His life and the life of gangs in the area have been captured in several books by his descendant, Brian McDonald.

Billy Kimber (1882 - 1945)

Kimber was born in Birmingham and led one of the largest and most feared gangs in the south of England, the Brummagem Boys. Most recently he has gained a new fame as a character in the BBC series 'Peaky Blinders'. The Brummagem Boys were a street gang whose reach extended from the North of England to London's underworld, between the 1910s and 1930. In this period gang warfare was focused on England's racecourses. The only gambling allowed in England was the races. The introduction of special excursion trains meant that all classes of society could attend the new racecourses around the country. Crowds flocked to the races and bookmakers followed looking to separate punter from cash. The role of the gangs was protection.

Kimber and the Elephant Boys formed an alliance in London which was broken only by the Great War. As gang warfare in the capital escalated post war, Kimber emigrated with McDonald to the United States in 1921. He returned in 1929 and resumed his criminal activities.

He died in 1945 in Torquay.

The National Sporting Club (NSC)

The National Sporting Club was founded in London's Covent Garden in 1891. No organisation did more to establish the sport of boxing in Britain than this club. It was co-founded by John Fleming and Arthur 'Peggy' Bettinson. The fifth Earl of Lonsdale, Hugh Lowther was its first president. Lonsdale, famously, gave his name to the championship belt worn by British champions and which they get to keep if they manage three consecutive title defences. The club's heyday was in the immediate pre and post Great War periods. The club was private with around 1,300 members. It sought to make boxing respectable. To this end, fights were conducted in silence.

By the late 20's the club no longer had the influence it had once enjoyed.

Jack Murray

Sam Langford (1883 - 1956)

Sam Langford, the Boston Tar Baby, has long been considered the greatest fighter never to win a world title. He fought at a time when there was a colour bar. This effectively denied him and other fighters like him such as Joe Jeannette and Harry Wills opportunities to fight for the titles their skills so richly deserved.

Langford fought at every weight from lightweight to heavyweight. Considering his size, he was reputed to be around five feet seven, his fight record in the heavier division is more remarkable. He fought the first black World heavyweight Champion, Jack Johnson, losing a decision over fifteen rounds.

Langford visited Britain on several occasions. He fought twice at the NSC in 1907. winning against Tiger Smith and Geoff Thorne. The fight described in this novelette took place in February 1910, not December 1909. He did fight Yorkshireman Iron William Hague. He won by knockout which was a great relief to his manager who had bet ten thousand on the outcome not realising that he'd bet in British Pounds not US Dollars. This would have put Langford's losses at $50,000 which was five times the purse he was to receive.

For the first few rounds, so overcome by the implications of the bet, Langford was beaten up badly by Hague. When he finally woke up to his predicament, he knocked out Hague with a single punch (see Bill Stern's Favourite Boxing Stories, 1948, Pocket Books).

The Kit Aston Novellas

AND OTHER STORIES

EXCERPTS FROM

THE PHANTOM (KIT ASTON BOOK 3) – THE MISSING DIAMONDS

THE FRISCO FALCON (KIT ASTON BOOK 4) – THE NINETEENTH HOLE

Jack Murray

Jack Murray

THE MISSING DIAMONDS

THE PHANTOM (KIT ASTON BOOK 3) - EXCERPT

February 11th, 1920: Grosvenor Square, London

Night crept into London's Grosvenor Square like a street urchin picking a rich man's pocket - stealthily at first and then all at once. The square was comprised of grand houses surrounding a large garden. The very richest in the land chose to live in this location rather as a fish should choose to live in the sea. It was their natural habitat and always had been.

Building work began in Grosvenor Square around 1721 soon after the South Sea Bubble burst to spectacularly impoverishing effect on its numerous British investors. The square took to heart the idea that an Englishman's home is his castle and made a jolly decent attempt at bringing this concept to reality. Perhaps an unintended after-effect, made manifest in Grosvenor Square, was the idea that investing in London property was rarely a bad idea.

On this night, young Ezra Mullins was, as his mum might have said, in a right state and no mistake. He was dressed in livery only marginally less stiff than cardboard, sporting a top hat that was one or possibly two sizes too big. The sight presented by the estimable young Mullins would almost certainly have induced paroxysms of pride in his mother and mirth in his father; such is the uncommon nature of women and the immaturity of men.

Ezra had recently been recruited as a doorman for an industrial magnate, one of the few men in England able to afford a mansion in one of the least affordable locations in London. Tonight, he was witnessing and bowing to a parade of the flushest and most powerful individuals, not just from Britain but from around the world.

A Rolls Royce Phantom attracted his attention as it drew up to the magnificent mansion. The chauffeur, another young man, stepped out from the front and opened the door. From the car emerged easily the most beautiful girl Ezra had seen all evening, if not ever. The lucky fellow with her, conceded young Ezra, was also a fine-looking gentleman. He couldn't help but notice the man's limp. It wasn't difficult to guess the reason why.

As the couple walked up the steps, the young woman glanced at Ezra. His attempts to disguise his admiration were sadly undone by a mouth that had dropped open and an inability to tear his eyes away from her face. She looked back at him; her blue eyes narrowed faintly, then she smiled. Moments later she was away and moving into the hallway of the mansion.

Dominating the hallway was an enormous malachite staircase which led from a black and white marble floor to a second-floor landing which housed an enormous Van Dyck portrait of a Dutch woman overlooking the whole scene with all the patience, bonhomie and good spiritedness of a wife awaiting her lord and master's return home from the pub.

The staircase was lined with footmen who smiled as the young couple walked up towards the drawing room. Inside there was already a large crowd of men in white tie. There were relatively few women, observed the young man. The raised eyebrow of his beautiful young partner told him she was thinking along similar lines.

Lady Mary Cavendish surveyed the room for a few moments. She noted, without caring too much, that many of the men aware of her arrival were surveying her also. She looked up at the man who was accompanying her and said with a smile, 'Two Prime Ministers, a former Prime Minister and a couple of cabinet ministers. Not bad. You do take me to all the best places, Lord Aston.'

Kit glanced down at Mary and returned her smile.

'Well, cooped up in hospital all this time, I thought it was the least I could do.'

'Lead on, Macduff,' ordered Mary sweetly. Up ahead she noticed a distinguished man absenting himself from the company of Prime Minister Lloyd George to have a word with a servant.

'He's rather good looking for an older man,' observed Mary.

Kit raised his eyebrow and replied, 'I happen to agree with you. That is our host.'

Mary put her arm through Kit's, looked straight ahead and said, 'Introduce us, please.'

Across the room was Lord Peter Wolf, the joint owner of Lewis & Wolf, a large industrial conglomerate. They were inside the drawing room of Wolf's mansion in Grosvenor Square. The room seemed to be the size of a small county. Overhead were two crystal chandeliers which competed unsuccessfully for attention against the *objets d'art* which included Renaissance paintings on the walls and a Canova bust situated at the end of the room.

Kit and Mary walked towards Wolf. 'How rich is he?' asked Mary nodding towards the wall housing the Titian.

'Clearly not in penury,' said Kit under his breath.

Wolf turned around just as the couple moved towards him. He was a tall man, around sixty, tanned with hair turning from dark to silver. His blue eyes crinkled into a smile as he saw Kit with Mary.

'I'm sorry, I didn't see you arrive. We've dispensed with announcing arrivals.'

'I'm glad,' replied Kit, 'It would seem like a relic from the last century.'

'I agree. After Flanders, I'm not sure it feels appropriate either,' said Wolf. Turning to Mary, 'Is this the extraordinary Lady Mary?'

'I wouldn't quite go that far, Lord Wolf,' said Mary modestly.

'I would. Your story caused quite a stir in our household,' replied Wolf taking Mary's hand and shaking it. 'What you did in going to nurse the men at the front was very much to your credit so you may count me amongst your many devotees. Although if the rumours are true, it seems you have one particular admirer.'

Kit laughed and admitted the rumours were true. Wolf looked at them, and his smile grew wider. They made a beautiful couple. Noble without superiority, intelligent without conceit and approachable without being over-familiar.

'My wife and I weren't fortunate enough to have children but, if I may say, I'd have been immensely proud if they'd been like you, my dear. Congratulations, Kit,' and Wolf took Kit's hand and shook it vigorously. The sincerity of Wolf's sentiments was clear.

'Thank you, sir, and thank you for the invitation to your…,' he searched for the right word to convey the fact that they were amongst many of Europe's leaders on the eve of a major peace conference in London. He settled on, 'soiree.'

This made Wolf smile and he said, 'I thought it appropriate you come given your escapade in Paris last year.'

Mary looked up at Kit proudly, 'Yes he's been somewhat reluctant to tell me exactly what he did.'

'There's a man coming towards us who should be able to elaborate,' replied Wolf.

'Lord Aston, Lady Mary,' boomed a voice rich enough in timbre to suggest a long and successful career on the boards. In fact, this was not so very far from the truth as the man was playing a role. The role was as fictitious as his playing of it was true.

Both turned around to be greeted by the sight of Percy Pendlebury, gossip columnist and, as of last year's unintentional involvement in 'The French Diplomat Affair', mysterious man of, well, mystery. Wolf rolled his eyes and made good his escape.

'Percy,' said Kit shaking the journalist's hand, 'How are you? Glad to see you're fully recovered.'

'Oh, completely, Kit, but enough about me. Now, Lady Mary, I don't believe we've met but I have met Lady Esther,' said Pendlebury fixing Mary with his full attention.

'Yes, I read the piece you wrote about her. You were very kind.'

'I should love to have included you also, my dear. My readers were bewitched by my series on what people such as yourself were doing during the War.'

Mary had nursed at the Front under a pseudonym for the last year of the War.

'I'm sorry. I didn't want to talk about my time there.'

Just for a moment Mary found it hard to breathe. Unhappy images of the appalling injuries inflicted on the soldiers in her care swam in front of her eyes. Kit was aware of Mary's grip growing stronger. He looked at her face and saw a change, almost imperceptible, but clear. He fell in love with her again for what seemed like the hundredth time that day.

Pendlebury, whose own intuition was as highly tuned as Kit's, also saw the change. He took her hand and smiled sympathetically.

'Please forgive me. I quite understand your desire not to discuss those heart-breaking days.'

He did. Unusually for a newsman whose prior career had principally involved the reporting of rich people being and acting as rich people do, he had travelled to the front to see for himself and report on the lives of the men and women serving.

'But am I to assume that you two wonderful young people, have some news to share with me and all my readers?'

Mary blushed slightly and glanced at Kit who returned her look.

'Yes, Percy. I rather think you can.'

'Is this official?'

'It will be when you break it,' pointed out Kit.

Pendlebury offered hearty congratulations before nodding to two older men standing in a corner, 'Well, Kit, I must thank you for this scoop, although I think we'll both agree you did owe me one. Ah, you'll have to excuse me on that happy note. I've just seen two Prime Ministers talking to one another. I shall see if I can hear what they're saying.'

The two Prime Ministers in question were Lloyd George and Francesco Nitti of Italy. Both were due to host the Conference of London the next day.

Mary looked up at Kit suspiciously.

'What did he mean by that, I wonder?' asked Mary. 'Is this another thing you've neglected to tell me milord?'

'I'm afraid it is rather a failing of our gender that we sometimes omit details in our desire to avoid boring to death the audience.'

'Or,' pointed out Mary, 'when said detail may not reflect well on you?'

'Especially that.'

Wolf returned and taking Mary's arm said, 'If I may, Kit, I'd like to take the most beautiful lady in the room to meet her many admirers.'

'That didn't take long,' laughed Kit relinquishing Mary's arm.

As he did so he became aware of a man ambling up beside him. He turned around and found himself looking at Gerald Geddes, a man he'd encountered last in Paris around the time of the Peace Conference.

'Hello, Aston,' said Geddes.

Kit nodded at Geddes, 'Hello, Geddes.' He tried not to look surprised at seeing a spy at the soiree. But, then again, it made sense. There were a lot of senior politicians and businessmen here this evening. There were bound to be indiscretions and when alcohol was involved.

'Working?' asked Kit amiably.

'Yes. You?'

'No, purely social. I'm with my fiancé,' replied Kit.

'Congratulations,' said Geddes before nodding a goodbye. This coincided with the arrival of a man Kit knew well.

'So, I gather congratulations are in order,' said the man, who was at least as tall as Kit.

'Yes, Lord President,' replied Kit to former Prime Minister Arthur Balfour.

Balfour nodded, and both men regarded Mary appreciatively. Then he turned back to Kit and said, 'I knew her grandmother slightly. She was also very beautiful. You must introduce us later. How are you anyway? You've had a busy few weeks if what I hear is true.'

Kit laughed. In the last few weeks, he'd solved the murder of Lord Arthur Cavendish, seen his fiancée almost fall victim to poisoning and solved a crime involving several murders connected to a conspiracy to assassinate the King and the Queen Consort.

'Yes, it's been somewhat hectic,' agreed Kit.

'You met my successor, Curzon, I gather.'

'Indeed,' said Kit looking at Balfour with a half-smile.

'Indeed,' responded Balfour in an equally neutral tone. Glancing ahead he saw Mary ensconced with Lloyd George and Nitti.

'Your intended may need rescuing. One Welsh goat and an Italian seem to be wooing her. If she's in any way attracted by power, you could be in trouble. If, instead, she values men of a more philosophical bent, I may throw a hat into the ring myself.' Both observed the Italian Prime Minister put a protective arm around Mary before noting his hand dropping further down.

'Normally I would say she can hold her own but perhaps, on this occasion, she's outgunned.'

The two men walked forward to rescue Mary, who glanced archly at Kit as he arrived. Turning momentarily to Lloyd George before looking again at Kit, she said, 'The Prime Minister was just telling me how you probably saved his life last year in Paris. I must say I'm looking forward to knowing more about my future husband, Prime Minister. He tells me nothing.'

'And the King's life this year,' added Balfour. 'By the way Lady Mary, I'm Arthur, as none of these gentlemen seem in a rush to introduce me.'

'Lord President,' said Mary smiling up to Balfour, 'I've been an admirer of yours for many years.'

'And I of you for many minutes,' replied Balfour nobly.

-

Around midnight, the main dignitaries had retired for the evening. Wolf suggested they withdraw to the library for a nightcap. The library, if not as large as the drawing room, was as impressive. Books lined the walls from floor to ceiling. Some wall space was occupied by paintings from the French Impressionists who were gaining in popularity and value by the year in England.

The room was lit by an enormous crystal chandelier which had, as Wolf demonstrated, several dimmer switches around the room. Mary had been subject to vigorous displays of what she and Kit later agreed was behaviour only marginally differentiated from a Gorilla beating its chest and a lot less impressive. All of which amused Kit and provided no end of entertainment to Mary as well as to her newfound friend, Arthur Balfour.

With the politicians gone, bar the indefatigable Balfour, the conversation moved on to the recent spate of robberies in the city. This brought back memories for some of the thief known as 'The Phantom.'

'You're not going to claim credit for that one also, Kit?' asked Balfour, with one eyebrow raised.

Kit laughed, 'No, I was just leaving for the War when the Phantom was captured. I do know the chap who caught him: Chief Inspector Jellicoe. Good man.'

'I must say, I was relieved when they caught him,' admitted Wolf. Upon saying that, he went over to a painting on the wall and moved it to one side. Behind it was a safe. Given that he was with men and women of unimpeachable background, Wolf felt completely at ease in what he was doing.

He opened the safe and removed a small black velvet pouch. From the pouch he extracted a diamond necklace. Mary gasped involuntarily. She wasn't the only one. There were over a dozen sizeable diamonds on the chain. It was beautiful and unquestionably worth a small fortune. Everyone in the room inched forward to have a better look at the necklace Wolf had placed on the table.

Just as Wolf stepped back, the lights went out leaving the room in complete darkness. Two of the women screamed and there were shouts from a couple of the men. The lights came on again after a few moments. When everyone looked down at the table, the diamonds were gone.

Wolf looked at everyone in the room, and said, 'Is this some sort of joke? If I may say, it's in very poor taste.'

Mary looked up at Kit and whispered, 'Do something.'

'Me?'

'Yes, you.'

Everyone turned to Kit.

'Oh,' said Kit, unsure of what was expected from him, 'Perhaps we should lock the doors.' Behind him the footmen in the room did as they were bid. Kit looked at Wolf. The room was silent as they waited for Kit's next words. And then Mary spoke.

'Well, clearly they're hidden up above. Who's going to look?'

Everyone looked up at the chandelier.

'Good thinking,' said Balfour smiling.

A young man volunteered, and space was cleared for him to stand on a chair and to root around the chandelier with his outstretched hand. All this time Kit kept his eyes on Wolf.

'I can't find anything,' admitted the young man.

'Oh,' said Mary, clearly disappointed that her first stab at detection had, on this occasion, been a failure. She felt a comforting hand on her elbow from Kit. She looked up and made a face. Kit had a faint smile. Mary frowned. She sensed what was coming.

'What are you thinking, Kit?' asked Wolf.

'A greater and, frankly, more credible detective than I once said that if you can eliminate the impossible then whatever remains, no matter how improbable, must be the truth.'

'Go on Sherlock.' said Mary, who made having a grin and frown at the same moment not only physically possible but very enticing.

'Well, with that in mind,' said Kit walking forward to the safe and looking inside, 'I would suggest that the necklace is back in the safe where Lord Wolf placed it when the lights went out.'

The safe was empty.

Wolf's face was non-committal. Kit turned to face the room. No one had moved except to look either at Kit or the empty safe.

'As you can see the safe is empty,' said Kit. He caught Arthur Balfour's eye. The glint suggested the former Prime Minister was enjoying this as much as he was fascinated by what the solution to the mystery might be. Mary was beside him. Her face now betrayed a degree of nervousness. With the safe empty, she was worried he was going to make a fool of himself. So was Kit.

'However, if I do this,' said Kit, pressing down on the base of the safe and extracting from the compartment underneath, a diamond necklace which he held up for all to view, 'then the diamonds reappear, as if by magic'.

Everyone broke out into spontaneous applause, none more so than Lord Wolf who was laughing in delight. Shouts of 'Bravo' filled the air. As the ovation died down one voice broke the silence.

'Of course, you're now in trouble,' said Arthur Balfour.

'Indeed, that thought has also just occurred to me,' admitted Kit.

Wolf and the others in the assembly turned to Balfour for an explanation, who duly provided it.

'Well Kit has, rather publicly, been proved right. I fear his delightful fiancée will, indeed must, make Kit spend a lifetime reflecting on how he chose to deploy his unquestioned intellect ahead of a piece of wisdom that has existed at least as long as humanity.'

'Which is?' prompted Mary, with something approaching relish.

'That women are always right,' finished Kit, shamefacedly.

Mary stepped forward and kissed Kit gently on the cheek. This brought a second round of applause. Kit glanced and saw Gerald Geddes looking at him quizzically.

'Any other party tricks?' asked Geddes. He was smiling but there seemed to be little humour in his tone. Kit was distracted by Lord Wolf coming up alongside him clutching the diamond necklace.

'I wouldn't want to be in your shoes when you go home, Kit,' said Wolf with a grin. The smile on Wolf's face changed in a moment to confusion. He stared at the diamond necklace and then looked back up at Kit.

'What's wrong, Peter?' asked Kit, looking also at the necklace. He looked back at the ashen face of Lord Wolf.

'It's fake. The necklace is a fake.'

Wolf went over immediately to the safe. He placed his hand down on the base which tipped down to into the hidden compartment found by Kit during the practical joke.

He turned to face the assembly. Incredulity was written on his face. Kit picked up the black velvet pouch and turned it inside out. As he did so, a small card fell onto the table. Kit lifted the card and showed it to Lord Wolf.

On the card was the face of a phantom.

Jack Murray

THE NINETEENTH HOLE

THE FRISCO FALCON (KIT ASTON BOOK 4) – EXCERPT

Troon Golf Club, June 1920

The golf ball rolled slowly towards the hole, wiped its feet at the entrance, then toppled forward like a drunk trying to pick a coin off the bar floor. There was no celebratory cheer despite the fact it was a birdie. Instead, the golfer walked forward briskly and whisked the ball from the hole. Another golfer stepped up and addressed his ball.

The putter drew back slowly and then after a short pause, he released the head. It clipped against the ball, propelling it forward. It rocketed past the hole like a cannonball.

'Blast,' said the man. Then he stood erect, attempted a smile, and walked forward, hand outstretched.

'Well done, Gloria. Two up. I didn't make use of the shots you were giving me here.'

Gloria Mansfield nodded curtly. She turned and walked over to her caddy, handing him the putter.

'Well done, miss,' said Hamish Anderson with a grin wider than the Irish Sea. He would earn a little extra reward thanks to his mistress's victory. He liked caddying for Miss Mansfield. She was generous with her tips when she won, and she usually won. The two golfers left the green quickly, followed by their caddies. There was a smell of salt in the air. And defeat. Humiliating, overwhelming defeat. By a woman, no less. But what a woman!

The wind was at their backs, coming off the sea. Soon it would be damn near unplayable. Miss Mansfield looked up at the sky and shivered involuntarily. She headed directly to the changing room.

-

Inside the clubhouse, Aldric 'Spunky' Stevens watched all that had taken place through a military telescope he had neglected to hand back when he returned from France.

'Yes, old chap, she's certainly has good form,' said Spunky, nodding sagely.

'She's single figure now,' said Reggie Pilbream, a young man of twenty-four, and that was probably just his IQ. He was a slightly built, pallid boy with short dark hair and a laugh that often ended in an unfortunate snort, the impact of which he was wholly oblivious to, but not the legion of women who had, sadly, tended to avoid romantic entanglement with him.

'I don't doubt it,' replied Spunky admiringly, his telescope travelling down the well-made body of the young woman. By no means slender, she was unquestionably a sporty young lady, whose outline matched her handicap of eight.

'I mean how on earth will I ever get a look in?' cried Reggie. 'A fella off twenty-six shouldn't really have any chance when the love of his life plays off seven or eight. She's hot stuff.'

'Certainly is,' agreed Spunky, puffing on his pipe contentedly, eyes glued to the approaching vision. At nineteen, Gloria Mansfield was attracting many admiring glances from the men at the club. This was less to do with her ability to draw a mashie onto the centre of the fairway amid a stiff nor 'wester than the presence of big blue eyes, surrounded by bubbling blonde curls and a healthy bank balance.

'I say, Spunky, dash it all, we're talking about the lady who's stolen my heart. She's not some sort of…'

'Understood old chap, but I think you need to open your mind to the rather singular reality that the young lady who has, as you say, stolen your heart, is rather easy on the eye. If you don't believe me then look at the pride of lions circling the prey on the practice green.'

'I see what you mean,' said Reggie, looking out the window. He collapsed to the seat, and drained Spunky's gin and tonic before his face took on a melancholic frown that would have been tragic had it not been so funny, at least to Spunky's one good eye.

'What's a chap to do?' he asked plaintively.

'It's the age-old question, from Socrates down to...'

'Wasn't Socrates a bit..?'

'Well yes, a bit, but it doesn't mean he didn't put his noggin to the mystery of goddesses or some such topic. Anyway, give me the skinny on this filly's form.'

Reggie looked up. He was a little put out at the somewhat frivolous attitude of his friend. He was, also, too miserable to give his old friend a piece of his mind which, he would have been honest enough to admit, was not of the first rank.

'Gloria Mansfield, the angel, is from the Berkshire Mansfields. I think she's a cousin of Tuppy Thomas. Anyway, this divine creature plays at Sunningdale apparently, and could be a starter in the British Women's Amateur soon. Plays off eight but she's been round Troon in scratch apparently. You see, Spunky, it's no use.'

'Well, I presume there's more to her than just golf,' pointed out Spunky patiently.

'Well, she's with that beastly boy. It's her young brother, George. Beelzebub if you ask me. Whiney little character.'

Spunky turned to Reggie. This was interesting. Brat kid brothers offered promising avenues of strategy for a man such as Spunky.

'Go on, tell me more about the little monster.'

'Of course, she dotes on him. Perhaps her only fault. Anyway, I've the little terror off scaring wild wolves and crocodiles while Gloria is playing golf.'

'Adventurous little sod then?'

'Rather,' said Reggie, emphasising both syllables.

Spunky sipped at his gin and tonic and gave the matter some thought. Despite the appearance of being a fatheaded ass, Spunky was, in fact, a highly valued member of British Intelligence. Such a role was not lightly bestowed nor was the Service likely to employ anyone with a deficiency of intellect unless, of course, it was accompanied by a soundness of breeding.

Owing to the loss of his eye during the War, Spunky's remit was mostly backroom where he applied a surprisingly mathematical mind to understanding economic pressure points in potential enemies of the empire. These days that seemed to encompass the rest of the map not coloured red.

A plan began to grow which, to Spunky's mind, was as devilish as it seemed logical. That it was, likely, devoid of any sign of good judgement was entirely another matter, and, in this case, someone else's problem. To be precise: Reggie's.

Spunky leaned forward causing Reggie to lean forward also. Taking another sip from his glass, he began to outline his plan. What he had in mind was strategically sound but posed some executional challenges.

'We need to imprison the boy, raise the alarm that he has been kidnapped and then, low and behold, Reginald St John Pilbream saves the day, rescues the boy and watches Miss Mansfield collapse gratefully into his strong arms.

Reggie glanced down dubiously at his arms. Never the most athletic of chaps, the prospect of a young woman, even one as attractive as Miss Mansfield, requiring physical support from him struck Reggie as overloaded, both figuratively and literally, with risk. It was with some trepidation that Reggie raised a finger to interject a couple of perfectly sound points around the plan being as illegal as it was immoral.

Anticipating such bellyaching, Spunky waved away any hint of complaint by reminding Reggie of what seemed to him the key fact to consider.

'You can't win the fair maiden's heart on the golf course. Not off twenty-six anyway. A flanking attack, mark my words, will carry the day.'

The soundness of this principle was unquestionable. Reggie's complaint was less about the underlying strategy than about the practicality of carrying it out. Realising that Spunky would not listen to sense, at least from him, Reggie tried his own flanking thrust.

'Shouldn't we wait until Kit arrives? He's a chap with a sound grasp of things. I'm sure he can think of something.'

Spunky shook his head and looked at his friend with patient affection.

'Reggie, old chap, when you look at Kit what, and follow my logic here, do you think a young woman might see?'

'Well,' acknowledged Reggie, a little uncomfortably, 'He's a good chap.'

'You miss my meaning. Let me elaborate. Kit is rich, correct?'

'Yes, he's certainly minted.'

'One has to admit, sadly I might add, he's not ever going to be mistaken for the back end of a horse.'

'No, I suppose he's rather good-looking too,' said Reggie glumly.

'Showed up well in the war.'

'A bally hero,' said Reggie almost on the point of tears.

Spunky realised he was pushing this idea way beyond the limits of Reggie's self-esteem. He quickly brought the train of thought to a juddering halt.

'Point is,' said Spunky with exaggerated patience, 'what does Kit know about trying to woo a young woman? My word they're falling over themselves to marry the damn fool.'

'You mean Gloria will fall in love with him, don't you?'

This was proving more of an uphill battle than Spunky had bargained for. There were times when his dear friend displayed all the imagination and daring of a hunting hedgehog. On the point of trying an alternative angle of attack he saw his friend's face register first surprise and then delight.

Entering the bar was a tall man, walking with a slight limp. The man smiled and waved over at Spunky and Reggie.

'Hello, Kit,' said Spunky with something less than his usual enthusiasm. 'We weren't expecting you until around dinner time.'

'Caught an earlier train,' explained Kit arriving at their table which instigated a round of vigorous handshaking.

'I say, Kit,' said Reggie, relief soldered into every syllable. 'You're just in time.'

'Oh, just in time for what?' asked Kit with a smile.

-

Kit sat silently staring at a faraway object through the window. Finally, he turned to Spunky and said, 'Yes, I can see how the plan might work.'

'You can?' exclaimed Spunky in genuine shock. This was close to a first for one of his schemes; they invariably crumbled under the onslaught of cold reality, which usually coincided with Kit's first exposure to them.

'Yes, certainly,' reassured Kit. 'Tell me, is that the little blighter over there?'

The other two men turned from facing Kit to look out the window. They saw a small boy of around ten or less, and a black Labrador. The boy was swinging a club and deliberately missing the ball. However, the poor dog, in expectation of chasing said ball, was tearing off in search of the phantom projectile before returning dejectedly to the source of his persecution, ever hopeful that the next strike would be the one.

'Charming little fellow as you can see,' said Spunky sourly.

'Indeed, and if I may ask, who are the other runners and riders in the field?'

'Sorry?' said Reggie completely confused.

'One other chap,' said Spunky taking over again. 'Name of Hugo Fowles. Bleater of the first rank. Fowles by name and__.'

Kit nodded. Their paths had crossed before. Spunky's assessment was surprisingly moderate. Reggie added a few other less-than-admirable qualities besides and soon a picture emerged of a man who not only didn't deserve to best Kit's friend in a duel of the heart but more pertinently, did not deserve the fair hand of the maiden who could drive a ball more than two hundred yards. Straight.

The rival soon arrived at the bar accompanied by Gloria Mansfield. He glanced swiftly over in Reggie's direction. A sly smile and a knowing wink. This was met with a round of "I Say's" sotto voce, at the table where the three men had been so happily discussing his downfall. The wink added another level of resolve to the participants in the plan.

Kit rose immediately to say hello to Fowles. Spunky and Reggie watched as the two men greeted one another like long lost buddies from a forgotten war. Kit's arrival gave Fowles the chance to fluff himself up even more. He introduced Kit to Miss Mansfield. Much to the Reggie's chagrin, it was abundantly clear that the young lady was very taken with the new arrival. So much so that at one point, Reggie was beginning to doubt the good intentions of his friend.

However, a few moments later he saw Kit pointing out the window in the direction of the putting green. This resulted in a hasty exit by Gloria Mansfield. Clearly Kit had squealed on the young tyke forcing his big sister to rescue the unfortunate canine dupe.

Spunky and Reggie watched Kit chat amiably with Fowles before collecting a round of G&T's and returning to the table. A few moments later, Fowles left the bar with a steely steadfastness set firmly in his eye.

Reggie looked up expectantly at Kit, but the great man shook his head and checked to see if Fowles had gone. Outside the window an amusing scene was developing. Gloria had arrived and was giving young George a severe ticking off that stopped just short of physical violence. Kit raised his eyebrow at Spunky, who had turned to him with a grin.

Gloria Mansfield then departed the scene carrying the poor dog who was breathing rather heavily by this stage having run several miles on the fruitless quests staged by the vile boy. The Labrador in question was as grateful for the lift as the viewing gallery in the clubhouse was impressed by the ease with which the young woman picked him up and transported him away from psychological harm.

'Two hundred yards off the tee,' said Spunky by way of explanation to Kit.

-

An hour later the cry went up, or perhaps more of a gasp. Where is George? Gloria, already on her third G&T, had suddenly realised she hadn't seen the little beggar for a while. After sending a young caddie off in search of the evil sprite, she was persuaded to have a final snifter before dinner.

The young caddie returned empty handed. This cued a few humorous comments from Hugo Fowles designed to calm the now slightly concerned object of his affection, highlight affectionately what a good-natured devil the child was whilst, at the same time, emphasising his good-man-in-crisis credentials. This seemed to be working after a fashion.

A little more time passed before Reggie arrived, looking somewhat bedraggled.

'Good lord, Pilbream,' said Fowles, wanting to highlight his love rival's appearance, 'You look like you've been dragged through a hedge backwards, old chap.'

Reggie's next comment started the panic and, inadvertently, ended with the heart of the fair maiden finding its hero.

'I've been looking for George. I can't find him anywhere.'

Gloria Mansfield's eyes widened as fear set in. She looked at the jovial countenance of the frontrunner, now sipping his fifth G&T. Fowles lowered the glass from his lips as he realised the impression, he was giving lacked some, if not all, of the man-of-action credentials that were needed in the developing crisis. However, he had an ace up his sleeve.

'Leave this to me. I will organise a search party,' he announced decisively. He pointed to the young caddie and ordered him to round up the remaining staff. With that, he set his G&T down, looked Gloria Mansfield in the eye and declared, 'I will find him.'

Reggie looked on, powerless in the face of such authority mixed with resolve, and a slice of lemon. He trooped sadly over to Spunky and Kit. He sat down dejectedly and put his hands over his face.

'It's over. I shall have to stand aside,' said Reggie, nobly acknowledging the likely success of his rival.

'What happened?' asked Spunky, completely confused.

'I went to find the evil little beggar to do as you suggested, y'know, to hide him away from kidnappers by locking him up somewhere, fake a massive bout of fisticuffs before rescuing said imp and winning the hand of my one true love. But fate has dealt me a pair of twos.'

'I see,' said Spunky, who plainly didn't.

'Are we to assume you couldn't find the child, hence you were not able to play out the scene you planned?' interjected Kit.

'Right on the money, old bean.'

Kit stood up and suggested they join the search party. In fact, he specified they look somewhere around the tractor shed.

'It's where I would put a monstrous little so and so if I was of a mind to get him out of the way for an hour or two. I suggest you make haste there, Reggie. We'll follow behind.'

There comes a time in a man's life when the truth of it being darkest before dawn becomes, well, true. A light that had gone out in Reggie Pilbream's eyes suddenly flickered again. Hope once more grew in the mind and, more importantly, the heart of that stout archaeologist. Before you could say Nefertiti, Reggie was out of the bar, a steely glint in his eye, which did not go unnoticed by Miss Mansfield, who had drained the rest of her drink and was preparing to join the search party. She called out to him as he passed, but Reggie was a man not to be held back.

Spunky eyed Kit wryly as they ambled out of the bar towards the early evening air. It was a beautiful evening. The sky was a purple-blue and seagulls played above, singing the joy of summer, perhaps.

'You don't seem in such a rush; old chap. Makes me wonder if this plan hasn't been adapted slightly from its original design.'

Kit looked at Spunky and replied, 'I'm not rushing because I don't want the stump to chaff my leg too much.'

'I see,' said Spunky. And this time he did.

-

Spunky's plan worked brilliantly.

The boy was found, and the hero duly sat beside his betrothed. Gloria Mansfield was a picture of perfect contentment. She had found her Lancelot, her Tristan, her Harry Vardon. Her life was almost complete, although the British Women's Amateur title would certainly put a ribbon on it. She glanced down at George. Children would have to wait a little.

Spunky looked at Reggie, with a smile redolent in affection mixed with no little relief. The young man was in heaven as he sipped a G&T. He looked across at his former rival, Hugo Fowles. A stab of sympathy pierced his triumphant heart. He gazed upon a face that could not have looked any more dejected than if he'd had a young child beside him continually poking him in the chest which, coincidentally, he did.

Such was dinner that night in the clubhouse at Troon. Spunky turned to Kit, removed a cigar from his mouth and said in a low voice, 'Well, bloodhound, I have to hand it to you. Some people work by the ordnance survey map of life, but not you. No, you don't just see the map, you see the whole damn milky way. In short you are a marvel.'

'Really, Spunky, your plan was flawless.'

'No Kit, you, sir, are a marvel. It needed your genius to unlock its real treasures.'

The two men looked across at Hugo Fowles again. His face was set in a rictus grin as the pie-faced sprite had now taken to punching his right arm. The simple solution, of course, would have been to swipe the evil imp with his other hand. However, it was currently holding the hand of his fiancée, Gloria Mansfield.

'You put that bleater up to imprisoning the child, didn't you? How did you do it?'

'I merely adapted your brilliant idea,' replied Kit. 'It seemed to me right from the off that the match was a mistake. It occurred to me that Fowles was better-suited for the young lady.' They glanced across the table at Fowles. He had just received a little peck on the cheek from the future Mrs Fowles, which seemed to put him in better fettle. So much so in fact, he accidentally clipped young George on the back of the head. He apologised profusely of course, but his heart didn't seem in it.

Kit, meanwhile, continued, 'I suggested to Fowles that the child had an active imagination and a message that sent him to the barn on some pretext of foreign spies might unlock an opportunity to, so to speak, get the frog-faced excrescence out of his poor sister's hair for a while longer. This would give him time to seal her fate and then act the hero to find him, should he choose to bother.'

'I'm sure he wishes he'd left hell alone.'

Reggie leaned over to his two friends, 'A near miss, methinks.'

'A near miss indeed,' agreed Spunky.

'I think I shall exit stage left tomorrow morning bright and early in case anyone has a change of heart.'

'Where will you go?' asked Kit.

'Off to Malta actually,' responded Reggie, lighting a celebratory cigar. 'A bunch of us are looking for some lost treasures of the Knights of St John.'

'Well, I think that merits a toast,' said Spunky, for whom any occasion merited such a cheerful response.

The three friends clinked glasses to the success of this venture and perhaps of the episode just passed.

Jack Murray

About the Author

Jack Murray was born in Northern Ireland but has spent over half his life living just outside London, except for some periods spent in Australia, Monte Carlo, and the US.

An artist, as well as a writer, Jack's work features in collections around the world and he has exhibited in Britain, Ireland, and Monte Carlo.

There are now six books in the Kit Aston series with the latest, The Bluebeard Club, just published.

Jack has just finished work on a World War II trilogy. The three books look at the war from both the British and the German side. Jack has just signed with Lume Books who will now publish the war trilogy. This means that although they were available on Amazon formerly, they have now been taken down in readiness for publication with Lume in summer 2022.

A spin off series from the Kit Aston novels was published in 2020 featuring Aunt Agatha as a young woman solving mysterious murders.

Jack is working on a new detective series featuring the grandson of Chief Inspector Jellicoe.

Visit Jack's Facebook page: fb.me/jackmurraypublishing

Or you can contact Jack: jackmurray99@hotmail.com

The Kit Aston Novellas

Visit Jack's Facebook page: fb.me/jackmurraypublishing

Or you can contact Jack: m.me/jackmurraypublishing.

Jack Murray

Acknowledgements

It is not possible to write a book on your own. There is a contribution from so many people either directly or indirectly over many years. Listing them all would be an impossible task.

First, a mention for key references used in this novel. I have been lucky to have access to great research material such as Margaret Macmillan's Paris 1919'. Highly recommended for anyone who wants to read of the extraordinary men who fashioned the Versailles Treaty and reshaped the map of the world. The Long, Long Trail website and The Imperial War Museum are excellent sources of material on the process of British Army Demobilisation at the end of the First World war

Special mention therefore should be made to my wife and family who have been patient and put up with my occasional grumpiness when working on this project.

My brother also helped in proof reading and made supportive comments that helped me tremendously. Kathy Lance provided invaluable help in improving errors that dogged an earlier edition of this book.

My late father and mother both loved books. They encouraged a love of reading in me also. They liked detective books, so I must tip my hat to the two greatest writers of this genre, Sir Arthur, and Dame Agatha.

Following writing, comes the business of marketing. My thanks to Mark Hodgson and Sophia Shaikh for their advice on this important area.

Finally, my thanks to the teachers who taught and nurtured a love of writing.